RIE LEE

VESSEL

Prickly Pear Books
Pasadena, CA

Prickly Pear Books
Pasadena, California

Cover credits: Front cover photograph "Candles on shoulder" by Manuel Gamboa (https://studiofocalmagic.com), used under open license from Pexels (https://pexels.com/license). Back cover photograph "Rural cottage window decorated with potted houseplants" by Maria Orlova (https://orlovamaria.com), also used under open license from Pexels.

Cover and book design by Rie Lee.

Author photograph by Laura Beth Stelling.

Fonts: Garet, Code, Daniel, Bell MT, Bodoni MT, InkFree, Constantia.

Library of Congress Cataloging-in-Publication Data

Name: Lee, Rie, author.
Title: Vessel: a novel / Rie Lee
Summary: In a ravaged world where survival depends on blind faith, Paige has one chance to escape an arranged marriage to a boy in her post-apocalyptic cult: by becoming the town's human sacrifice.
Library of Congress Control Number: 2024917499
Genres: Fiction—Science Fiction—General | Fiction—LGBTQ+—Gay
Subjects: Cults | Religious deconstruction | Coming out | Spiritual abuse

ISBN 979-8-9913862-0-3 (paperback)
979-8-9913862-1-0 (eBook)
979-8-9913862-2-7 (hardcover)

10 9 8 7 6 5 4 3 2

For Luca and Nora

DIRECTORY

WHY I GAVE YOU THIS BOOK

an excerpt from the Statutes of Equality

THE SCREAMS OF OUR ancestors echo across the empty desert plains surrounding our small town; there is no one left but us. We refuse to fall prey to their temptations; it was their weakness, their selfishness that nearly removed us all from Earth. This community is the lone survivor of a destructive war, and therefore peace is taken very seriously in our town of New Standard. History has taught us, then, that peace is in our hands. And I tell you, Friend, that the key to peace is love. Take solace, Friend, and keep sweet. You are part of my community, and I exercise love[1] towards you.

We have learned from our ancestors: the experience of one individual is so much less significant than the community as a whole. We have learned that goodness rewards the faithful, especially in times of suffering. Here in New Standard, love is prevalent, because love is everlasting, love is peace. We stand firm in our keeping of our love, of our peace. We cling to our faith and we cling to each other because they let us survive on a crumbling Earth.

Join me, Friend. Take my hand. Take solace in the love found in our community, because there is room for nothing else.

---

[1] **Love, *v*.** To exercise mindfulness toward a fellow Friend emphasizing patience, kindness, goodness, faithfulness, and self-control, without envy and without boast, without pride and without rudeness. To love is to center your whole mind around your fellow Friends, to be selfless, to value your community above all else, and to always put others first. You are only one part of this community; it can only thrive if the Self does not get in the way of the Whole.

AMBROSIAL HOURS BEFORE DAWN

P AIGE THOUGHT ABOUT SLEEP. She concentrated on relaxing all of her limbs, letting the muscles in her wrists go when she noticed that she was holding them stiff under her pillow, but every time she relaxed something, she tensed something else. Only a gauzy fog of light from the torches outside actually passed through the window, barely breaking into the darkness in Paige's room, but even the darkest night wouldn't let her sleep.

She usually felt satisfied after an Ascension, as if she'd just showered and cleaned out the dust hiding in every crevice of her body; she imagined the dust long-nestled in her diaphragm flying off into the wider unknown, allowing her to breathe fully once again. She felt satisfied now, in the aftermath of tonight's Ascension, too, but it was like her freshly purified soul had a tiny black speck on it because of the uncertain feeling that Chang had caused with her . . . *outburst.*

It had started off wonderfully enough, like it did every year: Everyone gathering in a swarm of cream-colored Ascension robes at the bottom of the Renewal House, anticipating the protection of age-sixty souls as they found their way back to their respective ancestral lands—their Afterlands. In the air, led by a trio of qeej players, the spread of song started toward the front of the crowd, rippling toward where Paige stood in the middle and spreading far beyond her, until everyone in the entire community was singing together. It was one the Ancients had sung, one of Paige's favorites in its slow, sweet melody, sort of sad like a lamentation—

> *Hashivenu, hashivenu, av kad'mon elecha*
> *Venashuva, venashuva*
> *Hadesh, hadesh yamenuke ke dem*

Everything had gone as normal, to start. In a long, plain, cream-colored gown, her feet covered so that she seemed like she was gliding, the Matriarch had swept forward and introduced the Ritualist. Paige knew her: a quiet girl who had been in the cohort above Paige's whose name was formerly Agatha, escorted by two Civil Servants onto stage in front of the Renewal House with her infant child, swaddled in a blanket, nestled comfortably against her chest. There was something otherworldly about the Ritualist, like the last year had transformed her into pure spirit itself rather than a human manifestation of spirit. Last year, she had been just-Agatha, ridiculous and silly and unkempt hair flailing everywhere; tonight, she stared blankly out into the crowd, standing in front of everyone as their key to survival.

Paige's heart had swelled. This was why they had been spared: to save humanity from its own destructiveness, together. This was why they were still here. This was her home, and these were her people, and maybe next year, they would let her lead them with her Light.

The usual phrases had been uttered:

The Ritualist is the Light. The Matriarch, leader of all of New Standard, proclaimed this in front of everyone. And everyone murmured, in congregation:

She is the Light within me.

Maybe Paige could have ignored what Chang had shouted into the night if she hadn't been watching the Ritualist's face so closely. Something looked off—nothing big, maybe just the moonlight making her cheekbones seem sharper. Her elbows, too.

The look of her was startling, really: her collarbones like blades pushing up from under her skin, her face hollow and empty and cold. But the Matriarch had pressed on.

She guides our ascending cohort. She is a lamp unto their feet and a light unto their path.

And again, everyone had replied:

She is the Light within me.

Paige closed her eyes now in her bed. She shut them tight. Willed her body to relax into the mattress. The scene from earlier that night replayed, moment by moment, in her head—the Matriarch replacing the Ritualist's baby with a candle, the infant producing a splitting cry as it was taken away from its mama and given to the Civil Servants, with each of the CSes trying not to wince at the necessary tragedy of the part they played; the Ritualist lighting her candle and passing the light to someone in the crowd, who passed it on in an exponential broadening of warm flickers; and then Chang's wild shriek in the night, her disheveled yellow hair stuck to her face in a panicked sweat, insisting—

THIS ISN'T LOVE. IT'S A LIE. THEY JUST WANT CONTROL.

And the two flashes of trailing light and smoke at the front of the crowd—CSes with torches, moving quickly together.

She stood by her family and watched as the CSes dragged Chang away, pitying Chang's obviously out-of-control illness. She craned her neck to see if Chang's spouse, Pierce, and their two-year-old son were following after her, but Pierce and the baby stayed put. Paige couldn't help but think she might have done the same, if her spouse had an outburst like that. That was the whole point of living in a cooperative community—other people could provide services if you weren't available, and Pierce was certainly not available in that moment. Not when he was now solely responsible for making sure that their son was present to witness the salvation of the entire human race.

How long had it been since Paige had been in bed? Five

minutes, an hour? She rolled over to catch a glimpse of the clock on her wall, its glow-in-the-dark hands ticking ever-louder into new minutes: one-fifteen. One-sixteen.

She should have dismissed Chang and her actions. Forgotten all about them, like the Matriarch had told them to do. The things Chang had said were ridiculous, and she was ill. Of course this was love. Of course this was real. But no one had ever interrupted the Ascension before. No one, in such a delicate, crucial moment, would ever dare.

But Chang had. And Paige couldn't stop thinking about it.

The rest of the Ascension had gone by without incident. The CSes on the stage grabbed gentle hold of the Ritualist's arms to lead her to the Renewal House. For a moment, the Ritualist flickered her eyes over to her parents in the front row, but everything else remained the same, lips pursed tightly, nose pointed and upturned. Paige watched the Ritualist's back as the Matriarch led her into the Renewal House, as the Ritualist was seated in the chair in its cozy home of sheet metal, as the Matriarch closed the pyramid door. Paige had always longed to be able to see that moment from the Ritualist's perspective—to be able to watch, in real time, the magic that only the Ritualist ever got to witness: the Afterlands meeting the earth, healing the whole world.

The Matriarch pressed the button on the outside of the door, and then it happened.

There was heat, and light, and smoke—pure energy consuming the Renewal House and, inevitably, everything within it. Paige had imagined over and over again what it looked like from the inside: the painfully beautiful opening of a portal in space and time, like a mouth yawning open to beg for sleep; how the light must bleed through the portal opening, blisteringly bright; the ghostly hands of the Ancestors reaching through to finally make contact with the hand of the only person pure enough to touch them. Then, finally, being pulled through into the Afterlands, a few hundred age-sixties behind her, into a place of eternal luxury and peace and rejoining family who migrated there long ago.

The world around Paige darkened as the light faded, leaving a dark silhouette stamp of the Renewal House in the air in front of the crowd. The silence of what was left of humanity—six thousand dedicated followers of the Statutes of Equality—watching in complete reverence rang, deafening.

The Matriarch, now holding a small wooden bowl, had stepped up again and recited a favorite line of Paige's from the Statutes: *"Death is not the opposite of life, but the birth of a pure spiritual existence."* An apt quote, marking the end of the most beautiful, magical event of the year. Paige watched as one by one, the Matriarch dipped her thumb in the bowl, then placed a dot of oil on each person's forehead, then each of their cheeks. One by one, they stepped toward the Renewal House and opened the door, revealing the same chair in which the Ritualist had sat, now empty. One by one they sat in it with peaceful expressions on their faces. A nearby CS closed the door, pressed the button, and the light flashed again. And one by one, when the CS opened the door again, the person sitting in the seat was gone. And Paige let herself be doused in witnessing the moment's beauty, clinging on to the satisfaction that usually clung on to her.

They just want control.

She couldn't shake the feeling that she was somehow to blame for the look of sheer, genuine terror on Chang's face, now imprinted eternally in Paige's mind. Chang's words and the look on her face echoed through Paige's head all the way home. She reminded herself that Chang's perspective really wasn't the most reliable of perspectives. Chang had probably been hallucinating to be so doused in fear. She was constantly plagued by nervous ailments.

None of that helped Paige sleep.

She let out an aggravated sigh now and sat up in bed. Everything in the small room was as it should have been: wardrobe in the opposite corner, desk right next to it, a vertical stack of two box-shelves filled with books about biology and insects under the window.

She probably just needed some water. She got up and creaked her door open, tiptoed down the five feet or so around the corner, and was about to step into the kitchenette except that she saw the silhouette of what used to be light.

A speedy exhale and a rustle of paper.

And the smell of smoke from a blown-out candle.

Paige froze. There was a person in the dark behind the coffee table. The person didn't move, and neither did Paige.

She heard breathing.

The breathing was shallow; eventually the shadow recognized how loud it was and quieted.

The person was just waiting to strike. A hidden weapon in a corner. Waiting for her to move so she'd turn her back and the Theorist offender could make his move.

That was all it could be: a Theorist. They were the only dangerous people in the community and no one knew much else about them. Paige had never heard of one committing assault, nor entering into someone else's tetriplex without their permission, but with the figure right in front of her now, so very real and so well hidden by the shadows that not even her eyes adjusting to the darkness revealed who it was, she wouldn't put it past them.

To her left, there was the CS alarm button that outfitted every room. Two steps and she'd be there. She hesitated, waiting to see if the intruder was going to make a move, but there was no motion.

She took a step.

Then—

"Wait, it's me," whispered the figure.

Paige frowned, her hand just hovering over the CS button. "Sol?"

She dropped her arms to her sides, trying not to groan. She was a complete idiot; of course it would be her little brother, Solomon. He lived here. Was she really so paranoid about Theorists that she was going to ignore the basics of rationality and assume that someone had sneaked their way into her tetriplex unit for malicious intent?

Apparently.

Then again, who could blame her? Theorists would be the undoing of the entire community, and Chang's outburst had put Paige on edge. They threatened the end of everything in New Standard—and since New Standard was the last existence of humanity on Earth, the end of humanity, too.

"What are you doing up?" she asked, pouring herself some water, slowly because her hands were ever-so-slightly shaking. She tried to calm them down.

"Couldn't sleep," said Solomon. Paige waited for him to offer more explanation, but he didn't.

"Me neither." She leaned against the wall, sipping her water, studying him. She was calming down now. He was sitting on the floor in front of the coffee table, and he'd moved something out of sight. "So you're what, calming your not-sleeping by way of . . . sitting?"

"Meditating."

He said it quickly. Too quickly?

No. She was reading into it because of her mental state. She took a deep breath to calm herself, then let it out and smiled.

"It doesn't look like it's working," she said casually, taking a seat on the old couch across from the coffee table. "I couldn't sleep, either."

"Yeah?"

"Yeah." She swallowed some more water and carefully placed the glass on the coffee table. "Just—the Ascension—"

"*Yeah*," said Sol, like Paige had hit on something he'd been too afraid to say but could now. "It was . . . scary."

His face was more defined now that she was closer, but still his normally bright features were masked by the night. Solomon tended to be reluctant to admit how he was specifically feeling, more likely to follow the energy of the people he most looked up to, their next-door neighbor and Paige's best friend, Mott, being the most common one. Around Mott, Sol was always thinking up new jokes and doing funny dances and she was always encouraging him to be more lighthearted; around their Mama and Papa, he tended to mute himself.

But with Paige, he was honest. Maybe it was because she was his protector in their home, the person he went to when Mama and Papa wouldn't stop fighting and they were sure, for the thousandth time, that their family was going to fall apart. Or maybe it was because she had done everything she could to be worthy of such trust through her strict practice of the Statutes, memorizing every word and following every bit of guidance so that she could be the magical vehicle who would save not just Sol, but all of New Standard.

"Oh, Sol." She put an arm around him and he let his head fall onto her shoulder, an easy habit. The Statutes said that the best way to reassure people was to be honest, so honest she would be. "I thought it was scary, too. I couldn't get her voice out of my head."

"Me, neither."

"The Statutes tell us to listen to our neighbors, you know? To listen for the call of the Ancestors, since it can come in unusual ways."

Sol hesitated. When he spoke, it wasn't with the teenage confidence he'd been trying on for size lately; it was with an age-eight,-tell-me-it's-all-going-to-be-okay vulnerability. "So maybe . . . maybe Chang was speaking for the Ancestors?"

"Well, maybe." Absolutely not, but a good leader didn't tell others outright that they were wrong. Paige placed her head on top of his; the feeling of his fine, soft hair under her cheek soothed her. "*Or* maybe it was a test of faith for us."

As she said it aloud, she felt her heartbeat calm back into its familiar rhythm. This made sense: the anomaly wasn't an existential question of whether Chang was right or wrong, but whether the New Standardites who witnessed Theorism firsthand would choose the right path.

"So the Ancestors *wanted* us to challenge Chang," said Sol.

"Exactly." Paige stroked his hair out of well-practiced habit, like she did every time Mama and Papa fought. "The Ancestors have to test us every so often to regulate us, you know? There's too much at stake for New Standard to falter in its doctrine. Especially when there's been so much change lately."

"Change?"

"Like the three-child rule that the Council is considering. Yeah, it's good that we're expanding population, as far as the human species goes, but we have to make sure we're not falling into the same habits that the Ancients did. So we don't make the same mistakes."

She didn't say: *so we don't set the world on fire again.*

"It's a lot of work," Sol said.

"That's true. But it's important work. And it's worth it."

"Mm."

She could feel Sol relaxing against her, like he normally did when they sat on the couch like this, holding each other when it seemed like Mama and Papa couldn't stand each other anymore, and by proxy, couldn't stand the life they'd created together. This pattern of him relaxing was familiar; soon, he would fall asleep, and she'd watch him snore for a few minutes before gently shaking him awake and sending him off to bed.

"I'm tired," he murmured. Paige turned her head to look at his face, expecting to see his eyes drooped and sleepy, but he was staring intently at the window in the wall in front of them.

"Go to sleep, love," Paige said.

Sol didn't move for a moment, but he finally let out a huge sigh—like he'd been holding it in for years—and removed his head from her shoulder, finally sitting up. Paige un-crossed her legs and pressed a hand on the floor behind herself to push herself up.

Crunch.

Huh?

It was paper. Two sheets of paper, filled with words scribbled in tiny print all over them, front and back. The writing was hasty, nearly illegible, the print was tiny.

"Oh, thanks," Solomon said, taking the papers from her.

"Journaling again?"

He shrugged. "Just working out some feelings."

That's what Sister Nadine's there for, Paige didn't say. Solomon had a difficult time expressing his feelings (then again, Paige did, too) and wasn't always comfortable talking to people about them because he easily got confused about them. And in a town like this, there was always someone listening, wasn't there? She understood.

"You can talk to me, you know," she told him. "It's okay."

"I know." His voice was so warm. He folded the papers into squares and shoved them in the pocket of his pajamas, then capped the pen that was on the coffee table. "I should pretend to get sleep, at any rate."

"Yeah, probably."

"Night, P," said Solomon, heading back to his room.

"G'night, Sol," said Paige. And then, after a moment: "It's going to be okay, you know that, right? The Council will make sure of it."

Solomon sighed in the hallway and took a moment before he reached for his doorknob. He seemed to be staring at it intently, but that could have just been Paige's eyes not functioning in the darkness.

"They always do," he said finally, and headed in to sleep.

FINDING THE AFTERLANDS

an excerpt from the Statutes of Equality

CLEANSE YOURSELF, FRIEND, FOR those who came before us were unclean. They cared not for the survival of their home, littered the Earth with their dust and debris. Their numbers grew swollen, Earth overpregnant with unwanted scum. Eight billion, and then ten billion, and then eleven, all because of the avarice of those people, our Ancestors: they believed they had the right to superhuman longevity, that their lives should last longer than others, and they all fell down.

It did not take long to reduce their numbers. How feeble was nine billion. How strong, six thousand. These people, this community, geared for survival, built for success.

Life itself consists of two parts: the Present and the Afterlands. The Present is a gift; the Afterlands is a refuge. We refuse to make the same mistakes as our ancestors; we limit our neighbors and ourselves to a productive life on Earth, and then give ourselves freely to the Afterlands. In both places, there is no pain, no suffering; though where there is suffering on Earth, there is also love. We go with our neighbors into the Afterlands as we go with them through life on Earth.

And in the Afterlands the world shall be unlittered: no dust, no debris. Only peace and love[1]. Only the

---

[1] **Love, *n.*** A principle prioritized as the center of life. It is through love that we do all things, that we think all thoughts, that we live all lives. We pull the following principles of love from our foremothers' old-world thinking:

Love is patient.
Love is kind.

pure can enter; only the clean shall pass through.
After this land, you must renew.
     Peace be with you.

Love is understanding.
Love does not envy.
Love does not boast.
Love is not proud.
Love is not rude.
Love is not self-seeking.
Love is not easily angered.
Love keeps no record of wrong.
Love does not delight in evil.
Love rejoices in the truth.

TAHARAH

Paige saw blue. Blue trim on the windows of her Afterlands cottage, framing the incoming bright sunlight and clean air. Blue trim lining white walls. Blue beneath the skin in the tips of Solomon's fingers dangling below his body as he floated in the air in the middle of the room.

She was looking up at his back, standing directly beneath him. Gravity draped down his arms but hovered the rest of his body. He wasn't moving. She couldn't see his chest to see if it was rising and falling, but his eerie stillness suggested that it wasn't.

Between Paige's bare feet, on the ground: pieces of crumpled-up paper. Paige picked one of them up. It read:

> We slaughter our own
> for a fable

A buzzer went off a few feet away in the quaint kitchen. The smell of baked, thick yeast filtered into the experience of blue. Paige ate the crumpled-up paper. It was sticky in her throat, pasty; it choked her. She started coughing. She couldn't stop. She couldn't breathe.

Water? came a voice.

Papa stood there in front of her, offering her a glass. She took it, gulped it down, and then she could breathe again. Everything was okay. Solomon was gone and Papa was there, in her After-lands cottage, and she'd just been dreaming about Solomon, but she was awake now, and this was reality.

The front door clicked open, then shut. Paige hurried to retrieve the bread rolls from the oven as Mott came in, said hello to Papa, and came up behind Paige to snake her arms around her waist, looping her fingers together in front of Paige's hips, and in one motion that was familiar and foreign at the same time, placed a delicate breath of a kiss on Paige's earlobe.

Felicity, don't, said Papa.

She was salivating, though she couldn't tell if it was because of the promise of the freshly baked bread or because her whole body was tense with pleasure at Mott's touch. She knew how this ended. Hadn't she already been cleansed?

My dad is here, Paige protested to Mott, holding the tray of bread.

No, he's not, said Mott.

She guided Paige's hands to move the tray onto the counter and turned her around, then picked up a bread roll, breaking it open slowly so that the steam warmed her hands and Paige could watch the bread resist Mott tearing it apart, glutinous tendrils clinging together for dear life.

Mott dipped one end of the bread in a jar of honey, the delicious drip of clear amber a steady stream of sugary rain.

Open wide, she told Paige.

And then it hit Paige's tongue, gloriously coating it in just-enough-sweet and just-enough-salty, and she bit down and chewed. And just when she swallowed, Mott stroked Paige's hair, then stopped with her hands on the back of her head, and slowly brought her face toward Paige's for their lips to meet. And when they did Paige couldn't resist the draw any longer; she kissed Mott furiously, pressing her stomach against Mott's, their gravity pulling them together like they had never meant to be separated in the first place, and she let Mott's tongue part her lips gently open and she ran her hands over Mott's shoulders—

had they always been bare? Had Mott always been wearing this thin white slip, acting less like a protective barrier and more like an invitation to slip one of the straps off of her shoulders and feel the true warmth of her skin and her breath and her body against Paige's own?

Mott pulled her face back but never let go of Paige.

You're my favorite, Mott said.

She was holding Paige—no, clinging to her, like a tornado was expected to hit and Paige was her anchor to the ground. She felt wanted and solid and whole.

We can't have favorites, Paige said, but she didn't believe her own words.

And then Papa was shouting behind her.

YOU DID THIS.

He said it over and over again, breaking Paige and Mott apart until Mott wasn't even there anymore, and Paige was reeling from the absence of Mott's body and staring at Solomon's body now on the ground, his eyes wide open and unblinking at the ceiling, like there were answers there if only he looked at it long enough, if forever was long enough.

Save him, said Papa. *Take him with you to the Afterlands. You owe me that much.*

And the cottage disappeared around her. She stood in the middle of a deserted Serenity Park, Solomon in front of her laying on a large slab of stone. The Renewal House gleamed just behind Solomon and Paige rushed toward it, reaching for the entrance, except there was no way to open it. No handle on the door, no way to slide it open, no access.

SAVE HIM, said Papa.

I can't, Paige said.

SAVE HIM.

Paige grasped at every corner of the door, tried to dig her nails in the sleek silver siding, but it burned her.

I can't. It's burning me.

So let it!

She threw herself at the Renewal House, letting it blister her skin, the burning white-hot, decomposing as she became part of it. But she knew she wasn't part of it; it was rejecting her. It was burning her alive on its outside and not its inside; she wasn't worthy, because the Renewal House knew what Paige had been doing with Mott just now, it knew she wasn't pure, and because of it she couldn't save Solomon, and it was her fault for desiring another girl, for desiring the pleasure of sex; because she didn't believe enough for herself to be saved, just like Aunt Felicity.

Her feet were wet. Sticky. She looked down and saw the pool of blood that spread from behind her, saw it leaking out of Solomon's body, dribbling down his eyes and out of his mouth and getting stuck in his hair, and Paige tried to scream but she couldn't force out any noise. Her mouth opened over and over and crickets jumped into it and she choked, and she choked, and she coughed loudly as she sat up, sweating, in her bed.

—

PAIGE CLICKED OPEN THE top of the tea kettle. The enamel of the kettle's body clicked neatly—comfortingly—against the triggered handle and the sound of the water filling it up tied Paige to her current reality: the kitchen, the large window letting her watch the twilight bleed into the sky behind the row of tetriplexes across the street. Too soon, the kettle was filled and Paige could only stand there, staring outside the window, for so long before it seemed ridiculous for the water to not be heating up, and finally she placed the kettle onto its induction hotplate and leaned against the corner of the counter to wait. The faintest of clicks came from the hotplate, like old joints cracking for the first time of the day, but other than that the room was silent and still and Paige found herself staring at the bottommost shelf in the bookshelf across the room, not two feet away from where she and Sol had sat only a few hours ago. The family photo albums resided in the corner of that shelf—isolated in the hopes that they would be forgotten, but still there in a reluctance to destroy history.

Finally, she couldn't take it anymore. She left the tea kettle alone and—after glancing into the hallway that divided the living space from the bedrooms to make sure no one else was awake—strode across the room and grabbed the faded-rose, canvas-covered album off the shelf.

She turned to the back. And there it was: a photo of Papa and his family—his brother, his parents, and their siblings—from when Papa was around Paige's age. Paige looked so much like him—the high cheekbones casting a shadow onto her golden-undertoned skin; the thick, dark eyebrows that gave her a look of perpetual concentration; the long nose that pointed into a delicate tip; the shoulders hunched forward ever-so-slightly, unclear whether this was standoffish or shy, but closed off either way. In this photo he must have been only an age-sixteen, because—underneath a dried flower petal taped on top of the photo that Paige now lifted up—Aunt Felicity hovered just above him, flinging her arm around their mother.

Aunt Felicity seemed like a quiet woman in the photo, unlikely to make the trouble that she did. Her thick, black hair was brushed straight into a neat ponytail, the collar on her impressive Council-Medic shirt pressed to perfection. She couldn't have been much older than Papa, maybe a year or two. Not a few weeks before she was cleansed, probably. She was beautiful and her smile glowed brightly; she'd heard whispers—from when people gossiped but thought no one was listening, but never from Papa himself—that she was kind and friendly and that no one saw her cleansing coming.

The kettle started a tiny whistle, working up to its loud wail. Paige snapped the album shut and took it with her to the kitchen, taking care not to destroy the petal that covered Aunt Felicity's face.

The ritual of making tea calmed her: chamomile leaves in a strainer, hot water, honey, the mug warming her hands; it rooted her in reality. She wasn't Aunt Felicity, the woman who'd shamed their family as a sexual miscreant, loving some unknown woman in secret; Paige was the heroine who would make up for all of that. She was the one who would forever turn her family from a family who needed to be saved to a family who saved everyone else.

Not Aunt Felicity, whose name she was never supposed to speak. Paige. She sat at the counter and sipped her tea, flipping back to the last page of the photo album. The flowery hot water of the tea washed over her tongue and warmed her throat when she swallowed, the faint hint of honey sticking around in her mouth long after the tea settled into her belly. She'd done all she could, unlike the woman in the photo. She'd done everything possible to be the Ritualist: maintained her marks in lessons, gone to every meditation session she could, volunteered in the Audit House with Sister Nadine. The Council of Elders had even asked her to submit a written interview for the Ritualist responsibility, a surefire sign that she was in their top five, at least. The *New Standard Gazette* had written a brief article on which rising age-seventeens to keep an eye on for the job, and she was named in it, without even a single reference about her family's relation to the streaky-black scandal of Aunt Felicity, who suffered, a faux-martyr, the punishment for two individuals. And if Paige was chosen, if she was *actually* chosen . . . it would be like Aunt Felicity never even existed. The stain of Theorism on her family would finally be erased.

And maybe that would be enough relief to her parents to get them to stop fighting. And maybe Sol's life would be calmer after she was gone. She would save him, too.

In the distance, the clock tower by the Edufice tolled six o'clock. Paige set her mug down on the counter and flipped the album closed, heading for the washroom. She'd hadn't noticed the kitchen brighten over the past twenty minutes or so, but the day seemed to want to press forward. Her heart fluttered uncomfortably; she tried to deliberately take her time—washing up, combing the tangles out of her hair, selecting her best dress for the Peace Festival birthday party after the Rite of Responsibility—but still she was ready well before six-thirty.

So was Papa, stepping out into the kitchen as Paige nervously tidied up the room. He was fully dressed, shirt crisp with his worn copy of the Statutes neatly arranged in the shirt pocket.

"This is it," said Papa. He smiled brightly, though she could see the exhaustion in his eyes from his fight with Mama the day before. "Nervous?"

"A bit."

"Don't be," he said, closing his eyes. He sat at the counter and patted the seat next to him; Paige placed a mug of tea for him on the counter. "You're going to be wonderful. You've always been wonderful. And wherever they put you, it absolutely will be the right place. *'A purpose for everything—'*"

" *'—and everyone,'*" Paige finished. She patted the pocket of her dress to make sure that her own Statutes copy was there; it was.

Papa smiled. "You've put your faith in this town your whole life. It's provided for you. For all of us. Today is no different, yeah?"

The confidence that Papa had in her sparked a spread of warmth across her heart. She was going to miss this if she was Ritualist: having tea with him before the day started, where they could share their stupid biology jokes and read a morning devotional together. But the memory of Papa's face in her dream stirred up the fear she'd tried to swallow down with her tea.

"Yeah."

Quick footsteps pushed away the quiet. Pajama-laden, hair pushed up against one side of his head and flattened against the other side, Solomon raced into the room and started moving pillows out of the way in a panicked search. "Have you guys seen my bow tie?"

Paige's gaze flickered up to his eyes, his hair, the floor. No blood. She felt ridiculous for looking, but it didn't matter. She had to know he was okay, dream or no dream.

Papa shook his head. "No, but I recommend you put it in the—"

"—same spot every day, I know, I'm working on it."

It took all of Paige's strength not to interrupt Solomon's search and hug him tight and never let him go.

"Good morning to you, too," she said instead.

"Morning," Solomon mumbled. He headed directly back into the hallway, having exhausted the nooks and crannies of the living room.

"Your brother . . ." Papa rolled his eyes.

Paige gave a half-laugh, mostly because that was what Papa seemed to expect. She busied herself with taking the strainer out of her tea and emptying the leaves into the compost. Solomon had nothing to worry about.

"*Your* son," Paige shot back.

"Touché," said Papa.

Paige glanced back under the coffee table. No papers.

Good.

—

THE THOUGHT IN PUTTING all of the female members of the now-age-seventeen cohort together in a room to change into their Rite of Responsibility garments was well-intended, Paige assumed. No temptations, no distractions. Despite this, Paige was spending a disproportionate amount of time trying to figure out how to avoid displaying her own bare body.

"You're not changed yet? Dude, we have, like, two minutes." Mott, garments slightly wrinkled but securely fastened, her thick hair thoroughly combed despite how long it must have taken her to get through all of its tight curls, rolled her eyes and steadied Paige by her shoulders. "Eugh, you look terrible."

"Thanks."

"Here, let me unzip you."

And before Paige could say anything, Mott had spun her around, hands at the top of Paige's zipper, pulling it down as it followed the length of Paige's spine.

At the bottom, before Mott let go, Mott accidentally brushed her knuckles against one of Paige's vertebrae. Paige felt her skin tighten, the hair on her arms standing on end, her nipples hardening against her bra in a way that made her push her shoulders inward to cover her breasts. Despite the appearance of chill on her skin, the inside of her body was flushed with warmth, like bread fresh from the oven, steaming and dipped in honey. She felt sick.

"Hurry up," Mott said, already tucking the garment's blouse into its long skirt.

Paige shook her head to clear it. It was wrong, this feeling was wrong, and feeling it was like breaking Mott's trust even without doing anything. These were not the pure feelings she was supposed to have during one of the most reverent times of the year—of her *life*. And Mott would probably be disgusted if she knew Paige had dreamed about her that way. Pretty much everyone would be disgusted. Sexual pleasure was a reward for attempting to repopulate the world; you didn't get rewarded for *not* repopulating it.

It's not real, she told herself. *It was just a dream. You're not Aunt Felicity. It was just a dream.*

Paige took over tucking her own blouse into its skirt as quickly as she could, hoping the protection of sacred clothing would be enough to chase away the feelings. And then Mott grabbed her arm and pulled her into the queue of shortly-to-be-age-seventeen girls. Shortly-to-be women.

It all moved faster than Paige thought it would. The door opened and they were off down the hallway. Paige followed Mott and kept her eyes lifted to the familiar tight black curls on the back of Mott's head, hair just short enough to reveal the deep-brown skin of Mott's neck. Paige's own hair was pulled back and up, her neck feeling naked and propelling the chill throughout her body despite the warm day making the dining hall facility feel stuffy and dry at the same time. They met the queue of boys coming from the opposite end of the hallway in the middle, and Paige breathed deeply.

This was it. Only a few moments away from being presented with the responsibilities they'd take on for the rest of their lives, until their own Ascensions as age-sixties. Not long until they learned who would be the one who wouldn't Ascend with the rest of them, the one who would be the savior of this year's Ascending cohort, the one who would be the savior of all of New Standard. Of literally all that remained of humanity.

But no pressure.

Instead of doors leading to the stage, there was a white curtain. Two by two, an event administrator invited them through the curtain, where Council members stood on opposite sides with a bowl of water each, a small ceramic ashtray next to it. The Council members poured the water over the hands of Paige's cohortmates: three times on the right, three times on the left, once together, then a dab of ash pressed into the middle of their foreheads. Then quiet murmurs of peace to one another.

It felt like no time at all before Mott was the only one ahead of her. They'd be going through together, at least. Just before the event administrator pulled the curtain aside, Mott whirled around and gave Paige a hug, a swift kiss on her cheek, and whispered, "We've got this."

Paige forced a smile on her face and nodded at Mott, too nervous to say anything back. Her cheek tingled where Mott's lips had been, and the sick feeling in her stomach deepened.

Then they were walking through the curtain. Paige's heart beat so wildly that she was genuinely afraid it might bruise the inside of her ribcage. She'd never seen a Council member this close up. They were all former huérfanos, grown into leaders of the entirety of New Standard, supposed to have the age and wisdom that came with distance from the community and family units that could guide the world forward in a productive way so that humanity wasn't wasting its limited time. They were the guardians of the future, and one of them—a bony older woman with silvering hair and a nametag reading FLORENCE—was washing Paige's hands, making her clean.

The water was cool and welcome; Paige closed her eyes, breathing the sensation in. Elder Florence pressed her thumb to Paige's forehead with the sacred ash, then bowed her head, whispering to her:

"Peace be with you."

Paige opened her eyes, earnestly bowing her head back to Elder Florence. "And also with you," she replied.

And with that, Elder Florence had rid Paige of any past impurities. Paige felt relief. There was a peace in just saying it, her mouth soft, breathing peace into the recipient by talking alone.

That peace settled over Paige's heart now as she followed Mott to their seats on the women's side of the stage. Mott grinned at her as if to say, *See?* And the peace settled over Paige's heart was so powerful that, in relief, Paige grinned back.

Soon enough, everyone in their cohort was on the stage, and then the Matriarch walked toward the microphone on the left side.

"Let us rise together," she said to the audience.

Everyone stood up: everyone there was at the Ascension last night, except the Ritualist and the age-sixties. Paige's heart beat faster, remembering that her parents were out there, and Mott's parents were out there, and Sol and Mott's sister Rory were out there; she breathed in, two, three, out, two, three. The moment was here. She was either the new Ritualist, or she wasn't.

Trust that you've done enough, she told herself. *Trust that you are enough.*

A young huérfana, probably an age-twelve or age-thirteen, walked toward the center of the stage to meet the Matriarch.

"We will now follow our Friend Lane in singing our anthymn," said the Matriarch while adjusting the microphone height for the huérfana, "in celebration of this New Year of Peace in 2140." And together, the entire town sang:

And then it was time. The huérfana stepped off the stage and the Matriarch readjusted the microphone.

"Neighbors and Friends of New Standard," she began, more toward the age-seventeen cohort than the audience of the rest of the community, "we welcome you to this sacred space, and hope that you will find joy in serving in the home of our community this day. You may be seated."

Finally.

"The age-seventeen cohort here today has been washed, anointed, and clothed in the protective garments of our community. You have been washed and pronounced clean, or that through your faithfulness and dedication to the Statutes of Equality, you may become clean from the blood and errors of this generation and those of the Ancients, who led humanity into such a place of devastation that they nearly destroyed the entirety of the human race in their arrogance and avarice."

Paige sat up a little taller. She'd never seen the Matriarch this close before, and now she was only across the stage from her.

The Matriarch seemed radiant as she spoke, slivers of gray in her dark, sleek hair glowing brightly as they fell against the dark brown of her skin.

"You have been anointed into this sacred space into this productive community, and with this anointment, you accept the blessings, responsibilities, and traditions of atoning for the sins of those who came before us, of serving as proof of the resilience of human nature, and as resistors to the concept that humans simply want to destroy each other."

Paige tried to find Sol in the crowd. It was such a large crowd and it was nearly impossible to find him by way of something easy to spot, like the color of his hair, because almost everyone in New Standard had dark hair. She looked for a pattern of a short woman and a medium-heighted man and a slightly-taller boy in between them, and when she finally found them she saw that Solomon was looking away, out the window.

"With this anointment and initiation into the adult responsibilities of this community, you accept this mission and commit to building a better world for the humans who come after you. To confirm your acceptance of this responsibility, please respond 'I do.'"

"I do," said Paige, along with the chorus of age-seventeens around her.

"If any of you desire to withdraw rather than accept these obligations of your own free will and choice, you may make it known now by raising your hand."

Of course, no one raised their hand. Paige had never seen anyone raise their hand during this portion. To raise your hand would be to be labeled a Theorist; to be labeled a Theorist was to be tried and cleansed.

"Last night," continued the Matriarch, "we kept our covenant with our Ancestors, who stand at the gateway to the Afterlands."

This was it. Paige's pulse pounded steadily throughout her body. She was going to be the pride of her family. She was going to save them all.

"We maintain our commitment to this lifestyle by sacrificing one of our own, one who gave birth to a new observer of how we live, who in turn will grow into an Elder and become part of our governing Council. We ask all members of this cohort who have the ability to grow and birth a child to please stand."

Paige stood with the rest of the women's side, except for one or two of them. She felt bad for the seated girls; they didn't even have a chance.

"On your garments, just over the left breast, there is a small triangle embossed into the fabric. Each of you bring your right fist to the triangle."

They did.

"Will you solemnly promise before the Ancestors, your cohort, and these witnesses that—should you be selected for this highest responsibility of Ritualist—you will observe and keep the covenant of our land, as contained in the Statutes of Equality, in order to preserve our world and extend all of human existence, as has each cohort of women has done before you?"

And Paige's nervous energy melted into something resolute and proud as she said, with the rest of the functionally-bodied girls in her cohort, "We accept this covenant."

And the huérfana who sang earlier came forward with a beautiful silver robe, the shiniest thing Paige had ever seen in New Standard except for the Renewal House itself. Paige imagined how soft it might be on her arms, how radiant she would feel to put it on. Any moment now, they would say her name.

"Humbly, to accept this greatest of responsibilities, we ask Ingrid to step forward."

Paige blinked several times in rapid succession.

Ingrid.

Ingrid had been chosen as Ritualist.

Paige stood still in place.

It wasn't her.

RESPONSIBILITY, KNOWLEDGE, CONTROL

an excerpt from the Statutes of Equality

COME WITH US, FRIEND, to a place beyond survival. We have survived; that war is won; and now we are the ones who have remained. And why should we have remained? The greediness of the Ancients was rampant and infectious—so why were our predecessors unaffected? How did they resist the seductions of the tangible world?

We remember our founders with the utmost gratitude, for they had the foresight and faith to think of our species as a whole. From various faiths they came, and together they collaborated with the commonmost of their values, and together they ensured the continued existence of our people. And thus, from the widespread destruction we saw during the near-extinction of humanity, our founders— the Spared—ensured the continued existence of *all* people.

It is not chance, Friend, that the Spared found each other in the same place during such a devastating time. They came from everywhere and found their home here, each Called for a different internal purpose; and yet we see now what their purpose truly was: to bring together a broken world. They beheld the Truth: that the suffering of one is so much less than the suffering of the many. So they gave up the seductive comforts of the world that destroyed nearly everyone; they surrendered their desires for the benefit of humanity's survival.

And in this vein we persist: we feel the same Calling. Where else could that communal Calling be from but somewhere unknown to humans on Earth?

Through this legacy we have the privilege of living, of being Chosen to perpetuate the best of what humanity could be; we have the perspective missing from millennia of human history. In this life we will do nothing short of saving the world. In this mission we must not fail.

IN THE BOSOM OF FOOLS

Iₙ NGRID STEPPED FORWARD WHILE Paige's hopes crashed into the ground.

Paige couldn't see Ingrid's face but she'd spent enough time sitting behind her in class, staring at her thick, dark, wavy hair that Paige could recognize her from the back of her head. Her long spine made her seem even taller than she was; it propelled her to walk calmly, evenly. Like a Ritualist should walk.

All together, the community chorused:

"Oh Ancestors, hear the words of our mouths.
Oh Ancestors, hear the words of our mouths.
Oh Ancestors, hear the words of our mouths."

Paige's lips moved along with everyone else's, her words drowned out by the collective voice of New Standard.

She wasn't good enough.

She hadn't been clean enough.

She felt Mott's hand grabbing her own, Mott's warm touch rooting her in reality. But Paige was already making a list of how her life would go now, and realizing that she hadn't prepared for it. Not like the other girls in her cohort had. She hadn't even thought about whom she might want to consider for a spouse, and she hadn't daydreamed about having sex so that she could get pregnant—and the last time she'd thought about that was when she'd asked Mama in the living room after a game of Tlenga a few weeks ago—

Do you like Papa?

Of course I love him, Mama had said, without missing a beat.

No, said Paige, *I mean, do you like him? Like, are you—* She hesitated, unsure whether the question was appropriate, unsure whether she actually wanted to know. *—are you* attracted *to him?*

Mama paused a moment. There wasn't anything else to tidy up, but she pretended to anyway, wiping off invisible dust from the corner of the cabinet or the handle of the faucet.

You know, Paige, attraction is a funny thing. Fleeting. Doesn't mean much in a spousal arrangement, I think.

So, no.

Why? Mama's voice was abnormally gentle. *Are you worried about that?*

A little, Paige admitted. *I just—in order to have children, you have to—*

Saying it out loud made her want to throw up a little.

Mama's eyes went wide and she ventured toward Paige, reaching out to hug her. Paige stood still at first in surprise—Mama didn't hug often, and when she did it was hardly ever this earnest, this soft and warm, like cuddling into a super-soft blanket on a cool night—but eventually relaxed into Mama's chest, the way she'd done when she was a kid and she'd had a bad day, when Mama's inhales and exhales would buoy her head and and Mama used to tell her that everything would be okay. It was warm here, and safe and comfortable, and Mama smelled very much like herself—a little bit like vinegar, a little bit like lavender. Paige felt guilty for staying here so long, being comforted by her mother when she was on the brink of adulthood like she was that child again. But she didn't want to let go.

You know, P, said Mama into Paige's hair, *it's true that boys only want one thing. All these New Standard boys—they might have taken their celibacy vows, and they might be nice, upstanding citizens*

Paige nodded slowly as Mama let her go. She was embarrassed to even be having this conversation with Mama, but the Edufice had always encouraged kids to have conversations with their parents about such matters. But Paige was nearly shaking, internally, whenever she thought about it.

Maybe she could be paired with a friend—maybe Adam. He was nice enough, she liked him enough to be comfortable sharing a living space with him, and probably would even be fine raising children with him.

But the thought of having to be *naked* with him was absolutely horrifying. She didn't want her skin on his skin. She didn't want her nether regions anywhere near him.

You okay, P? asked Mama.

Paige looked up at the crow's feet around Mama's eyes, surprising for someone her age. Typically those skin creases didn't happen until people were at least age-forties, or age-forty-fives. Mama looked startlingly tired, human instead of mother; Paige released her and nodded with as much of a smile as she could muster.

And now, in the dining hall, Paige didn't want to look into the audience to find her.

She'd disappointed them all. And now she was going to have to figure out how to deal with some boy's genitalia for the rest of her life.

There was a point at which you could *stop* having sex, right?

"Ingrid of the Cohort of 2123," said the Matriarch, "do you enthusiastically accept and embrace the honored responsibility of Ritualist?"

The Matriarch beckoned Ingrid forward to reply into the microphone. The audience took on an extra layer of silence while they waited.

As if Ingrid were going to say no. If she said no, she'd be on a straight path to be cleansed. At that point, you were going to go out in literal flames either way; might as well go out with honor instead of treason.

"I do."

The audience erupted into applause, whooping and getting to its feet. The mood lightened in the dining hall from anticipation to celebration, the energy contagious and spreading onto the stage to the other cohort members. Paige smiled, applauding with everyone else. Her palms felt chalky and sweaty at the same time as she smacked them together.

I'm happy, she told herself. *Ingrid deserves this. Now I get to stay.*

An Administrator appeared on the other side of the stage with a small object—a triangular pin, Paige knew, reminiscent of the Renewal House—and handed it to the Matriarch, who pinned it over the stitched triangle on Ingrid's garments, and she returned to her seat among congratulations and excited whispers from the other girls. Paige moved her smiling lips in a way that she was pretty sure actually formed the word *congratulations*. Mott offered Ingrid a high-five.

"All rise," said the Matriarch, though everyone had started to stand anyway. "Without further ado—I present to New Standard the new age-seventeen cohort! Welcome, Friends."

The applause continued while two Event Administrators—Paige recognized one of them, EA Davis, who had been an EA as long as Paige had been alive—pulled some baskets with pins and scrolls in them toward the microphone.

"Adam," said the first one, the audience still applauding, though it faded into politeness now, folks taking their seats again now that the peak of excitement had faded. Adam's family whooped for a moment in encouragement, and Adam laughed as he walked forward to meet the EA, shake his hand, receive his responsibility scroll, and be pinned. Ever efficient, EA Davis announced from the other side of the stage, "Alice," and the same pattern followed.

Paige lost herself in the low rumble of applause, drowning in the enthusiasm that wasn't reaching her. She had expected to be selected, and that had been her mistake. She dared to look out into the audience now, searching for Solomon—and when she found his face and made eye contact, he looked so relieved that he might cry.

It was like he was thinking, *thank you for not leaving me.*

And Paige gave him a sad smile. As if she'd had a choice.

But it was going to be okay. She was going to be there until she was espoused, and she still had a year before she could apply. Solomon was an age-fifteen as of today—only two more years until he got his responsibility, so at least they'd overlap for a couple more years at home and he'd find peace in that.

Even if she wasn't Ritualist, she could provide peace to Solomon. For a moment, that made Paige's smile genuine.

Mott nudged her shoulder. "Hey, guess what. You're stuck with me for a really long time now."

And with that, Paige's heart lightened. She was grinning now, genuinely so, and she rolled her eyes at Mott. "Ugh," she said, "I thought I was getting away from you."

"You couldn't escape me if you tried."

"Challenge accepted."

Mott laughed. "Sure. Go hang out at the borders and tell me if you want to leave on your own."

Paige shuddered thinking about it. Beyond the borders was a big load of nothingness—debris and waste and starvation and ugliness. To go there without a crew was certain death without the opportunity for redemption, no passage into the Afterlands. Worse than being cleansed. And if you got caught, you'd be cleansed anyway. "I'll pass. This time."

Mott had dragged her to the borders a couple of times "just to see," and they only ever were at an open spot of the border for thirty seconds before a CS was on them to make sure they didn't go beyond it without proper equipment and supervision. Mott brazenly asked all sorts of questions that Paige had always wondered but never dared to vocalize: what was out there? Why couldn't they go out? Were there any other people? To which the answers were obvious to the naked eye: the air beyond New Standard was only clean and safe for a few hours' journey before it started to thicken up and choke you to death, and everything else, beyond the salvaged concrete that made up New Standard's sidewalks and the succulent-lined dirt pathways where concrete couldn't be filled for lack of legacy supplies, was a wasteland. Dilapidated tree branches and tall, monstrous-looking weeds made up an odd forest of sorts, and Paige couldn't imagine ever getting lost in that. In the aftermath of the Paterazm, the drought had only intensified; New Standard couldn't afford to be anything other than diligent about its water practices, so outside the border there likely wasn't any water for days. Even if someone made it beyond the CSes, they'd be dead by the end of the day. It would be a slow and filthy death, dry and miserable and alone.

"Mott," said EA Davis, and Mott bounded up.

"Ta ta," she said, prancing over to the microphone to receive her pin and scroll. Mott's family was the loudest set of whoopers; Mott pumped the air with her fist and took a bow after she got her pin, grinning and blowing kisses into the crowd. Paige laughed. Mott could always make her feel like things were going to be okay.

Too soon, they were at the Ps.

"Paige," said the other EA.

She barely remembered going up to the front of the stage, watching the sea of community members watch her. Maybe it was a good thing she hadn't been selected as Ritualist; she wasn't comfy on a stage in front of people. Solomon let out a singular whoop, but Paige's parents remained their reserved, quiet selves, showing their enthusiasm only by—maybe, Paige wasn't close enough to tell—clapping a little bit louder.

The EA shook her hand, fastened the pin on her garments, and handed her the scroll—and then that was it. Paige was an adult.

. . . cool?

She stood up a little bit taller. Took a deep breath in. Smiled. There, that felt much more adult.

Totally.

And if she didn't think about it too hard, she could believe that all of the expectations that came with adulthood were imaginary.

Paige's and Mott's families were waiting for them outside the dining hall in the sun after the ceremony. Mott's family was practically bouncing up and down; her mother had all her weight on her toes and nearly tried to snatch Mott's scroll out of Mott's hands to read it.

"What does it say?" Mott's mother practically burst.

"Xenia, chill," said Mott's father.

Xenia ignored him. "Open it, open it."

Mott laughed, peeling the wax seal off the scroll and opening it.

"Archaeologist," said Paige. "I'm calling it."

"No way," said Xenia. "Gentry and I have our bets on Excavation Crew."

"Isn't that the same thing?" said Mama.

Xenia shook her head. "Archaeologists are moreso in a lab, Excavation Crew does more of the border expeditions and discovery—"

But Paige was watching Mott's face as she opened the scroll and read it. Mott squinted at it, turned it over to make sure she had the right scroll with the right name on it.

"Age-Two Caretaker," she said.

"Oh!" said Papa, though he was the only one of them with an audible reaction aside from Mott's sister, Rory, who said, "Ew, like diapers?"

"Well, she's got to learn eventually," said Mama.

"I guess that's a *kind* of exploration adventure?" said Solomon.

But then Mott's family caught up with the surprise and started whooping enthusiastically. "AGE-TWO CARETAKER!"

they shouted in unison, enveloping Mott into a group hug. Mott's confusion melted into laughter.

"What does yours say, Paige?" asked Papa.

Paige picked off the wax seal absently. In all honesty, she was just glad that her parents weren't showing huge signs of disappointment. She couldn't tell, yet, if they were just putting on a show or not right now; it seemed like they were, to save face with Mott's family by not being judgmental, but then again maybe she'd underestimated them. Maybe they really were okay with her not being selected as Ritualist. Maybe they really didn't think she'd let them down.

She took a deep breath, then peered at the paper.

"Architecture Refurbisher," said Paige.

"Oh," said Mama. She was quiet for a moment, but then she spread a smile on her face and said, "That's great, P."

"We're so proud of you," said Papa, grabbing Paige's shoulders in an awkward side-squeeze.

Paige nodded absently, focused on the schedule in front of her. Training: oh-six-hundred hours, starting tomorrow.

This feeling was too familiar. It was like those times when her parents had got into a huge fight and Paige and Solomon got in the middle of it, and Paige tried to scream at them to stop and they would get mad at her for interfering when all she was trying to do was say it didn't have to be like this, and how could they be such hypocrites and practice the Statutes outside of their home but inside it was like patience and kindness went totally out the window. And they would wash her mouth out with soap for talking back, and she would gag on the soap, and then half an hour later they would all have to go to meditation together and she would have to put on a cheap smile and pretend to be happy. She glanced over at Mott and her family, chattering excitedly like Age-Two Caretaker was the title Mott had always wanted.

Paige shrugged. "I was hoping for something biology-oriented. Research Scientist. Oh, well, I guess."

"Being an AR is like house-biology," Solomon offered.

"Sure," said Paige. But after a moment, she ignored the scroll completely and wrapped Solomon into a hug. "I'm just glad I get to stick around with you."

Sol hugged back, his bony arms squeezing her waist almost tighter than he ever had before. "Me, too."

"That's the spirit!" said Mott's father. "You girls—"

"*Women*, Gentry," said Xenia.

"Women, I'm sorry. You *women* will be friends for the rest of your lives, and you'll grow old together, and you'll have babies together, and you'll learn together. Your parents did that with us. It's a great life. It's not even about the responsibility you get, you'll see. It's about the people."

"Absolutely," said Papa, and Paige felt a bit more relaxed now that the conversation was flowing.

"Now," said Papa, "can we go get some cake?"

"CAKE, YES," said Mott, "Bye."

And before their families could protest, Mott grabbed Paige's hand and led her toward the picnic that had been set up on the lawn in Serenity Park.

"Eat some greens first!" Papa called after them. And the further Paige and Mott got from their families, the closer they got to the Peace Festival picnic—to New Standardites settled on blankets on the wide-open field, the sweet smells of barbecuing eggplant thickening the air—the better Paige felt.

It was like everyone had forgotten about Chang. The picnic served giant amounts of food like it did every year, enough for people to go back for seconds, and there was a birthday cake at the end. Musicians were already setting up by the dance floor set up in the middle of the lawn; brightly colored papier-mâché decorations hung from the poles that usually held the lanterns for the Ascension. As kids, Paige and Mott had loved volunteering for the decoration-making crew—Paige because of her penchant for assembly and order, Mott because she was given license to dig her hands into sticky things.

Paige kept herself from staring longingly at a group of younger girls jumping rope next to the picnic blanket where their friends were sitting. The large, pyramid-shaped Renewal House shone in the distance behind them: a beacon of the Statutes of Equality and everything beautiful they stood for. The girls were on the third verse of "Firetruck Red," singing:

"The sky was blue, the trees were green, and all our lips were red,

But a mushroom cloud cried blackened rain and now we make our beds."

Paige and Mott and their friends had been those kids, once. They had run around on the lawn playing tag and hide-and-go-seek and jumping rope, singing the same nursery rhymes, probably even jumping with the same rope. But they were adults now. They sat politely together—Dorothy, Pepper, Adam, and Beck—on one of the blankets provided by the set-up crew, eating their lunches, childhood a long whisper away.

"So!" said Beck, a bite into his cornbread. "Let's leave the mystery behind, what did everyone get?"

"Event Administrator!" Pepper announced, smudge from beans drying on the corner of her mouth.

"Those are going to be the messiest events in New Standard's history," Mott said.

"You're one to talk," said Pepper.

"Yeah, but I'm not an EA. I'm a Caretaker."

"Really?" Beck said. "Me, too! What cohort?"

"Age-twos."

"Heyyyyyy, me too." Beck high-fived Mott. "I can't believe they put two newbies together."

"Well, the age-twos are a rowdy bunch," said Pepper, "they've got like twice the Caretakers that most of the other cohorts have. *And* they'll be growing in size as that new three-child law's passing. You think we're all going to get to have three kids?"

Paige's gaze lingered on Mott's hand from where it had made contact with Beck's palm. Mott and Beck got along well, constantly on the same page; maybe they'd get espoused together.

Maybe they'd have kids together, came a thought, accompanied by an uncomfortable jabbing feeling in her stomach. Three of them.

Beck shrugged. "If the law passes in time. Amendments take a while."

"I hope it passes in time," Adam said. "I'd love to have three kids."

Three kids. Having to have sex three times. At least.

"Ugh, you're one of *those people*," Pepper said, grinning. "What'd you get? Caretaker, too?"

Paige didn't like how she felt when she thought about Mott and Beck having sex together. There was something dark worming its way through her gut, maybe infecting her vital organs.

"Research Scientist," Adam said. "I was hoping for a Caretaker spot, but I guess they were already full."

"Trade you," Paige said, the worming darkness making its way to her heart. Jealousy. It was jealousy. She tried to bury it, only to find that now she had guilt about being jealous. It made sense when it came to Adam getting the responsibility she wanted, but jealousy about Beck having sex with Mott? Did that mean *she* wanted to have sex with Beck? She watched as Beck finished his cornbread, licking his fingers through his big lips and wiping them on the picnic blanket, and thought maybe that was sexy.

"Why?" Adam said. "What'd you get?"

Paige rolled her eyes. "Architecture Refurbisher."

"That sounds awesome," Dorothy said. Paige was startled by her clear voice; Dorothy hardly ever spoke up when they were in a group, and when she did, it was when she was right next to Paige and she could lean over to mumble something quietly. "I got Historian."

Paige lit up. "You get to be in the history museum? With all the bug models and the artifacts?"

"That's what the page says," said Dorothy, tilting her head toward her scroll on the blanket beside her.

"Just don't let Pepper in," said Beck.

"What!" Pepper protested. "Why not?"

"Remember that time you almost broke the replica of the Pandora?"

"Okay, that was *one time*—"

"It's *one replica*!"

"Yeah, but it's a *replica*, they can make another one—"

"So not the point—"

"GUYS. THERE IS CAKE. FOCUS," Mott insisted, popping up.

"I'll go with you," Paige volunteered.

They meandered toward the end of the queue. Mott stretched her arms behind her head as they walked, pressing her chest out forward; though they had changed out of their garments and back into the clothes they'd selected in the morning, which were *more* modest than the garments, Paige found that the feeling she'd had from her dream re-surfaced.

She shivered.

Mott smirked at her, then squinted at the blazing sun. "The cold's getting to you, huh?"

"No, I just—I was remembering something."

"Something?" Mott raised her eyebrows. "Well, isn't that mysterious."

Paige shrugged.

She wasn't going to be Ritualist. She wasn't going to be a research scientist. She had a responsibility, and it wasn't completely what she'd wanted, but who cared, it was a way for her to serve the Statutes. What mattered now was her family—building one of her own? If she could just have Mott be her family, it would be so much easier.

"Seriously?" Mott nudged, grabbing a plate for the cake. "You're not going to tell me about this mysterious thing you're remembering that makes you shiver in the middle of a heat wave?"

Even if she did want to talk to Mott about it, there were people ahead of them and behind them in the queue. "Maybe it's the sweat."

"Sweat isn't a thing you remember and are subsequently afraid of."

Paige shoveled a piece of cake onto her plate, saliva already collecting into a pool under her tongue. She was definitely coming back for seconds. And then, in a moment of guilt remembering Papa's words, she forked a couple of pieces of eggplant on her plate, too.

Mott fished two forks out of a bin at the end of the queue and, before Paige could veer them back to the picnic blanket where the rest of the crew sat, led her to a bench behind the playground.

"Sit," she said.

Paige sat.

"Talk."

Paige shoved a bite of cake into her mouth in defiance. It was delicious, overly sweet and doused in honey, some kind of frosting on top. She remembered the way honey had dripped in her dream in an unashamed, sticky amber drizzle right onto the bread, how delectable it was when she swirled it around on the tip of her tongue.

"Something happened," Mott guessed. "That's why you were so weird this morning."

"No." Paige sighed, set her plate on the bench's attached table, criss-crossed her legs under herself. "I had a dream. And if I tell you about it, you can't laugh at me."

Mott lit up. "Ooh, an embarrassing dream. I like it. Was it a sex dream?"

Paige took the opportunity to place another bite of cake in her mouth. Her heart pulsed like it was trying to get out of her body, like the flames batting at the insides of the Renewal House, only ever getting released as smoke. Mott gasped, grinning triumphantly.

"You have. I knew it. Who with?"

" 'With whom,'" Paige corrected.

"It's me, isn't it?" Mott gleefully settled onto the bench across from her, preening. "I'll bet you've had dreams about me."

Six times. She'd always woken up with a flush over her whole body, a pleasant high in her head, a distinct longing that she had to push down with a few meditative breaths.

"Oh, gross," Paige lied.

"See, now, that's just rude."

Paige ate a bite of cake. Mott's smile faded.

"Wait, *have* you?" she said.

Paige paled. "Have I what?"

"Had dreams about me."

Mott's gaze was so deliberate that Paige dropping her own eyes would be an instant admission of guilt. Paige felt powerless, like she did in the dreams where she'd been unable to fight against her own terrifyingly intense desire to grab Mott's face and pull it toward her own. Or worse: not unable. Unwilling.

"They're just dreams."

"It's okay, Paigey," Mott said. "It happens to all of us." She reached out to gently tuck a strand of hair behind Paige's ear like she had a million times before, on their first day of school as age-fours and on Paige's porch in the middle of the night when she could hear her parents from down the hall, articulating each other's names as if that would somehow make their argument superior (*Why are you always so obsessed with how you think we look, Na-o-mi; Because I care about our continued survival,* Phil-*lip*) she couldn't sleep. The spot Mott had touched behind her ear burned hot, spreading warmth everywhere.

How far was Mott from her now? She felt like she could feel the steam from Mott's breath in the thin air between them. For a moment, everything else faded away; it was only them, the two of them in time and space and history, and nothing else mattered. The warmth spread itself into a blanket over Paige's heart, and she believed Mott. It was okay.

Mott dropped her hand, letting it fall into her lap.

"Haven't you?" Paige asked.

"Haven't I what?"

"Had any—any sex dreams?"

She didn't like how her voice faded unintentionally at the word *sex*, like she was some age-six on the playground spelling out the word to avoid saying it. She traced the edges of her dwindling cake with her fork.

The few seconds after Paige's question it felt like forever, like Mott was avoiding the question. She was unusually quiet, like there was a possibility that she would admit something egregious. Like owning up to having the dreams that 'happened to all of us' was an unforgivable crime after all. Like maybe her dreams were so close to home that if she verbalized them, some vulnerable organ inside of her would bleed out.

"Good cake?" said a voice.

It was Adam, flushed and sweaty from either the dancing or the heat. The delicate pressing Paige had felt from Mott was gone now, and Paige couldn't tell what the cold feeling rushing through her digestive system was.

Relief, maybe.

When she glanced back up at her, Mott looked like she always did: wearing her usual goodnatured grin, seemingly amused by Adam's mere presence, like she saw everything around her but never got sucked into it herself. Paige gestured to her empty plate and licked the crumbs off her fork. "Great cake."

There was the delighted screech of two children chasing each other on the nearby grass. Paige yearned to be that young again, when the games of Tetriplex, picking a pretend spouse and serving mud pies to friends together, were limited to just games and not speculation.

"You want to get another helping of vegetables to balance out the sugar, don't you?" said Adam.

Paige forced a grin onto her face, and within a second—maybe from the training she'd gotten her whole life from Mama—it felt real. "I'm resisting the urge."

Adam laughed and shook his head. "Predictable," he said.

"Oh, yeah? You're just jealous of my super-clean arteries."

"You got me." He took a final bite of his cake and set the plate down on a nearby table. "Wanna dance?"

Paige glanced back at Mott, raising her eyebrows to communicate a *holy-matriarch-I'm-getting-asked-to-dance,-several-exclamation-points*.

Mott waggled her own eyebrows back, as if to say, *well, aren't you in high demand,* and everything was as it should have been.

Paige grinned. "Sure."

"Yeah, okay, you kids have fun, now," Mott said, waving them off.

Adam offered his hand and Paige took it after some hesitation. Adam's hand felt strange in hers, and there was something intimate about the palms of your hands touching when not engaged in a handshake and Paige resisted an overwhelming urge to recoil. But he lifted up her arm and placed his other hand on her back, and off they went on their polka.

She was touching a boy. She was touching a boy. She was touching a boy and it felt so . . . *weird*.

He guided her firmly with rigid arms, his footwork well-practiced and confident. Paige wasn't as graceful, her choppy movements a strange accompaniment, but together they offered an air of precision, of classic New Standardite tradition.

"You're not half-bad at this," Paige told him, though she was barely keeping up.

Adam beamed, straightening up his spine a bit further. "Were you expecting me to be bad?" He led her in a guided turn. "I'm offended."

"No no, sorry, I didn't mean—"

"Paige, I'm joking."

She supposed she knew that, but she and Adam had never been this close before, close enough that her smaller nose might get bruised by his bigger one if he tried to kiss her.

She kept talking just in case he thought to try. Not that he would—the Statutes strongly encouraged modesty, and 'planting one,' as Papa would say, in the middle of the town-wide Peace

Festival birthday party, would be ill-advised, at best. "Well, I was, too."

Adam laughed. "I can tell."

A gentleman, Paige thought. If this was going where she thought it was going, she'd heard of worse men.

The conversation fizzled out, not for lack of things to say but because the dance was fast and cardiovascularly inclined. Through the dance, she grew more used to his touch, and soon it was nothing but practical, something to keep her upright. Paige had read once about the fastest animals that had existed before the widespread nuclear fallout that was the Paterazm, and among them was a fascinating animal called the cheetah. As babies, cheetahs had looked like delicate, fuzzy creatures with whom she might have wanted to share a nap, but as they got older they turned into impossibly fast predators with sharp teeth that could easily cut flesh. Paige was always baffled that, fast as they were and dangerous as they could be, they hadn't survived what the Ancients had unleashed upon the world.

They would have been the first creatures she would have looked into if she'd been placed as a Research Scientist. A wave of disappointment rushed through her as she thought of Adam getting to wear that lab coat instead of her, "RS Adam" on the name badge instead of "RS Paige," but she swallowed it back down. This was why they hadn't selected her as the Ritualist, probably—her penchant for jealousy.

Adam bowed to Paige as the polka ended to thank her for the dance, and she bowed back. She laughed, more at-ease again; they exited the dance floor to catch their breath.

"Wanna walk for a minute?" asked Adam.

Paige hesitated, understanding—this *was* going where she thought it might. She felt part-flattered, part-nauseated.

Courage, she told herself. *You're going to have to buck up sometime.*

And another voice, less-welcome:

Boys only want one thing.

But Adam's hands were neatly tucked into his pockets. She'd known him for years. He seemed safe enough.

"Sure."

They walked in heightened silence along the well-worn path that lined the park's field, away from the crowds. Paige had always loved this path: it was composed as an art project in the early days of New Standard by the Saved and their followers. The path itself was a mosaic of different relics from the rubble of the Paterazm, broken and flattened into tiny pieces in catharsis of the sick world they escaped—pieces of shiny data discs catching the light between smashed bits of the fine china and plastic fibers of haute fashion and crumbles of unnaturally life-elongating pills, *poisons*, that the Ancients prized over their fellow humans; paper pulp from books that celebrated avarice in all its many, disgusting forms created a binding agent. Walking on it reminded Paige of all the work she'd done to distance herself from the Theorists who wanted to revert back to such a horrible, heartbreaking time—people who dared to undercut the Statutes for their own pleasure without a thought to the few humans who ensured the survival of all of humanity. It was noble work, saving humanity. But they were called to do it, and do it they would.

A few parents with younger kids ran around on the field, chasing the kids; Paige's gut panged with jealousy again. It had been so long since she and Sol had done that with Mama and Papa.

"I feel like I'm staring at my future," Adam said.

It didn't feel that way to Paige. She was staring at her past, her family's dirty legacy that she was supposed to fix, that she could have fixed if the Council had let her. But she said, "Yeah."

"Actually, I wanted to talk to you about that."

There it was. Paige's heart pounded as she yanked herself back into the moment here, with her friend. A boy.

"About . . . your future?"

"*The* future. Our future."

Our. Paige's spine became very rigid. Adam seemed nervous.

"I've been meaning to ask you," he said, staring at a particularly interesting hair at the top of her head, "Would you consider me?"

Paige blinked and stopped walking.

The word *consider* rang through her head on a repeated echo; she understood what he was asking her, had anticipated it, but it was impossible.

Consideration was for special people. Paige wasn't special.

She was average in every way and had never imagined that anyone would ever ask her to consider him, and that she'd simply mark "no preference" on her spousal application when the time came.

"I've wanted to ask you for a while," Adam babbled, scratching the back of his neck, "but I thought for sure they'd pick you as Ritualist, so I didn't want to get my hopes up . . ."

She couldn't process anything that was happening except in microimages that seemed to be overly elongated. Somewhere, in the back of her own head, she had felt words bubbling up while they were delivered out of Adam's mouth, the same way her hands would come up to brace herself if she were falling, about to hit the ground.

Adam *liked* her, in more than a friendly way, and she had an overwhelming urge to tuck herself beneath her skin and hide there. Everyone said that considerations were just for people who thought they might be good partners—nothing was guaranteed in a spousal application—but even Paige knew that considerations were really used to show interest in someone.

Interest of the sexual variety.

Adam wanted to have sex with her.

Only one thing.

Paige was going to be sick.

She supposed she should feel flattered. Why didn't she feel flattered? She felt like she was totally naked in front of him, despite that she was fully, modestly clothed. Her body felt too big for those clothes, like she'd been gluttonous and she'd been caught, like her stomach was bursting and even her skin couldn't stretch enough to cover it, leaving her organs exposed to oxygen.

She shouldn't have eaten that piece of cake.

A nearby a group of younger girls jumped rope in the lazy afternoon sun, chanting the nursery rhyme that had shaped Paige's own childhood: *Firetruck red, firetruck red, sound the warning bell.* The large, pyramid-shaped Renewal House in the distance behind them collected the sun with its solar panels, glimmering in the light: a beacon of the Statutes of Equality and the sheer beauty of everything they stood for, everything Paige wanted to be but was now sure she wasn't.

HOW TO ACHIEVE HAPPINESS

an excerpt from the Statutes of Equality

For many centuries, Friend, people have sought happiness. They have pondered, too, the differences in the influences of nature and nurture. They blamed their lack of self-control on the raw, animalistic violence of human nature. They also blamed the parents of a renegade for their failures, the communities around them for abandoning the needs of their citizens.

Some said that happiness could not be achieved because human nature made people competitive, and that competition led to motivation of the destruction of anyone who tried to get in the way of another's success.

Do not imitate the mindlessness of these lazy non-believers! Their penchant for blame removed their own responsibility for their own shortcomings. They lived in a community in which they were the only members. They were alone, and they were unhappy, for how can happiness be achieved without togetherness?

But, Friend, we have learned.

We know from their mistakes that collaboration is the path to pure happiness.

We know that happiness does not wear a mask of dishonesty but rather resides in the bases of our souls, only discoverable by working together in earnestness.

We must be honest about our failures, for it is through this that we can lift the blanket of guardedness to expose our vulnerability for happiness. Our nature as humans may be competitive, Friend, but the nature of happiness is vulnerable collaboration. It is only together that we can achieve our personal happiness; it is only through individual happiness that greatness can be truly attributed to a group of humans.

Therefore: We reject the plague of individualism that infected the Ancients who came before us, which led to the near-complete destruction of the world.

We commit to our firm belief that we have been chosen[1] to ensure the longevity of humankind on this Earth, and for the stewardship and repair of the Earth itself.

We pledge ourselves to our community, even and especially when it is difficult, and understand how crucial we and our philosophy are to the thriving and prevention of destruction of our neighbors.

And we promise to provide emotional and physical and spiritual support to any neighbors who might falter in these beliefs, for if they have faltered, we have failed.

Though we must heed caution in our trust that these neighbors will accept our help. For if they reject it repeatedly, we must accept that they have been infected by the same sickness of the Ancients. This sickness is a plague that we must not allow to infect our community. Therefore:

"It is better that one man should perish than a nation should dwindle and perish in unbelief."[2]

---

[1] We know ourselves to be the last set of humans that reside on this planet. We are a small community—only six thousand—and we have grown from a small but hardy team of founders who were spared in the midst of the massive death toll in the Paterazm that followed the Immortality Pandemic. The Paterazm destroyed the lives of everyone who sought immortality (and everyone around them) and dared to try to live beyond what a village could support and what an individual body could support.

Researchers have long searched for an alternative answer to how these Spared were able to survive. Historically, perhaps, "luck" may have been credited; but the Spared cited their daring act of trusting one another in an untrustworthy time as the reason they survived.

To this day, over a century later, we have not seen any other survivors. We can only operate by what we know worked for our Ancestors: the audacity of trust in one another, which translates into Love.

[2] From *The Book of Mormon*, 1 Nephi 4:13. This ancient religious text was hugely important to a large group of pre-war residents of our town. The passage quoted here tells the story of one man who is commanded by his deity to kill another man. At first glance, this story may seem violent, very much unlike New Standard's set of philosophy. But within the context of this story is that same trust of a being that guaranteed the protagonist's life, who protected that protagonist. That deity was a parent protecting all of its children, and children who disobeyed that deity were putting the other children at risk.

Come, Friend.
Let us be happy together.

Our Ancestors were spared for this very same purpose: to ensure the survival
not only of themselves, but of the future of all of human existence. In all
this time, there have been no others; therefore, we must not fail in our
quest to rebuild our species. We must succeed—or risk being completely
destroyed, with nothing left but our ashes to tell the tale of our history.

SEEK NOT AFTER YOUR OWN HEARTS AND EYES

Paige's insides squirmed with a burning, moving dissociation, her whole body high above her, watching the whole thing happen.

How long had he been thinking about this? Did anyone ever say no to these requests? Did anyone ever deny a potential shot at *choosing* their spouse, however slim the chance may be that the Council would agree that it was the right fit? She and Adam had been friends for a while; he was a known entity. And having a spouse meant eventually having sex with them, and as violating it sounded to have a boy's hands on her body, his fingers making their way over her hips and his penis between her bare legs, populating her body with sperm—she managed to refrain from shivering at the thought—she'd rather have Adam do that than someone she had hardly ever spoken to.

The jump-roping girls sang:

"Come on, Mama, come on, Papa, if you want to stay,
Speak your mind but I think you'll find that Theorists hold the blame."

She had to do this. She wasn't a Theorist. She wasn't Aunt Felicity. She was a regular, normal, age-seventeen now-woman and a boy was asking her to consider him and the discomfort she felt was nothing but nerves.

"Yeah," she said, pressing a smile into her cheeks. Maybe if her face made the motions, her neurons would push confidence through her body. "Sure. Let's do it."

Adam grinned more broadly than she'd ever seen him grin before. "Aw-awesome," he said, a little shakily—surprised by her answer, maybe?—like he'd been holding his breath. "Yeah. That's great."

He was kind of handsome like this, kind of sweet, his arms dropped by his sides awkwardly like he didn't know what to do with them. And the more she thought about it, the more she felt like it probably *would* be fine. She was now in a consideration, and so was he, and there it was: proof that she wasn't a Theorist, after all. Proof that she was nothing like Aunt Felicity at all, that her dream was nothing more than wisps of Paige's needless paranoia manifesting themselves into her psyche.

"Paige! Adam! Hey!"

Paige's stomach clenched as she recognized the voice as Mott's. She whirled around and saw Mott running swiftly up the path behind them; still, Mott's breath was totally even by the time she caught up to them, where Paige and Adam seemed slightly out of breath even though they'd only been standing there.

"I've been looking for you two," Mott said. "Your dad's looking for you."

"My dad?" Paige asked.

"No—Adam, I meant Adam. But if *you* want to head home, I'm about to walk in that direction."

"Oh, thanks." Adam's smile slipped. "I'll . . . take that as my exit, then. Congrats to you both, and peace be with you."

"You, too," Mott said, while Paige automatically replied, "And also with you."

He lingered there a moment more, staring at Paige like he wanted to say something else but couldn't gather up the courage. Then—before Paige realized what was happening—he took a step to close the gap between them and leaned his face into hers, pressing his lips briefly on her cheek in what felt more like a slightly-wet stamp on her face than anything else.

"I'll see you," he said when he pulled away, his smile spilling over his whole face, and he spun around to run back to the Peace Festival birthday party.

Mott was watching Paige carefully. Paige studied the corners of Mott's big lips—stretched over her teeth in a smile that didn't entirely seem like it was reflective of Mott's happiness—and the constellations of freckles spread across her nose and spattered onto her cheeks like a set of wings.

"What?" Paige said, hand reaching up toward her cheek on instinct. She touched the spot where Adam's lips had been gingerly, as if checking for blood.

Mott shrugged, closing her lips over her teeth, careful to not let the smile fade. She offered her arm to Paige in what was probably supposed to be a playful display but seemed . . . half-hearted, somehow. Like she was . . . disappointed? Angry? Unnerved? Disapproving? Paige wasn't sure whether she *should* take Mott's arm, but it seemed like a bigger deal if she didn't. She slipped her arm through Mott's and they linked elbows out of habit, but the inside of Paige's elbow seemed to burn where it touched Mott's warm skin.

"What do you mean, 'what'? That. *That. You* just got kissed. You just got *kissed.*"

It sounded incredulous; it felt like an accusation. Paige started sweating, felt her breathing shallow up, and not just because of the hot, early-spring sun. She tucked her hands in her skirt pockets as they started to walk alongside the buck brush, white flowers swaying airily in sidewalk planters. Thick, drooping clusters of poppies hung over the planters' sides, begging for a trim, reminding Paige of the weeds that grew longer and more unruly the further from the town borders they got.

Mott had once dared Adam to see how far they dared to go into the threat of residual radiation they'd heard so much about, even though it was pretty much all gone in the immediate vicinity. No one knew, for sure, what was out there beyond the invisible line marking the border that expanded further each year as the Excavation Crew cleaned up more and more land. They'd heard rumors of real, live animals, maybe mutated from what they looked like in history books; there were ghost stories of people who'd traveled from across the continent to find life, only to hear that they were rabid and wild by the time they met the border-CSes, and had to be put down. Mott had beat Adam then, getting within a hundred feet of the CS on duty there; Adam stopped at the abandoned storage yard across the cracked asphalt of Bullard Avenue, not daring to step over the obsolete arrows once-painted to tell automobiles where to go. Adam had bowed dramatically at Mott while Mott flailed her long limbs in a victory dance, and within thirty seconds the CS on duty was hollering at them to back away from the border for their own safety.

"I did," Paige managed meekly. Like she was also informing herself.

She stared at the ground, not sure what else to say. They were nearly to the edge of Serenity Park now. Her life felt surreal, like she was hovering somewhere above herself, watching a stranger in her body go through real, adult milestones.

"Well?" Mott demanded.

Paige hesitated; she'd rather listen to the shuffle of their feet on the ground. But finally she relented. "He wanted me to consider him."

"Consider him," echoed Mott.

"For espousement preference?"

"I know what consideration is."

It was said more sharply than Paige had been expecting. She squinted at their growing shadows on sidewalk. Mott's elbow felt stiff linked with her own.

"You sound annoyed."

"What? No." Mott shook her head, but when Paige looked up Mott's smile seemed glued on and her voice retained its edge. "It's just weird, I guess. What did you say?"

"Weird how?"

"What did you *say?*"

"I said yes."

There was no way Mott didn't know this. She was there when Adam had kissed her cheek, she'd watched it happen, but still for some reason she wanted Paige to confirm it aloud.

"You're being weird," Paige accused.

Mott fell quiet. They passed a group of kids sashaying in a circle with their hands joined in a classic Peace Festival game, singing,

"Round and round the Fresno trees, a CS chased a Theorist,
The Theorist died and nobody cried; next time we'll cleanse 'im!"

Paige shoved her hands into her dress pockets as they walked, remembering the tingling feeling of Mott's fingers at the zipper over her spine. Adam's kiss hadn't felt anything like that, which had been disorienting and guilt-inducing and strange, so maybe she'd really made the right choice. If a kiss didn't make her feel like her insides were wrenching themselves apart, then it must have been right. It was just lips on a cheek.

"It's just odd that Adam asked you now. It's like he's—I dunno, calling dibs on you or something."

An invisible metal rod jammed through Paige's heart, cold and hard. Mott was looking at something in the distance—at the old freeway overpass beyond the neighborhood, maybe. They were at the end of the street, turning the corner from McCaffrey onto Vartikian, the old sign of their street bearing the new white letters of its preserved old name.

Calling dibs. Dibs, like he owned her, like Chang had said the other night at the Ascension; Paige contained herself for the length of the time it took them to walk past the two tetriplexes before theirs, but once they got to the old door of their tetriplex she couldn't stop herself from yanking her arm away from Mott and cupping it protectively against her side.

Mott stood startled, her own arm hanging awkwardly out in an empty, broken diamond.

"What?"

Paige took a deep breath. And another one. She swallowed down her instinct to lash out at the one person who was always on her side no matter what, the one person she trusted her whole self with, who happened to be poking at insecurities beneath Paige's skin during the time Paige needed encouragement the most. She thought carefully about her words, took another breath before saying them. "No one *owns* me."

Mott stared at her a moment, big eyes carefully studying Paige from under thick eyelashes. Then she sprayed a harsh laugh through her teeth.

"Does Adam know that?"

The rod jammed deeper, splitting Paige's spine apart. She yanked open the door and started climbing the old, carpeted stairs, not caring if the door shut Mott out of the building. The smell of dusty carpet was familiar and comforting in a way that Mott wasn't right now.

But the door didn't slam behind her, and she could hear Mott's footsteps definitively behind her, the stairs giving muffled creaks with every step they took.

"Why?" she asked over her shoulder, marching up the stairs. "Why are you being such a—a—" She paused at the top of the stairs and whirled around. "Are you *jealous?*"

Mott narrowed her eyes at her from the penultimate step up. "Jealous of what? Your early, loveless, *blindly* devoted espousement? I think not."

Every word burrowed into Paige's gut deeper and deeper, tugging forward as if it aimed to turn her inside-out. Mott's tetriplex unit was the door to Paige's left; Paige's was the door to her right, and she could just walk away, only an arm's reach to the handle. But she rooted her feet into the ground a moment longer. Mott was supposed to be her best friend. The only person who knew her, who really loved her for who she was.

"You know what I think?" Paige said, trying not to let her voice shake, but Mott crossed her arms over her chest—

"I don't care what you think," a bald-faced lie, her shoulders hunching forward to prove it, so Paige barreled on, not trying to practice the patience she'd learned from the Statutes, because *screw* patience when the only person other than Sol she loved more than anything was hurting her on purpose—

"I think you're not as brave as you think you are. I think you're jealous and you're too scared to admit it. I think you're as nervous about espousement and responsibilities and crap and you're pretending not to be, but it's all a lie, and I think Adam is being a better friend than you're being right now, because at least he's trying to give me a *choice.*"

Mott's lips thinned out across her face as she pressed them together in a pitying smile. Between blinks, her eyes shifted their hardness to something softer, but distant.

"None of this is a choice," she said. She quietly pushed past Paige up the final two steps, opened the door to Paige's left, Mott's right; she stepped through and closed it behind herself with a definitive *click.*

Paige stared at the empty stairwell in front of her and her knees buckled. She grabbed the banister for support as she lowered herself to the ground, curled her knees up to her chest and smushed her face to her knees, salty tears coating her face and her legs at the same time.

She should be happy, she reminded herself. Happy whether she was chosen for Ritualist or wasn't. Happy to be have someone she knew ask for her consideration.

Be grateful, she told herself. *You live protected.*

She'd seen the old photos from the Paterazm of bodies littering entire cities. She had life, and there were so many who had died.

She breathed in a long breath—five beats—and then held it for five more beats, and then exhaled for another five, repeating the sequence over and over until her heart rate slowed and she could think. The quiet, only interrupted by the sounds of her own deep breathing, pressed waves of calm over her shoulders.

Ocean breath, they called it during meditation. But it was all theoretical. Paige had never heard an ocean.

What would Adam's feet sound like on the floor of their would-be tetriplex? Would they have a couch like Mama's floral sofa, for which Mama'd spent years collecting luxury coupons? Paige couldn't even imagine what Adam might spend his coupons on. The truth was: even knowing him for all these years, even growing up together, she barely knew him at all.

Who did she really *know*?

Mott.

And there it was. That flicker of pain again that caught her breath in her throat and pushed further tears down the middle of her face and swept them back into her nostrils as she tried to catch her breath. It was something about— about rejection, maybe. Like somehow Mott was rejecting her, only she hadn't actually said anything to that effect.

She hadn't said *anything*. She'd let Paige talk, let her say stupid things that never should have been said, and then shamed her for doing what she was supposed to do.

Paige wiped the tears from her face. She let the furious energy rise up within her chest, hot and smoky.

But it died as quickly as it came up. It took too much energy to be angry. It was Peace Festival. A time of rest. So she would rest.

She stood back up and brushed herself off, let herself into her unit, and headed straight for her room. It was the middle of the day, but who cared? She could afford herself a nap. She didn't need Mott. She didn't need anyone. She could take care of herself until she was an age-sixty and ready for Ascension. And then, in the Afterlands, she could do what she wanted to do, be what she wanted to be, and no one could stop her.

When she woke, groggy and disoriented, the sky outside her window was dark, maybe around four or five hours after midnight. So much for a nap. Dawn still nestled behind the distant valley mountains, but even without the the sun the town still trapped the heat, suffocating and stagnant.

Her underknees were sticky with sweat. Her shoulders and hips ached from too much sleep, from trying to find a comfy spot even after she could sleep no more. How many hours before she had to report for administrative functions for her new responsibility? Three? Four? She couldn't possibly stay in bed that long.

She got up, let herself out onto the porch that connected the two top units; at least here there was open air, however little actually flowed.

But Mott had beaten her to it, already leaning over the railing in hopes of any sort of slight breeze washing over her face. She snapped her head around at the noise, fixating on her for a moment with an empty gaze.

"Hi," Paige offered.

Mott turned back around to staring out over the railing. "Hi."

This was their ritual: if they couldn't sleep, they met on Paige's side of the balcony that connected their two units and watched the candles blow out in the windows of the tetriplexes lining their street—except now all of the candles were long extinguished, the quiet street waiting for the sun to start a new year. Mott had long stopped trying to convince Paige that she wasn't going to get in trouble if she climbed over the railing to Mott's side of the balcony, especially when the rest of their neighborhood was asleep; for Paige to be outdoors at all was already a test of her courage. It didn't matter how many times Mott told her that there was no Statute that required that they stay indoors at all times after curfew, or reminded her that it was *her own balcony,* where she *lived.* Mott let it go most of the time because she was a good friend, because she knew how important it was to Paige to become the Ritualist and redeem her family's past.

Mott did not move. She would not look at her, even when Paige leaned against the railing next to her in a move of proposed reconciliation. Mott kept her face and body forward, angled away from Paige, and Paige had the distinct feeling that the restless girl she'd always known and loved no longer squirmed under the skin of the stranger next to her.

"You're up early," Mott observed instead.

This was good. She was talking to her.

"You are, too," Paige returned.

"Couldn't sleep."

"Yeah."

Silence while Paige worked up the courage to say what needed to be said—

"I'm sorry."

She felt better saying it. But Mott waved her apology aside. "I was being a jerk. Isn't there a line in the Statutes about that? *Jerks beget jerks?*"

"I believe it's, *the jerk hath been begotten by the jerk.*"

Mott laughed. It was a soft laugh, a short one, but it was gentle—nothing like the harsh one from a few hours ago. The prickling on Paige's skin lessened completely now; she could feel the hole inside her closing up, healing.

How many times had they curled up together on this balcony under the blanket on the back of the loveseat behind them now, watching the stars move like they had endless time left? Mott usually said something stupid like "wow, you rebel" whenever Paige answered the secret knock by coming outside. It was a joke, but Paige would puff herself up with pride and reply, "rebel without a cause," even though she barely knew what that meant.

Mott sighed loudly and with her exhale went most of the tension between them. Paige turned to grab the woven blanket from the loveseat and drape it across her shoulders and Mott's as they leaned over the railing together once more. It was thin and had worn a few holes onto its perimeter, but it had been around for ages. Papa had spent a few luxury coupons on it when Paige had first been born, but it exclusively sat out on this balcony, and no one used it other than Mott. It even smelled like Mott, whatever she put into her thick, tightly-coiled hair to keep it soft. Some sort of nut oil, probably, warm and half-sweet. Paige could smell it now as she let her head fall on Mott's shoulder, the rest of the tension between them gone when Mott reciprocated, laying her head on top.

"I guess this is it. Here we are, in adulthood. Charging forward."

"Into the vast unknown," Paige murmured.

"Yes, so unknown," said Mott. "We have *no idea* what's mapped out for us in our highly prescribed future."

"Look," Paige said, "just because we're moving on to ECPA doesn't mean there won't be surprises. Or that we won't be amazing at it."

"Ek-pah?"

"Espousement, childbirth, parenthood, Ascension."

Mott snorted, lifting her head up to look down at Paige with a mock frown. "Don't abbreviate things. It's weird."

"Oh, what, I can't be cool?" Paige shimmied. "And hip? With the kids?"

This time, Mott's laugh was wholehearted. "Oh, mercy, please never shimmy again."

"I will shimmy if I like."

Mott was still laughing, throwing her head back like she'd never laughed before. Paige was laughing, too, and it was like all the muscles in her body were finally relaxed, and everything was normal. She felt warm with a mounting security, a tingling calm all over her brain. She shimmied into Mott's face but didn't anticipate Mott whipping her head back up right at that moment, both of them stopping as they realized there wasn't more than an inch between their noses.

Mott smelled a little like honey.

"Oh, sorry," she said.

"I'll stop," Paige replied, breathless, expecting Mott to pull away, or to say something again that felt like more rejection.

But Mott didn't move.

"Please don't."

Paige's fingers felt prickly and she couldn't look away from Mott and the air was warm but she was hot, uncomfortably hot, and part of her wanted to throw up but most of her never wanted Mott to go anywhere else.

Mott ran her tongue over her lips and a sheen of saliva spread over them and memories of their childhood flooded Paige's head: of rain, and of ice pops, and of tea, and of how nice all of those things were when combined, how safe it all felt, alternating between licking an ice pop and sipping tea while sitting on the balcony under the roof in the rain like they did when they were kids, watching the rain douse the world in its protective shimmering veil, the perfect balance of hot from the warm ceramic and cold from ice that melted into juice at just the right moment when hitting your tongue—

—and all of those things with Mott—

The heat that Paige felt now radiated from Mott's skin. It was so nice, neurons firing around in her brain in a pleasant breath; she tried to look away from Mott but couldn't. Mott kept eye contact, even as she lowered her face toward Paige's and Paige could have cried because this was exactly what she wanted in her life, and she couldn't help but wonder why she couldn't just be espoused with Mott instead, they could be so good together—

But why not?

She'd been rejected as the Ritualist. She'd done something wrong. What was the point of even being the good little community member anymore? If she was flawed enough to not be chosen, then she was in need of redemption, and she might as well lean into the need for that redemption in the first place.

Every inch of her body was on fire. She didn't breathe. Mott was moving slowly, and Paige was, too, on nothing but instinct alone, and she closed her eyes to inhale Mott's fresh-linens-and-almond-oil scent, to taste it as their lips began to meet, to graze together in the gentlest, most magnificent touch that Paige had never known she wanted but now knew she didn't want to live without—

And then—

A blasting, blaring alarm, an explosion of sound, and it was everywhere, so loud that she saw Mott mouthing something but couldn't hear what she was saying.

What? What did you say? Paige tried to say, shouting as loud as she could, but no sound made it through the drowning wail of the alarm pulsing through the loudspeakers throughout the town. And in between pulses, a disembodied voice instructed, with no room for argument:

"All citizens report immediately to the dining hall. Repeat: all citizens report immediately to the dining hall. This is not a drill."

THE SOLACE

a handwritten note

the screams of our ancestors echo
across the empty desert plains
there is no one left but us
we refuse
to fall prey
to their temptations
it was
their weakness
their selfishness
that nearly removed us all
but history has taught us that
peace is in our hands and i tell
you friend that the key to peace is

the key to peace is

BLESSED ARE THE PURE

Someone had seen them.

Except, no—no one had seen them. No one was even outside right now. It was dark. No one *could* have seen them.

Guilt instantly festered in Paige's gut—*you're going to be cleansed, you're going to be cleansed*, it said to her—but she forced it out. She was just a regular citizen. She wasn't a troublemaker. Everything was going to be fine.

Except that there was an emergency.

There had never been an emergency before in all of Paige's life. She'd always done drills. Drills for fire, for an earthquake, for an external attack even though no one had ever come from outside the borders before, but nothing real. Always just-in-case.

Well. Here was the case.

"Shit," said Mott. "If your parents ask, we were just having tea."

A plausible explanation, and something they'd done a hundred times, so Paige was sure her parents wouldn't ask, but a stray worry that they didn't have any mugs out there tugged at her brain. But there was no time to think about it. She felt the panic radiating off Mott, too. She felt it crawl under her own arm hair and sneak under her epidermis.

Paige grabbed Mott's arm, held her steady for a moment with a calm she'd never known she had.

"Hey," she said. "It's going to be okay."

Mott looked like she was about to cry for a moment, but then the look disappeared and her voice came out annoyed. "I know."

Defensive Mott. *Now* who was terrible in a crisis?

Paige would have rolled her eyes at this, but her heart hammered in her chest, her whole body tingling from the almost-kiss and the potential of getting caught and her mind spinning from trying to find some sort of plausible excuse as to why her mind had even thought about kissing Mott in the first place. Her parents and Sol came out, half-dressed, and then there was Mott's family, too, and all the tetriplex porches and balconies in the neighborhood flooded with people, all of them shouting uselessly to be heard over the noise and the fear, and Paige could see them mouthing things like, *Are you okay?* and *What's going on?* and *Is this a drill?*

"THIS IS NOT A DRILL," the voice on the loudspeaker repeated.

She tried to push down the thoughts that this was the moment they'd been dreading, that Theorists were attacking and they could be anywhere, anyone. Sol grabbed Paige's hand and Paige squeezed it tight and Mott and her family rushed alongside them; together they waded through the frenzy of panicked neighbors down the sidewalk and back toward Serenity Park, funneling in through the four sets of doors leading into the giant hall, the alarm still loud and blaring and everywhere. People had given up talking, just tried to find seats as EAs ushered them all in and scrambled to arrange the last of the very chairs they'd put away only hours ago from the Peace Festival.

The hall filled in minutes. Paige found a seat between Mott and Sol, Sol squeezing her hand even tighter. They'd had enough drills as a community that everyone knew what to do, everyone cooperated and listened and filed into their seats in an orderly fashion, despite the ringing chaos of the noise. Some of the littlest kids made faces at each other to entertain themselves, like they normally did in drills. But their parents' faces did not contain the calm they would have in a practice.

As the last of the citizens fell into their seats the Matriarch stepped onto the stage, her whole face open and wide. She seemed to float, a ghost in white, only ghosts weren't real and this apparently was.

The alarm finally stopped, the hush that followed deafening for a moment until broken by squeaking chairs and crying babies. One young man in the row in front of Paige whispered something into his spouse's ear and handed her the whimpering baby he held; the spouse nodded and cradled the baby in the corner of her elbow and swiftly lifted her shirt, pulled down her undergarment to expose her breast, and shoved her nipple in the baby's mouth. The Matriarch adjusted the microphone on the stand. It whined in feedback, but the baby didn't seem to care; it sucked hungrily on its mama like a leech.

"I'm sorry for waking you all up," said the Matriarch, rubbing her face like the whole community was a headache she couldn't shake. Paige had never seen her so unkempt before, her single-lidded eyes bloodshot and tired, her dark, straight hair pulled back in a low ponytail with flyaways instead of the sleek, voluminous mane that usually framed her round face.

The Matriarch paused, and in this pause Paige was able to see her leader's hands shaking. Whatever this was, it was bad.

Theorists. It had to be Theorists.

And the Theorists were herself and Mott.

Paige felt sick: it was Aunt Felicity all over again. She'd fallen into it despite her best efforts, despite trying to cram the delicious safety and comfort and general wonderfulness of being around Mott down, way down in the pits of her body, in places that never saw the light of day. This was why she hadn't been selected as Ritualist: they knew she would crack eventually, and now she and Mott would serve as exemplars for the community. They were going to be cleansed.

Paige held her breath. Next to her, Mott was perfectly still. Paige didn't dare reach out to hold Mott's hand.

The Matriarch clasped her hands together, each palm clinging to the other. An EA hurried up the side steps to the stage to hand her a piece of paper, and the Matriarch bowed her head in thanks and held the paper—forcing her hands to be steady—up to her eye level, covering most of her face.

" 'This morning, at approximately oh-four-hundred hours, we received a report that the Ritualist was missing from her residence. Civil Servants promptly performed a thorough search of the town and within five miles of the outskirts and found no sign of her.'"

Ingrid?

Missing?

Where was there to go?

No one said anything, but the tension was audible in nervous feet, restless wringing hands. She and Mott were safe.

But what about the whole community? Was Ingrid even alive? How were they going to survive without a Ritualist? How would their souls be saved? How would they gain entrance to the Afterlands?

" 'One canteen of water was stolen from the emergency pack in her family's residence. She is presumed to have run away, and if she is not dead already, we assume she will be within three days from dehydration.'"

She didn't even take the whole emergency pack?

Dead. Assumed dead. It seemed too clinical. Just facts, only words. Everyone around Paige seemed to be processing in individual whispers among their own family units and neighbors, as if they could no longer trust anyone not in their immediate vicinity, the speculation bubbling and taking over like too much soap in the laundry could drown a whole room.

Theorist, she could hear in the hush of fear. The hissing *s* sliced through the dining hall, like the word was a sword that could cut through the threat before them. Like it was a shield that could protect them from infection.

Theorist.

But out loud, there were rituals to be followed. Words to be chanted. One person started saying *mercy*, and the rest of the community peppered in, "Mercy rest—"

"We will *not* wish mercy for the soul of Ingrid-of-2123," the Matriarch declared, looking up from the paper. Paige was half-startled, half-impressed by the power the Matriarch had to command the crowd in an instant. The Matriarch's face had changed from exhausted to fierce, eyes determined and alert now, her wide mouth strictly downturned. "She has abandoned her responsibility and betrayed her community. As a community, however, we will offer our love and support to her estranged 0-family, and lift them up together."

There was a confused pause. Then a solitary voice started to say, "We lift them up," and others haphazardly joined in.

"We lift them up," affirmed the Matriarch, gaining speed and rhythm, lifting her chin up so the tendons in her neck seemed sharper and more powerful, "and we persist through this time of trouble. We value their contributions to our community, the wonders they have provided us as a whole, and we offer them as much peace as we can muster in unity."

"We lift them up!" declared the community together. Paige felt the words somehow escaping her mouth on an inhale, the rise in energy levels throughout the dining hall happening so quickly that she could only process the moment by being swept up in it. She'd been abandoned. Ingrid had abandoned her. She'd been betrayed, but everyone else had stayed. So what if the Ritualist had gone? Together, the citizens of New Standard— herself included—could achieve the impossible. After all, their founders—the Spared—had made a functional collaborative society in the faces of those who doubted them.

There was a part of her that was terrified about the loss of Ingrid's soul in addition to her own. Ingrid's betrayal meant that she would be lost forever, into the abyss with the Ancients, and her soul would never remain intact like the rest of New Standard's followers' would. It would disintegrate, becoming nothing but dust. She and everything she had previously lived for would cease to exist. What was the point of living if your soul was to become nothing when you died? It seemed like wasted time. Wasted energy. And Paige and the rest of New Standard had a higher purpose than that.

" 'It is in this unity,'" continued the Matriarch, looking back at her paper, " 'that we are good neighbors, now more than ever. We do *not* crumble. We do *not* die. We create opportunity: in this case, the opportunity to make each other free through love.'"

The crowd clapped.

" 'Despite her sin,'" said the Matriarch, her voice quiet now, the audience freshly hushed, " 'We thank Ingrid for her life. Her death is precisely what we aim to eliminate: the horrors of having to die alone, in a traumatic situation, without the love that our dedicated community provides like a neverending fountain. This form of death that she chose for herself is filled with terror, fear, and unimaginable pain. We, the community, regret not having been able to utilize the Statutes that we practice to provide for her, to relieve her pain.'"

More clapping, and a few people shouted, *yes!* in various locations throughout the vast room. It was betrayal, but betrayal was a tragedy. A failure of the community's system. A rejection of the love that provided for them all. Paige felt the guilt resurrect in her gut—partially because underneath the fear that Ingrid was not okay, there was a persistent, lurking relief that she and Mott were. She was still sitting between Mott and Sol, the latter of whom was very still. Paige squeezed his shoulder, but Sol only managed a wrenched quarter-smile.

" 'But we will not fail in continuing to provide for the rest of our brothers and sisters. Per the Statutes: Should a Ritualist be unexpectedly deceased, the Council shall make a new selection. It is imperative that a Ritualist offers herself as a sacrifice to the Afterlands each year. Therefore we, the Council, have decided on a replacement for Ingrid.' "

Replacement?

" 'The Council has therefore chosen a Ritualist to take Ingrid's place. We announce our new Ritualist to be Paige.' "

Paige craned her neck to look around herself, waiting for the new Ritualist to stand up.

But no one rose.

People from her cohort began to turn in their seats to stare.

At her.

"Paige, will you please come forward?" said the Matriarch.

Paige blinked. She'd thought she'd heard her own name in the echo that followed the speech, but she was sure she'd imagined it. The stares flushed her face with heat as she started thinking about whether she should walk up there or stand for a moment and sit down again, and whether anyone would resent her for taking Ingrid's place, or whether they thought her capable of such a thing, since apparently she'd been too flawed to be selected in the first place. She dared not seek Papa's pleased honor now, lest anyone else should see what would surely be his excitement in the midst of a tragic moment, especially not with this rising nausea that came up in waves again and again.

She had almost betrayed her community, too. She had almost lost her faith. She had almost become completely impure.

Did this mean she was pure after all?

Second-best pure?

Pure with a few flecks?

The worst part was that she didn't know what Mott was thinking, and now her guilt over the near-kiss with Mott was overtaking her body like a swarm of fire ants. She hadn't abandoned her Statutes after all, no matter how much she wanted to. She could still be the savior of the community.

Now she had the reality she'd wanted all along.

The Matriarch's fingers, long and spindly, clutched the paper like it was keeping her alive. Slowly, Paige stood. Her feet started moving. The ground was thick beneath her, very solidly attached to the earth.

She should have been honored that they thought her so strong. So worthy. Honored that she could be Agatha's and Ingrid's replacement, stepping onto the same stage where a person of such dignity had, every year, been glorified with the early light of the Afterlands.

There one moment, gone the next.

Mott did not grasp her hand as she stepped away from her row and into the aisle. Paige supposed she should be feeling elation, acceptance, pride—but all she could think about was how distant Mott was now, how distant she would be, how she'd escaped her fate with Adam but had to shove down everything within her that she and Mott had nearly admitted to each other that they felt, too.

She should have been happy.

The only noise in those few moments was the nearly silent brush of her own footsteps as they carried her toward the stage, heel-toe, fingers grasping at the hem of her sleep-shirt, and if she'd been able to move any part of her face without crying she would have laughed to herself at the thought that she'd almost believed that freedom was a thing she could have.

ON THE STRENGTH OF THE MIND

an excerpt from the Statutes of Equality

Take notice, Friend, how your body responds to your mind. They are both one and the same and separate from each other, and you have control over them both. Think, and you shall do; act, and you shan't think.

And it is because we control our minds that we provide this static control over ourselves. When our bodies respond to instinct we stop them and remind ourselves that instinct is what brought us war. We separate individual desire from what is best for the Whole.

We give our selves to each other, Friend. And here I tell you that you have the divine power to say no. When your body tells you it would prefer not to wake up, you command it to rise; when it tells you it would rather love another of the same sex, you remind it that is not wise. The best method for survival is logic and calculation—and the love that supports it. That love is selfless and kind. The pleasure of selfishness is irrelevant and must be ignored.

Take that pleasure and push it away. Grind it under the dirt beneath your feet and dust it with the ash settled in the Earth's ruins. For pleasure is not what moves us along; pleasure is what keeps us behind.

AS IRON SHARPENS IRON

IT WAS EVERYTHING PAIGE had ever wanted and all she could do was observe the emptying dining hall as people swarmed out like ants to go back to bed. Blank wall behind her, simple brown trim on the bottom of the walls; open, and empty, but somehow heavy as fewer and fewer people filled it up, without the sunbeams that would start piercing through the window in an hour or two. She stood on the stage in the dining hall, the EAs stacking chairs and clearing the microphone system off the stage, the triangle Ritualist pin she'd coveted for so long *finally* pinned to *her* shirt—her sleep shirt, but her shirt nonetheless—and she could do nothing but breathe and blink.

The Matriarch approached her quietly. Like a dream. She said something, but Paige hadn't understood.

"Sorry?" Paige said.

"Are you okay," the Matriarch repeated.

It wasn't a question. Paige shrugged. She couldn't process anything. She didn't have a real answer.

And anyway, did her answer matter? She was the Ritualist now. The last Ritualist was dead at best, a Theorist at worst. Paige *had* to be okay.

"Sure."

The word seemed to be swallowed by the echoing, empty acoustics. Six thousand people had fit in this room, albeit tightly;

they were gone now, and it was all up to her to protect all of their souls from hate. From death.

From destruction.

Mercy *hell*. Just when she'd decided that she could own up to the feelings that had been plaguing her.

Where was that sense of purpose? Why was it covered by something grossly sticky, something she couldn't identify—

Or she could identify it, but she didn't want to, because it was shameful: ref

Disappointment.

She eyed the door, out of which the last stragglers were trailing. Her body's flight instinct was burning, burning, urging her to move, but she made herself stand still. Mott had been one of the last people to leave, had given her a meaningful glance as she made her way out the door—one that said they would be talking later. Everything inside Paige vibrated frantically and she forced her body to stay, clenched her tendons tight, so that she wouldn't act on the wild fantasy flooding through her brain right now: catching up with Mott and grabbing her and getting out of this place together, finding some sort of time machine, rewinding to an hour ago when Mott was about to kiss her and she was about to kiss Mott and pick a different ending. Ignore the alarm. Wait for everyone else to assemble to the dining hall and kiss Mott soundly, to hell with it, who was even sure salvation was really possible in the first place? And then they would run away from the community, beyond the borders, into whatever radioactive remainders still plagued the outskirts of New Standard, letting it turn them to ash because Paige was certain that would be worth the momentary elation of being able to acknowledge the feelings she'd had for Mott, call them what they really were, and have them returned in reality.

It felt strangely freeing. Like she didn't have to press a misshapen rock down her esophagus when she felt that tinge of something delicious, an extra slice of cake. Attraction, she guessed it was. What else could it be? She wanted to go into that moment with just Mott and her on the balcony and no one else; to ignore everything and everyone and block out the world and exist in that space by themselves forever.

This was what Aunt Felicity must have felt like.

The wave of guilt crashed over her again—they had the wrong girl. If she loved Mott like that, she was a Theorist, and she deserved to be cleansed for the good of the community. She would have to sacrifice herself.

But then again, she could hear Mott arguing, wasn't serving as the Ritualist a sacrifice, too? Wasn't it exactly in line with what the Statutes said about filtering your instincts but still acknowledging them? She felt a certain way, but she wasn't acting on it, and that was how she was going to be pure. That was how she was going to earn her own redemption from these sticky, impure feelings.

The last person left and closed the door behind him. The hall was empty now except for the Matriarch and Paige. The Matriarch stared over at the window, sighing impatiently. Paige had always had a hazy, glowing dream of meeting the Matriarch in this very situation: witnessing the Matriarch's impossible perfection up close, learning from the great Statutes wisdom she might bestow upon Paige if she ever had a chance to meet her alone.

But here the Matriarch was now, in the flesh, quiet and silent and distinctly ordinary. She seemed weary: her otherwise dark, sleek hair was interrupted by slivers of gray here and there; her milky skin was a little oily in some places and flaking off in others. Her words seemed unremarkable, too. Ordinary. Unmagical.

"We don't have much time," she said—practical, unceremonious, human. "The sun will be up in three hours, and we need to be starting the Procession around then." Her attention snapped back to Paige, looking as though the whole situation and the whole world around them was one giant mess for her to clean up herself. "Go home. Gather up your personal items, say your goodbyes. One of the CSes will be by your tetriplex unit to pick you up in thirty minutes."

Thirty minutes. It seemed like a joke. Thirty minutes to say good-bye to the forty-two years she'd never have, years she hadn't cared about up until an hour and a half ago. Then a year of constant supervision, and then Ascension—without anyone she loved.

Then the waiting.

Forty-two years before Mott could join her in the Afterlands, until they could be together. Paige would wait. She would be patient. She'd wait, in her crisp, clean Afterlands cottage with all sorts of books to keep her company, and she'd read them, and re-read them, and re-read them again, until their pages were stained and torn and falling from broken bindings, until she couldn't be patient anymore, and just when she was about to crack from forced eternal happiness, she'd read them again.

She wondered whether she would feel the time pass in the Afterlands or if it was a space of timelessness. It seemed suffocating that way, but she didn't know what to expect. No one ever talked about that part. But time was just an obstacle. It would pass eventually. Eventually Mott would be there.

Eventually she'd come.

———

AN UNCOMFORTABLE QUIET SETTLED on the surface of the carpet in the tetriplex living room. Mama collapsed in the rocking chair in the corner as soon as they had got in the door, silent except for the weary wooden creaking of the chair as she rocked it, self-soothing. Solomon looked even more gangly than usual with his hair plastered to his face like it was now from the heat, stood halfway between the door and the kitchenette, hesitant, hovering. Papa was beaming.

"My little girl," he said, reaching his arms out toward Paige. She obliged and leaned into the hug; he held her close to his chest and she melted into the nostalgic comfort, like he had when she was little, when she'd fallen off the slide and skinned her knee, when someone had made fun of her for being *so* devout. "I'm so thrilled."

He released her and held her at arm's length. She forced a smile.

"Happy to serve my community."

Solomon swallowed a drink of water. His mouth said: "Congratulations."

His face said: *You're leaving me.*

Paige pushed the guilt away, trying not to look at Solomon. A line from the Statutes appeared clearly in her head. It rang incorrect, though she knew it was right:

The suffering of one is so much less than the suffering of the many.

"Thanks," she said, though she didn't want congratulations. She didn't want ceremony.

Mama remained silent.

Wasn't she happy? In twenty-two minutes, Paige would be the symbol of the community first, their daughter second. As their child, she had been obedient and practiced Love; as the Ritualist, she would do the same thing.

"This is it, I guess," Mama said.

"I'm so *proud* of you," said Papa, flitting around the kitchen to put on a kettle. "*Ritualist.* You *did* it."

Paige pressed her lips together in a forced smile. "I think I'm going to go lie down."

"You can hardly believe it, either," Papa said, laughing. "I understand."

He didn't, but she didn't correct him.

"You don't want to play a last game of Tlenga?" said Sol.

If the way Solomon looked at her were physical, it would have been his arm darting out and grabbing hers, bruising the skin above her humerus in the process. Her lungs felt like they were shriveling like grapes in the sun, leaving behind nothing but a tiny, sad, black husk of the fruit she used to be.

"Sorry," she said, fighting back tears. "I'm exhausted."

"Let her rest, Solomon," said Papa. "She's got a long day ahead of her."

Paige nodded. "Yeah. Thanks."

To the credit of Sol's self-restraint, he didn't follow her when she turned and headed into her room and shut the door behind her. She leaned her back against the door, sliding down onto the ground, and tried not to think about everything she was about to lose.

So *had* she been pure enough after all? Or was she speckled with flaws, and they thought that was better than no Ritualist at all?

She could hear her family murmuring through the door.

"Go to your room, Solomon," she heard Mama say.

"Why? All I said was—"

"I know. You didn't say anything wrong. Just go somewhere else."

"It's dark outside. Nothing opens for another hour—"

"*Out.* To the park, the lights are on there. With Rory. Whatever. Anywhere that isn't here." The patience in her voice chipped off crisply, and she seemed to be trying to swallow her weariness.

The front door opened, then closed sharply. Paige heard Mama sniffling, like she was allergic to something and it was getting into her eyes. Only Mama didn't have allergies, and even if she did the medics would have given her an injection already, because that was what medics did. They fixed broken things.

"She's—" Mama said, giving up now.

Crying.

Mama was crying?

"I know," said Papa.

"She was supposed to—"

"I know."

"It hardly seems—"

"I know."

"You know. You know. You're just going to stand there and tell me you *know.*" Her voice old honey, worn rags. "I'm so tired."

Papa didn't say anything. Mama sobbed into the quiet. Paige didn't hear Mama cry often and it was startling now, a break from the firm, no-nonsense way she normally handled other people, like she was invulnerable to anything they could throw at her. This was the side of Mama she hardly saw, the Mama whose persistence wasn't unending after all, the Mama who was not the perfect practitioner of the Statutes but who struggled and challenged and failed.

She'd caught a glimpse of that Mama when they were on their way to the Ascension the other night. The soft Mama, the one who rarely showed public displays of affection but who'd looked at her that night with the strangest expression and kissed the top of her head.

I am so lucky to have you, you know that? she'd said.

Paige put her hand on top of her head now, wanting to feel Mama press another kiss in her hair.

"You're grieving," Papa said, "It's okay. This is a natural part of practicing love."

Paige thought that if she shut her eyes tight enough she could bring Ingrid back from the outskirts, from the dead, make all of it go away. There was something wrong about Mama crying. Paige wanted her nagging voice back, her croons of *Smooth your hair out, Paige,* and, *Your shirt is untucked, dear,* and *Where are your Statutes? Did you leave them in the laundry again?*

"Fuck you, Phillip."

It stung Paige's ears. Hit her chest. She'd imagined that. She had to have imagined that. Papa was silent.

"*Natural.*" Mama laughed like she was spitting out dirt. "You think this life is natural?"

"Keep your voice down."

"You know what's natural, Phillip?"

"*Naomi.*"

"Animals. Natural selection. Murder."

"Remember your Statutes, Naomi."

"What, *keep sweet? Hold thy tongue? Shove thy head up thine own ass?*"

"Naomi, shut *up.* You don't know who can hear you."

"What does it matter? Our daughter's getting taken away from us and all you can think about is what the neighbors will think? It's Xenia and Gentry. They're practically Theo—"

"How they decide to live their lives is not our decision. We lead by example."

"And just what sort of example are we setting for the rest of the community, hmm? 'Let them take your child after they've lost someone else's'? And what sort of Statute would that lead to?"

"And just *what* do you suggest we do about it?"

Paige hugged her legs, grateful for the door supporting her back. This she was used to, one of her parents finally outshouting the other, or both of them giving up when they had exhausted themselves. She had already decided that when she was assigned a spouse, she was going to do things differently. But now it didn't matter.

Now Mama was talking like she'd never talked before. No talk of Statutes-come-first. No beratements of shirt-tucking. Just rage. Anger at an injustice. Accusing the Council of said injustice.

Mama had gone wild.

And Papa talking about Mott's parents like that—like they were misguided children due for a visit with Sister Nadine—

They were just words in her brain. Everything was just words in her brain.

"We're capable of moving beyond our instincts, Naomi. That's what makes us human."

"Then I should just let her go, then? I should leave her without a fight?"

"Careful with that terminology—"

"*Fight* is not a dirty word, Phillip. It's a laugh. There's no fighting here, sure, except with us, huh? No freedom, either."

Freedom. It seemed like such a faraway concept. None of the world around her even seemed real. Paige was floating above them all, watching everything happen from a distance.

"You're sounding like Xenia—"

"Like a Theorist, you mean. *Say it.*"

"I didn't say that."

"Theorists are just mothers who love their daughters, Phillip. There's going to be another war, if that's how the thinking's going. All this work for nothing. And you—you're going to be the one to invite it."

Mama loved her?

More than the active way they were all supposed to love everyone?

So much that it made her cry?

"Naomi—"

"Fuck this. Fuck all of this."

For a moment all the noise stopped. Then the door opened again. Then it shut again. Then there was nothing.

Paige sat there in the nothingness. The silence was still; the air was still; she was still. Here, in the stillness, she was safe.

She heard Papa shuffle down the hallway into his and Mama's room, the gentle *click* of the door closing behind him. This wasn't how it was supposed to have happened. She was supposed to have come home and played a game with her family. Tlenga, sure, or some Ancients game named after places that were just rubble now—Texas Hold 'Em, Egyptian Rat Screw. Places that used to have presidents and governors, places with people who hated each other, eventually, so much that they all just crumbled.

Hate was a strong word. The undoing of everything. Forbidden for a reason.

A tapping on the window interrupted her stillness. She jerked her head up, startled.

"Open the window," Mott said, muffled through the glass.

She was holding something in her arms, something bulky, and Paige felt like she was moving through water. Mott didn't wait; she sighed and dropped the object on the floor while she opened the door herself.

"You're here," Paige said, throat croaking and raw.

"And *you're* useless in a crisis situation," said Mott. "Come on. I'm getting you out of here."

"Out?" The CSes were going to be there to pick her up in seventeen minutes. This was her moment to say goodbye to Mott, to say everything she'd been waiting to say in the seventeen years of their lifetimes. There was no out. There was only time, and such a short amount of it that Paige couldn't figure out where to start.

"Of here. Come on. You don't need anything, we just have to go *now*."

"Yeah? Where're you gonna take me? The Afterlands?"

"The border."

"Good one."

Mott held up a burlap sack.

"I stole food."

Paige blinked at her. Mott hadn't been joking.

"You *what*."

"Enough to keep us going for a few days. Until we can get to finding an old radiation bunker or something. There's probably some canned goods there. And I've got a water purifier. And a can opener."

"Mott, that is a *crime*."

"Yeah, well, you know what? There are a lot of things in this place that aren't crimes and should be!"

"Shut *up*, someone is going to hear you." Paige stiffened, surprised at how easily the phrase had flown out of her mouth. She glanced back at the door, wary of the noise. Out loud, she heard how she echoed her father. She was so like him in so many ways. Including the pissing-off-people-he-loved part. Like his mom, when he'd told CSes that he'd accidentally walked in on his sister and her best friend's sister naked together in bed and got her sent to an auditing session that lasted an entire week. His mom had been angry with him until the day she Ascended, but Papa always said that he was scared that if he hadn't said anything, his mom never would have been able to Ascend. No one would have. He'd made a tough decision no kid should have ever had to make. And he'd done it to follow the Statutes, to keep everyone safe, and everyone was safe.

"I am *loud-whispering* at a *very reasonable level*," Mott hissed.

There was something confident about Mott's voice—but under it, a waver. Something she'd heard in Mama's voice. Something hurt.

Something desperate.

"You want to run away," Paige said slowly.

"And here I thought I was being subtle," said Mott.

"From New Standard."

"With you, yes, keep up."

Mott was breathless and earnest. Right there, in the bag in her hand, was evidence that she'd thought about their lives together, had thought about radiation bunkers. Had planned a future with her, however temporary. They wouldn't have to be apart.

Something dangerous and hot sprouted at the base of Paige's ribcage and spread through her chest. Her heart pounded so furiously that she could feel every pulse throbbing through her fingertips. None of it was logical. None of anything made any sense. This was a dream, and in a minute she would wake up— Mama and Papa would be drinking tea in the kitchen, Sol already at the first shift of breakfast in the dining hall. Paige would head to the second shift with Mott, and they'd jabber excitedly, among their friends, about their new roles, about the coming training periods, anticipation cloaked in the homey scent of breakfast patties and herbed potatoes.

And something inside Paige jumped at the sound of *with you.* There was something so storylike about it, so fantastical, calling straight from the Afterlands. She wouldn't have to wait forty-two years in solaced misery. She wouldn't have to go through NI-2, give birth to an huérfano, head into the Renewal House without any of her peers following behind her; her family wouldn't have to watch her burn. She eyed the dresser, calculated how many clothes she could fit into a small pack that wouldn't weigh her down.

What would a few days of rations and hunger mean in exchange for the unpredictability of time ahead of them? If she stayed, she was guaranteed to only have a year left, and most of it under direct supervision of the Council of Elders. But if she left . . .

Just as quickly as her hope had risen, it sank.

If she left, they'd take someone else to take her place.

Mott could see her processing through it, arriving at that conclusion; her face fell, her whole body sinking inward as if a black hole suddenly appeared in the center of Mott's chest. "You won't do it."

"I'd be a traitor," Paige pleaded. And what about the entirety of the ascending age-sixties she was supposed to lead to eternal life? All of their souls would be lost, denied.

Mott's face was closing up again. A cloud blocking the bright sun.

"So what?"

"So I'd have to live with it. Every day."

"It won't even be in front of you anymore. You won't think about it."

"Isn't that worse? That I'm blind to the suffering of my people?"

"What about the suffering of you?"

"*The suffering of one is so much less than the suffering of the many.*" The Statutes filled her head like a gas, a haze of comfort merely from being spoken.

"What about the suffering of two?"

"Two?"

"You and me."

"How would you be suffering?"

"Because I wouldn't be with you."

With you. Paige inhaled, afraid to let her breath go.

Mott dropped the bag to the floor and took a delicate step toward Paige. How long did they have left? Twelve minutes? Two? Mott took another step and Paige's head flooded with questions she couldn't verbalize. The hesitancy between them was unfamiliar and thick, and shouldn't have been there in the first place, but there it was. Mott didn't fling herself into Paige's arms and hug her tightly to say goodbye; she took another step, and another, and Paige was certain that if she exhaled the wind would take her breath out beyond the atmosphere and she'd never get it back.

Mott wasn't saying goodbye. Why wasn't she saying goodbye? Why wasn't she hugging her with everything she had, transferring a lifetime of hugs to her in that moment? They'd known this was a possibility. For almost four generations, every girl ever had known this was a possibility. They prepared for it. They made bon-voyage cards. They didn't steal food and try to escape.

"I can't ignore my duties to everyone else," Paige told her, though it was mostly automatic, words that had been branded into her brain year after year.

If Ingrid could leave, why couldn't she? Why couldn't all of them?

Death, or something, was the logical answer, but logic was an abstract concept lingering somewhere in the air above them, beyond the roof of the tetriplex, when under that roof Mott was standing right in front of her, almost nose-to-nose, her almondy scent pressing a wave of calm over Paige's shoulders. Mott's freckles stood out when she was this close, a constellation of high-melanin stars over the rest of her creamy brown skin. Everything about Mott was dark and warm, like the sun blanketing your skin as it set at the end of a hot, spring day while you sit on the balcony with your feet up and drink cinnamon tea. Paige could see every hair on Mott's impeccably groomed, thick eyebrows, could trace the shadow down from those eyebrows to the curved tip of her slender nose, just underneath which her normally-loud lips, quiet now and still so Paige could see the straggler freckle on the bottom one, parted ever so slightly to show the edges of her teeth—which Paige suddenly, desperately, inexplicably wanted to lick. To see what they felt like under her tongue, like that would give her access to know what made Mott Mott, the incredible girl whose skin couldn't contain her confidence, who always seemed to understand everything. It was like if Paige could touch her teeth, gain access to the inside of

Mott's mouth, suddenly she would understand everything about her and be cured of this insatiable wanting that pushed through her veins, her pores, her hair.

She wanted to kiss Mott. They were here, like they'd left off a few hours ago, and it was like the momentum couldn't be stopped now; against her better reasoning, she felt her hand reach out to hold Mott's face, tracing her jawline to her shoulder.

"Tell me you'll go," Mott whispered, leaning her forehead against Paige's, and Paige realized that she'd been wrong. *This* was everything she'd ever wanted. She curled her fingers in between Mott's with one hand, brought the other one up to tentatively touch Mott's neck, to run her fingers over the three vertebrae connecting her head to her spine.

"I want to," Paige whispered back.

"Then do it."

She was so close to saying yes. Mott accepted Paige for everything she was. She loved Paige despite Paige's insistence on subscribing semi-blindly to the New Standardite worldview; she loved Paige despite Paige's need to be right all the time and inability to let things go. She loved Paige despite Paige's high anxiety, conservatism, perfectionism. Mott loved Paige for being everything that Mott was not, and Paige loved Mott for the same reason.

She loved Mott. It felt so good to think it.

She loved her. More than she should love anyone else. More than was reasonable to love any one person. She saw Mott's face in her head and felt a sudden swarm of warmth in her chest, a burning that filled her heart and spread to her head and flushed on her face and didn't let her think.

A lingering hunger from deep inside her burst into unrest, a wild thing that clambered toward any opening it could find. It scratched at her throat and pushed at her lips to let it out, begging to be released, but Paige squeezed her eyes shut and shoved the it down with mental violence.

"I—I can't."

She could barely get it out. Her body slumped, exhausted from the battle, but she was sure that, despite the deep unhappiness she knew it would cause her, she had won.

But Mott's big eyes, an iridescent, unpinnable color that flitted between brown and green in the folds of the irises, like shadows on the underside of a mushroom, betrayed Mott's lack of conviction.

"Why not?" she demanded. Like it wasn't an acceptable answer. But mercy, it was so much harder to deny her like this. Paige didn't want to fight her. She wanted to give in, to let Mott's hands get tangled in her hair, to slide her own hands over Mott's hips, to have some visceral connection with her that would somehow, imperfectly, express the bursting, mixed emotions trapped under her skin.

Paige took a deep breath, let it out steadily, and refocused. She was the Ritualist, and if she didn't do this . . . "It won't stop with me."

"Meaning . . . ?"

"If I leave, they'll just pick someone else. What if it's Dorothy?"

Mott frowned and shrugged, as if this was obvious. "We'll bring her with us."

"You're not getting it. They'll pick someone else, too. We can't just take everyone with us."

"That's not your problem."

"It *is*, though." Paige could feel the tears welling up, spilling over the rims of her eyes, and she could recognize that the burning love spreading from her heart through her fingernails was intertwined with fear. "It is, because if I don't do this, it's my fault. It's my fault. It's my fault."

She had the talents. She had the skills. She had the calling from the Ancestors to redeem Ingrid's betrayal, to redeem Aunt Felicity's betrayal, to clean the stain of shame on her whole family, to purify the next set of age-sixties, and if she didn't, if she couldn't pull through, it was her fault. She sobbed, now, the weight of it all crushing her, but she couldn't let it. They'd picked her, and even if she was just second-best, they'd put their trust—their futures, their lives, their *souls* in her hands.

Mott relented, crying, too, the sight of her anger breaking into grief unfamiliar and unsettling; Paige felt the release within her breaking into clean pieces.

She waited for Mott to tell her it wouldn't be her fault. But Mott, who absolutely knew that no matter what she told Paige, Paige wouldn't believe her, didn't say anything. She cried silently and reached out to hook a piece of hair behind Paige's ears, her touch so gentle as it grazed her earlobe that it only made Paige cry harder.

Some tears caught on Mott's eyelashes; the rest of them dripped onto her cheeks. Paige could hardly stand it. Her throat tightened, too.

And she said, her voice wavering with the tears she swallowed back down, because maybe if she heard herself say it out loud she would believe it:

"My suffering will be less than everyone else's."

Mott let go of her hands to wipe her own eyes with her sleeve. "It's my suffering, too," she said.

But Paige was the Ritualist. Mott was a citizen. "It's easier this way," she whispered, pleading.

Mott backed away. Paige would guarantee Mott the forty-two years she couldn't guarantee herself. It was her obligation, she told herself as Mott's face fell and she hoisted the burlap sack onto her back. People would die if she didn't perform her duty. *Mott* would die. *Sol* would die. And her family would be twice as shamed as before.

Mott shot her an awful, gut-wrenching look at her as she wordlessly reached for the door. Paige wanted to take it back. She wanted to grab Mott and kiss her and forget about everything and everyone else. But she couldn't live with the entire community in shambles because of her selfishness to run off, taking her perfectly good ovaries with her, headfirst into death. So she'd have to die for it.

And she would do this despite the loss-of-warmth, the dy-
ing-of-magic from her soul as Mott sneaked back out the sliding
glass door, because that was selfless. That was love.

THE HEART

a handwritten note

the heart has four
chambers
left and right

    ventricle
    left and right
    atrium

        four places
        to store
        things that

                matter

JONAH MEETS WHALE

S OLOMON SAT BESIDE PAIGE on the sofa, watching Mama fuss around the living area as they waited for the CS to collect her. Mama straightened blankets and fluffed pillows; she scrubbed leftover tea mugs in the sink.

"I'm very proud of you, Paige," she said formally, but she kept her attention focused on undoing the tea-leaf strainers and sorting the wet leaves into the compost.

"Naomi, sit *down*," said Papa, holding in his patience like it was an insect trying to bite him. "You're missing out on this crucial *moment*—"

"Don't tell me what I'm missing out on, Philip," snapped Mama. She stiffened in the middle of scooping used tea leaves into the compost bin, her voice chilly. "Don't."

Papa held up his hands in surrender even though Mama wasn't looking at him. "I'm not *telling* you anything, Na-*o*-mi, I'm just *suggesting*—"

"Maybe keep your suggestions to yourself."

"I'm not allowed to suggest anything? What kind of partnership is this?"

Mama let out a loud, mirthy *hah*. "Partnership. You want to talk about partnership—"

Solomon sighed and rested his head on Paige's shoulder; she rested her cheek on top of his hair. She wondered if her new home would be calmer than this one.

Sharp knocks on the door cut through the silence; Paige and Solomon sat there for a moment as if they were only imagining them. If she got up and left his side, it was real. How long could she sit here and pretend that it wasn't?

The knocks came again. The CS even said her name. At least her name hadn't been stripped from her yet.

Not long, apparently.

"Coming," hollered Papa through the wall. He patted Paige's shoulders and kissed the top of her head swiftly on his way toward the door.

What did she really have that was hers, anyway? The bag she'd packed contained her Statutes, a couple of biology textbooks, and her small wooden box of special things—a dried dandelion necklace from Mott, a couple of years old; a paper crane from Solomon from the first time they'd built a fort in her room to create a place for them that was entirely their own; a tiny ceramic teacup she'd found in the relics shop.

She stood up slowly; Solomon snagged her hand before she could take a step. He didn't say anything—they both knew this was goodbye—and when she looked back at him he was staring at the wall.

She held his hand and squeezed it. He closed his eyes, clinging to her hand in the way he'd only ever held it if Mama and Papa were fighting—sitting in the dark on her bed, quiet, listening to the calculated words placed just right, calm and assured and sharper than teeth.

I'm sorry, she wanted to say, but Solomon stared straight forward. There were no words that would make this better. As soon as she walked out that door, he'd be alone.

There was another knock and then he let go; but it wasn't until he pulled his hand away that she realized he'd put a tiny, folded-so-tight-it-didn't-feel-like-paper-anymore piece of paper in between her fingers.

She frowned at him. "What—?"

He finally looked back at her, but only to gesture to her skirt pockets with one hand, put his finger to his lips with the other, and only for a moment.

And she couldn't ask anything else, because Mama swept her into a tight hug at that moment, planted another kiss into her hair, and whispered—so quietly that only Paige could hear—the words that were only ever supposed to be applied as a statement of action, a verb instead of a state of being—

"I love you."

—and then she released her and handed Paige her bag, ushering her toward the waiting CS, away from her.

—

THE CS ACCOMPANYING PAIGE to the Council building—CS Holly, her nametag read—had the good decency not to ask her if she was excited to be selected or how her day had been. In fact, she didn't say much of anything. She seemed like someone who'd been doing this a long time, someone whose tiny pieces of frizzy hair falling out of her otherwise-neat bun implied that she'd seen the face of every Ritualist in Paige's lifetime up close. Like she'd escorted every one of them from the Council building to the Renewal House when it was their turn to die.

The tiny triangular wad of folded paper hit her leg every other step through her skirt pocket, like it was building up a rash on her thigh. She tried to stay in the present moment: listened to the crunch of dirty road under her feet, felt the uncomfortable sweat between her toes inside her loafers from the desert-valley heat. Before she knew it, they had arrived.

The Council building's most prominent feature was its set of four large, slatted circular vents facing the road. Paige had always thought of them as Ancestral eyes glaring at her as she walked down the street. Now, as she approached the building behind CS Holly, she was so focused on the vents that she didn't notice a large crack in the concrete, and consequently stubbed her toe.

She sucked in her breath and swallowed the pain. If the Ancestors were watching her, she couldn't let them see her be brought down by something as paltry as a toe stubbed in a crack in the walkway.

She couldn't help but think that Mott would have made a big show about the pain and sat down in the middle of the walkway until she felt ready to move on. Paige would have laughed to herself if she hadn't still felt the wrenching, tender ghost of her own refusal to Mott's offer.

Forward she persisted along the walkway lined with thriving giant agave, new sprigs of lavender sprouting up in between, training her eyes above the entrance at the century-old faded sign that read CITY OF FRESNO in large red letters and below it, in smaller print, FIRE STATION 14. CS Holly led her through the double doors with the large "N" painted on the left one and an "S" painted on the right, past a Receptionist who scrawled notes on a log madly as he saw her enter (were they tracking her whereabouts already?). Down a long hallway with smooth beige paint and a single framed piece of embroidered cloth hanging on the wall, reading: PEACE RELIES ON LOVE. Underneath it hung a small tapestry of a brown man and a yellow woman holding hands and looking down at the two children on either side of them, both ornately stitched with speckled brown and yellow threads. And at the end of the hallway, CS Holly stopped her and knocked on the door on the left.

No answer, but apparently this was expected: CS Holly pushed open the door and wasted no time rummaging through the drawers. Paige followed her in.

"Put this on," said CS Holly, throwing Paige a long piece of fabric the same bleached-white color of textbook pages. Ritual-white. Paige only barely caught the garment before CS Holly headed out again with a dismissive, "The Matriarch will be by shortly."

And then it was just Paige, the fabric, and the unfamiliar room.

Her room? Was this where all the Ritualists slept? She eyed the bed in the corner of the room. How many young women had slept here, waiting to be impregnated and then set on fire for the good of their community? She thought she could smell them in the recycled-cotton fibers of the sheets, even standing an entire foot away from the bed.

This was—

It was—

Only one word came to mind, sneaking up on her.

Cruel.

It was like she was realizing it for the first time. No—this definitely was the first time.

The soft fabric felt weighty in her hands. She held it out at arms' length, then brought it closer again: a plain, run-of-the-mill, floor-length dress. Short sleeves, high waist, square neckline. Where had she seen it before—?

Oh.

Oh.

At the last Ascension.

On the Ritualist.

"Agatha," Paige felt compelled to whisper to herself, like that would give the last Ritualist a little more humanity, a little more peace now that her soul had left this world. Or just in case she could hear her from across worlds—then the last Ritualist— *Agatha,* she said again—would know that at least someone hadn't forgotten that she had been a person.

An individual.

Paige hoped the next Ritualist would think of her like that, too.

She dropped the dress on the bed and rubbed the gooseflesh that had started to sneak up her arms like exploratory ants. It had to be a totally new dress—obviously, Agatha had burned in the one made for her—which begged the question: how had the garment fabricators made one so quickly for Paige after Ingrid—?

She shivered.

They hadn't, she realized.

This one had been meant for Ingrid.

Despite the heat outside, an oppressive cold seemed to be filling every corner of the room and it pressed on her, abandoned, in the center. She shoved her hands in her pockets for a sense of familiarity.

And there was Solomon's paper.

She thought about opening it, but just at that moment, she heard a set of footsteps approaching.

She shoved the paper in the pillowcase on the bed—if the sheets were fresh, no one was going to check there, right?—and started to unbutton her blouse, holding her breath as she shoved the pillow further onto the bed with her hip.

What should she say if the Matriarch noticed something was off? If she demanded to see what was in the pillow?

The footsteps got closer. She expected a rapping on the door any moment now.

Just another couple of steps . . .

And then there was the squeak of a door hinge and the footsteps disappeared.

Paige frowned. She cracked open her own door to see what had happened. CS Holly peered through the crack after a moment and Paige nearly jumped.

"Something wrong?"

"I—no, I thought I heard something."

"Mm. Washroom's right across the hall from you. There's a private bath next door, but otherwise you share the toilets with Council staff and visitors." CS Holly frowned at her. "You're not done changing yet?"

Paige's face felt hot. "I—well, I was just getting acquainted with the space—"

"'Acquainted with the space'?"

"It's a thing I do," Paige lied. Or maybe it wasn't a lie. She felt like a new person—an angrier, more resistant one. Maybe this new person did lots of space-acquainting.

"Well, acquaint yourself a little faster. The Matriarch told me she'd be here in two minutes."

"Thanks."

Paige closed the door, relieved to be away from CS Holly and her crankiness. She finished removing her blouse, setting it neatly over the pillow, and stood in her garment top and her daily skirt staring at the spot with the pillow and the paper.

She glanced back at the door. Then back at the pillow.

Two minutes was enough time.

Just to look.

Against her better judgment, she opened the paper. And when she saw what it was, she immediately dropped it on the bed.

It was a page ripped from the Statutes, with something written on it. Ripped. The title at the top of the page read:

WHY I GAVE YOU THIS BOOK

Underlined would have been the phrase:

The key to peace is love

Except that "love" was scratched out so hard that the fibers of pulp from the paper shredded against the grain.

In its place was a scribbled-in question mark. And underneath, the words:

I REFUSE.

Paige's hand developed a phantom sting where it had touched the page. Her hand felt dirty but her heart felt defiant. It was like like someone had socked her in the stomach—the inconsistent, ragged pattern on the inside edge of the page, ripped so haphazardly that at one point it even interfered with the text itself with a triangular gap into the margin. To rip out that page from the Statutes was to reject everything she had ever known, everything that New Standard was, everything that had enabled all of humanity to survive up until this point, the entire legacy of the Spared.

But now—

Now, the universe was dealing with angry Paige. It had teased her with something she wanted and took away the two people with whom she felt the most safe in the world.

It had pushed her too far.

Solomon had *defiled the Statutes*, and Paige, despite a strong part of her soul feeling appalled, couldn't help but study the frayed paper in awe.

Creak. Creak.

Shoot. Footsteps along the weary floor outside. How quickly could she eat the note?

Two knocks. "Paige?" she heard through the door.

The Matriarch.

Paige's stomach beat like there was already a baby kicking inside of it. She couldn't chew that fast. She shoved the note in the pillowcase.

"May I come in?"

Did she have the power to say no? The power to say, *leave me alone?*

"Just a moment," she hollered at the door.

She wriggled out of her clothes, revealing her garments underneath. Automatic guilt resurfaced in her brain as she remembered her lustful dreams about Mott, how she'd tried not to look at her while she was standing next to her in the changing room before the Rite of Responsibility; the guilt traveled down her neck, crawled over her chest and over her nipples, down across her navel and into her pubic hair, then wrapped around her thighs and slid all the way down her ankle bones into the soles of her feet. She willed her garments to protect her from lust. She harried to dress herself in the Ritualist gown, as if that could brush off the ant-like guilt, as if the gown would make her clean.

The Ritualist gown felt too soft against her skin. It didn't fit right. The shoulders seams were wrong, her skin too old and dead for something so pure.

"Come in," said Paige.

The Matriarch slid sideways into the room with a sort of tentativity that Paige didn't expect. Her dark, straight hair was pulled into a ponytail at the nape of her neck; being able to see her ears like this made her seem disarmingly human. She gently closed the door behind her.

"Sorry it took so long," tried Paige, for lack of anything better to say.

The Matriarch offered her a small, reassuring smile. "It's okay. Takes a moment to figure out the clasps in the back of the dress."

Paige nodded, even though agreeing with the assumption was a lie. Never in her life would she have dared to lie to the Matriarch, but the guilt of Mott's almost-kiss—and the worse guilt of having to reject her—was enough to make her want to refuse something just because she could.

Her nod was resistance. It was revenge, defiance. It was only a nod, but right now it was everything.

"May I sit?" said the Matriarch, gesturing toward the bed.

There was kind of a lack of alternative seating options. Paige shrugged. "Go for it."

The Matriarch laughed softly, sitting right next to the pillow. Paige was annoyed by how lighthearted the laughter sounded. Like the world she was losing wasn't important.

She tried not to glance over at the pillowcase for signs of the folded-up paper, lest the Matriarch find something suspicious about it.

"I forget how young you are," said the Matriarch, "until I hear you all talk."

All?

"Sorry. I mean all you Ritualists."

You Ritualists—like Paige was in a class all of her own, one where there was no one else. No one to keep her company, no one to reassure her that they'd done this before and it was all going to end up being okay.

"It's just—I understand, to the extent possible by someone who's never gone through it, but as an observer for the past twelve years—the apprehension that comes with the territory of your position." The Matriarch seemed like she was tripping over her words, a sense of vibrant imperfection that Paige had never thought she would witness. "And I'm very . . . well, very *aware* that my experience of being seventeen was a long while ago, and it was . . ." She pursed her lips and frowned at the wall, her head somewhere far away. Finally, she decided on ". . . difficult."

The whole conversation felt surreal. Was the Matriarch really acknowledging the obvious distance between herself and Paige? Was she empathizing with her? Empathy was in the Statutes, and it was one of the most important practices in New Standard, but for some reason she wasn't sure that the Matriarch's empathy would feel this . . . real. This personal. This *honest*.

"I know this whole selection process has been stressful and confusing," the Matriarch continued, "but I want you to know that you're not alone here. You're safe. And you can talk to me about anything, okay?"

This felt like a totally different Matriarch from the one earlier today. Not a cold, unfeeling symbol of the community, but exposing her humanity. Waiting for Paige to respond.

Listening. Really listening.

"Anything?" Paige repeated.

The Matriarch nodded. Her face looked kind of like Papa's, except that the Matriarch's face was flatter than Papa's, her head rounder, the tip of her nose closer to her face. "It's scary, being on your own for the first time, and even scarier when you're the only one with your job. I get it. And I won't pretend to know exactly what you're going through. I know that isn't fair."

Paige felt her rising defenses pause. She waited.

"But what's similar about our positions is that we're both the only ones of our kind. The only way we're assigned our responsibilities is if someone else vacates the position by way of death. And we both spend our whole lives training for a responsibility we're not sure we'll ever have to take on."

Paige had never thought of it that way before, but it was true enough. New Matriarchs were selected from the pool of eligible female huérfanas by the Council of Elders. Paige couldn't be sure she wasn't imagining it, but the Matriarch seemed to carry distress in her eyebrows and the muscles that tensed up her jaw as she talked. She seemed to be talking more to herself than to Paige.

"And then there's this pressure for everything to go *right*. If something goes wrong, people start to ask why they're participating. And *you're* the one held responsible for whatever it is that went wrong. *And* they start to lose their faith."

The Matriarch clasped her hands carefully in her lap, like it was a skill she'd had to perfect.

"You see, Paige, citizenship in New Standard is a covenant. It's a contract, an exchange: a person gives themselves to the town, and the town gives itself to the person. Over and over again, history has shown us that this kind of symbiosis is the only peaceful way to live—and our past shows us that peace is the only way for us to survive. When New Standard started, we were *literally the only people left alive.* It's a lot of pressure."

Understatement of the millennium. But *symbiosis.* At least the Matriarch was speaking her language now.

"I know you know all of this already," the Matriarch went on. "But I want to remind you of this because I know, too, how tempting it can be to leave everything behind when someone else has already done it."

Paige shifted in her seat to face the Matriarch, curling one leg up beneath her. "You do?"

There was no way the Matriarch would ever consider leaving New Standard. She couldn't. She wouldn't.

The Matriarch nodded, pressing her lips together in a sad smile. "I'm ashamed of it now, of course. But when I was younger—about your age—I had a friend. Huérfanos spend most of their time here, as you know, so we don't make many civilian friends. But I happened to make one, and she and I were extremely close. Like you and your friend. The Caretaker."

"Mott."

"Yes, Mott. We were as close as the two of you are."

As close? Paige felt a shield swiping sharply into place over her heart.

Was that a legitimate comparison or a threat?

The Matriarch's trained her eyes on the wall in front of her, her mind lost beyond it, and Paige's understanding clicked into place. Something had happened. Something had gone wrong.

"What—" Paige cleared her throat, afraid to ask but compelled to anyway. "What happened?"

The Matriarch let her shoulders sag forward. Paige could hardly believe this was the same woman who'd taken control of an Ascension that could have gone in an extremely different direction. This woman seemed as listless as Mama, as breakable as herself.

" 'But be not dishonest about who you are!'" the Matriarch cited, as if in a trance, like the words were the only source of her comfort. " 'Filter your first instincts, but do not fail to acknowledge your initial intentions—' "

" '—for to deny the body of feeling internally is to rip the soul from the body,'" Paige finished.

The Matriarch smiled, finally making eye contact with Paige. "You know the passage well."

Paige shrugged, hoping that could pass for acknowledgment of the heat that flushed her whole body when Mott's finger grazed her back, of the doubt that penetrated her core Standards beliefs every so often. "It resonates with me."

The Matriarch took a deep breath; this close, with her hair pulled back and her clothes so . . . normal—the same kind of plain skirt and blouse that Paige and Mott would wear on a typical Wednesday—with her internal struggle was so apparent, and Paige could barely believe that she'd ever thought of the Matriarch as anything but human.

"I'll be honest, then, okay," she said. "I think, if anything, it's the least I can give you."

She exhaled, then began.

"I loved my friend more than anything. She'd just been assigned her responsibility in the Council building. She was a scientist, and she was adventurous. Always talking about the technology people used to have. And I mean *always*. She was excited by it, and I loved that about her. I loved watching her light up when she worked. She was extremely matter-of-fact, but when she was inventing, she was so *happy*.

"She invented one thing in particular that was intended to make crops resistant to radiofly saliva, which she tested out on a patch of strawberries one summer. Ruined a whole crop of strawberries that year, nearly killed her brother. That should have been my first clue, her insistence on breaking the rules, but I posited that she was only trying to break the rules to help people, so it was okay."

Something familiar tugged at the edges of Paige's brain, but she couldn't verbalize what.

"My first instincts—my honest ones, that I couldn't help but acknowledge—were that I loved her. More than I should have. And I didn't filter those instincts. I struggled, I struggled hard for such an *achingly* long time."

She looked at Paige meaningfully, but Paige was careful to keep her face blank. Her heart pounded into her intestines. She didn't know. She couldn't know. *Paige* hadn't even known until last night.

"But then the Matriarch at that time caught me with her, doing things we shouldn't have been doing, okay. She sent me to an auditor."

"Sister Nadine?"

"Like her, yes, but there's one who specifically serves huérfanos and elders, so I saw him. And he did a thorough audit, and it was—" she frowned, averting her eyes to the floor, as if considering something that was written there, "painful. Heart-wrenching, because I loved my friend so much, and part of me wanted to just forget everything about New Standard and live in the negative, indulgent behaviors I was engaging in. And the auditor helped me, okay, he helped me *so much.*"

She closed her eyes tight, shaking her head, and Paige could feel the relieved surrender as it swept through the Matriarch and into the top of Paige's mind. Paige wanted that, the sweet peace that the Statutes brought. She wanted to sit and let herself exhale. She could imagine herself having it, if only the Matriarch would tell her what the secret was.

"He helped me understand that passage—acknowledging my intentions for my friend, and the devious acts I performed with her—and showed me that the path to redemption was in that first part—*filter your first instincts.* It wasn't that there was anything wrong with me, okay. Just because I loved a girl didn't mean that I wasn't a New Standardite, or that I couldn't be the Matriarch. In fact, he told me—which *blew my mind* at the time—" and Paige felt a smile quirking the side of her mouth as she reflected on the fact that she was listening to the *Matriarch* say things like *blew my mind,* "People who are oriented for same-sex attraction are considered among the most pure—because it's a greater display of our commitment to New Standard. The Ancestors see that struggle, and they understand the massive amounts of effort it takes to restrict our physical displays of love. Which is why—to help other girls in New Standard going through the same thing— we tend to watch them closely, and why so many of them tend to be Ritualists."

And again she looked directly at Paige. Paige pulled her lips inward and pressed them together, providing relief from the unconscious clamping down of her jaw. It took all of her courage to stare the Matriarch down right back and not look away, but she forced herself to do it, and she did. She wasn't going to break the silence first. She wasn't.

Finally, the Matriarch broke it for them. "I knew that if I didn't follow the Statutes, I wasn't only putting myself at risk, I was putting all of New Standard at risk—including my friend. And I loved her too much to let her die.

"So I made a decision then—that that wasn't how I wanted to live. It's my duty to make sure everyone survives at all costs. Creating this community was difficult enough in the first place, and humans are finicky. One thing out of balance can wreck the entire ecosystem. The Statutes aren't just words on a page. They're regulations that legitimately keep us all alive.

"When you lead an entire people, Paige, they follow you. And if you can't protect them, then why are you in charge?"

Paige nodded slowly, processing. The doubt—that was the most powerful weapon against the beliefs that kept everyone safe. Ingrid's death was fresh on everyone's minds, and the loss of a Ritualist, of all people—it very well may have been the loss of faith itself. And because Ingrid had run away, there was no one to cleanse. And if there was no public punishment, others might feel emboldened, too.

Like Solomon.

The implications rang clear: if they didn't reinforce the community's faith in New Standard, more people could die.

"I understand," said Paige.

The Matriarch put a gentle hand on her knee. "Like I said: you're not alone in this, okay? *We're* in this. Together. Peace be with you."

Paige gave a small smile. "And also with you."

She felt guilty for her own doubt. But she had made the right choice. She'd been faced with her first huge test and turned out to be even more pure than she'd thought she was, even more suited for this responsibility than anyone could have expected. She hadn't fallen prey to the temptation of going away with Mott. She and the Matriarch were going to fix whatever they could in the community, whatever doubt that Ingrid's absence had sown.

She could put all of that behind her and clear her guilt and do what she was supposed to do: double down on her mission. Keep the world from collapsing.

Like she'd been destined to all along.

ON MODESTY AND DISHONESTY

an excerpt from the Statutes of Equality

I N THE FACE OF uncertainty, Friend, know this: your true intentions are your first instincts. We are an imperfect people, but we are subject—and obligated—to edit ourselves for the good of our community. Therefore, focus not on who you are but what you can make yourself, on the integrity of becoming your best self.

But be not dishonest about who you are! Filter your first instincts, but do not fail to acknowledge your initial intentions, for to deny the body of feeling internally is to rip the soul from the body.

A soul and a body are different; we have not control of how much light shines from our souls, but do have control over what we do with our bodies. Therefore: embrace your thoughts but restrain your bodies. Be modest, be honest: for honesty is love, and modesty is respect—and respect, too, is love.

FEAR NOT

A s an age-ten, Paige had gone to the history museum for a class field trip. The tour guide had said at the beginning of the trip not to touch anything in the museum, that everything was there *for looking only*, and Paige had done so well.

She walked by an old model of an airplane, dusty and broken, a relic of the old bomber engines this country had sent over another country. In the cockpit was an overly large wax figure, bright and shiny and flawed, sitting in the layers of skin he wore as evidence of his gluttony. She wanted to glide her hand over his belly, to see if it was as soft as it looked, even though she knew it wasn't.

But she'd been good. Hadn't touched anything. Moved on, even though she desperately wanted to know what the world-that-was had felt like, had smelled like, how all the sins of the Ancients had been supposedly so delicious that they simply couldn't resist all their temptations and their failure had led to the world-as-it-is. She'd kept her hands clasped behind her back as she looked at bullet shell casings and papier-mâché animals and models of how the world used to look.

But those were only relics. Fractured pieces of another world. They weren't even real.

The tour guide led them to the one real thing in the history museum: the Pandora, brought to the history museum from the

Council building only for special tours like this, for educational purposes. Despite its small size—a chest crafted from fresno wood no larger than a shoebox—and its plain design, it seemed to radiate energy. It had been built specifically to contain the negative energy and ashes from those who dared to negate New Standard's values. In it, the tour guide explained, were the ashes of the last person to be cleansed.

In this case, those ashes belonged to Yuri-of-2094, the baker who'd been cleansed a few weeks prior. Paige remembered his warm pats on her head when she would come into the bakery, the time when he let her taste a tiny bite of fresh bread from just out of the oven.

It had been delicious. He gave her some with honey, and that was even better.

He didn't want to be equal, said the tour guide, tilting his head back so that when the sun came in through the window, it created a silhouetted glow around his upturned nose.

Now, as Paige looked at the box that contained the person Yuri-of-2094 used to be, she felt regret in her belly—that tiny piece of bread rotting in her gut.

The Pandora trapped sins collected with other past sins, so that there could be no escape, but Paige wanted to see what Yuri-of-2094 looked like now. If she could put some of her skin cells in the Pandora, would it count for leaving her sins there, too? Before she realized what she was doing, she reached out to touch it. Just to see. Just to feel.

Now, Paige, said Educator Gail, pulling Paige's hand back from the Pandora, *I thought you were a better listener than that.*

Paige wanted to insist, *I am, I am.* But her hand had grazed the wooden box, and now it felt soiled, too, and how could she tell Educator Gail that she was full of sin without getting stuck in the box in place of Yuri-of-2094?

The clasp on the box seemed solid. Firm. There was no getting out once you got in.

"This way," said CS Holly, leading Paige and the Matriarch down the hallway where they'd entered.

Paige wasn't sure where they were going. She'd only ever visited one part of the Council building before—the court—which was a small room on one side of the lobby where families could talk to the Matriarch and the Ritualist once a week during visiting hours. From what Paige could tell, they were not going to the court. They were going to a room next to it, where the Procession participants were gathering and talking amongst themselves in a dull roar over instruments and singers warming up.

The Procession was more or less the same every year: students in a marching qeej ensemble, huérfanos performing a traditional dance, a small community mixed choir leading the watching citizens in song, the current sitting Council of Elders, and the Matriarch and Ritualist. Everyone wore brightly-colored woven shawls around their heads or waists, finely embroidered with patterns learned in childhood—luv tsev, jagged and precisely distanced; moj zeej, ominously shaped people; lub plawv, heart nestled with two mirrored spirals. The whole thing was magical: the second day of Peace Festival, the first full day that everything was different, and the energy around the town buzzed. Baking crews prepared for the Procession for weeks, assembling massive amounts of dough in order to be able to provide loaves and loaves of rich, multi-grain Procession bread to all the citizens lining the street so early in the morning just before the sun came out, clinging to their tea like it was a lifeline. Paige could still remember the subtle smell of agave syrup coming from Mama's mug. Those were the times when everything seemed like it would be all right, like even if Mama and Papa didn't really love each other like spouses should, they could still be a happy nuclear family, because love was a skill, love could be practiced.

A middle-aged man wearing thin wire-rimmed glasses stood on a step-stool at the front of the room. "I need the crowns!" he hollered over the noise of the room.

"I'm handing them out!" hollered back—

"Pepper?"

Paige had forgotten that Pepper had been assigned as an event administrator. Pepper turned to Paige, brightening, as she shoved a flower crown in an unsuspecting huérfana's face. "Paige!"

The huérfana—a girl probably around Solomon's age, maybe a little younger, with olive-toned skin and a slouch that indicated a lack of Procession enthusiasm—winced, but accepted the crown and wriggled a few more from the stash Pepper had wedged under her armpit.

Those painstakingly woven flower crowns were one of Paige's favorite parts of the Procession as a child. She knew they were wasteful—they would only last a day on people's heads—but then again, they would also last at least a few days as a table centerpiece once the members of the Procession passed the crowns on to younger children in the audience. But they were so beautiful, and she loved losing herself in their fresh scent, their soft petals, the way they made her feel radiant when she put them on her head. She remembered basking in the warm sunlight with her flower crown, ribbons dangling behind her as she chased Mott through the lawn in Serenity Park before school started, eating pieces of bread and trusting that everything would be okay.

That life was a wispy dream, now.

Paige tried not to stare at the huérfana; just because she and the other huérfanos were orphans who lived separately from the rest of the community didn't mean that they looked any different than anyone else. Still, Paige had never really seen one on her own, nor up this close for this long before, and the nature of huérfanos being more remote symbols of New Standard rather than ordinary citizens had always felt like an appealing mystery. Nobody knew about the procedures of huérfanos, or ever met them except if someone in the community died or disappeared, in which case an huérfano of the appropriate sex and a close-enough cohort was promptly placed in the missing person's spot.

Paige's mind was bursting with questions about who the girl was and how she lived and whether she was told that she was going to be the Matriarch someday or whether that was something the powers-that-be decided later on or whether that came down through some sort of divine inspiration from the Ancestors. But she heard Papa's teasing exasperation in her head—*calm down, kiddo, again with the invasive questions*—and kept her mouth shut.

Pepper launched herself at Paige and wrapped her in a hug with her free arm. "I was *wondering* when you were going to show up! I'm sure they've got you running everywhere. I at least got a smidge of training this morning before I became the complete expert you have the privilege of seeing before you."

Paige felt herself smile. Pepper might have been a ridiculous person, but that ridiculousness was a familiar, welcome comfort right about now. She could *do* this. She could be the savior New Standard needed. It wasn't an obligation; it was a calling. It was *her* calling.

"Color me honored," Paige deadpanned. "You look extremely professional."

Pepper swished her new event-administrator uniform skirt back and forth, grinning beneath her freshly combed, straight hair. "The trick'll be to keep it clean."

At least Pepper was rather self-aware. "Good thing it's black. Hides stains pretty well."

"That's what Adam said!" said Pepper, but then her preening smile faltered. "Sorry about that, by the way."

"About what?"

"Adam. He told me about his conversation with you. About how he asked for your consideration." Pepper pushed her mouth to the side pityingly. "Guess that's not happening anymore."

Paige tried her best to look disappointed. "Yeah."

"EA Pepper!" shouted the middle-aged man. "I need you to double-check the artifacts!"

"I'm *on* it!" Pepper shouted back casually, like she'd been doing this for ages and not for all of two hours.

"I need you to move faster!"

"I *am!*" Pepper gestured toward a corner of the room. "Walk and talk?" she asked Paige. But she didn't wait for a response; she headed over, dropping the rest of the flower crowns off with the hunched-shouldered huérfana and grabbing a clipboard hanging from the wall on her way as she expertly wove between costumed Procession participants. She was a natural; the Council had known what they were doing when they'd assigned her as an EA.

So they'd known what they were doing when they'd assigned Paige as Ritualist, she reminded herself.

CS Holly had left without any instructions other than 'wait and do what the EAs tell you to do,' so Paige scurried after Pepper, struggling to keep up with her long legs and somehow look dignified while doing it. Everything about Pepper was long, from her chestnut-colored hair to her pale, skinny arms; she was like the windmills in the distance you could see from the borders of New Standard, only not broken. She led Paige to the corner of the room with all of the symbolic artifacts that would be displayed proudly in the Procession as beacons of everything New Standard's existence and survival represented.

Everything that Mott had tempted Paige to leave.

"He told us the story and it sounded so *romantic,*" Pepper gushed, dragging a pencil tip down the paper on the clipboard in her scan of whatever list she had. Pepper's ability to multi-task in the midst of what Paige considered to be full-on chaos was impressive. "He told us he'd been thinking about it for a while, which of course all of us knew, because he's as subtle as the Renewal House on Ascension night, mercy. FENNEL AND SAOIRSE!"

Two of the dancers approached, and Pepper waved them over to the tapestry bearing the words LOVE THY NEIGHBOR in thick embroidery. But Paige was still lost in Pepper's words.

"Everyone knew?"

"Oh, yeah, I know, we weren't supposed to know, but honestly, we were all betting on how long it would be between the Rite and when he asked for your consideration—TANDIS! LEOPOLD!"

She handed the New Standard flag to two of the student band members, then turned to the hunched-shouldered huérfana, who had come back holding the remaining flower crowns. "Oh, Lane, good timing. Will you go grab the Matriarch? Tell her we're ready for the Pandora."

The huérfana—Lane, apparently (they were on a first-name basis? Or did you not have to use a title for huérfanos?)—glared at Pepper. "What, I'm your personal assistant, now? I do you one favor and suddenly I'm in it for life."

Lane departed in a huff, and Pepper grinned, hollering, "Thank you!" shamelessly after her. She handed one of the crowns to Paige. "This is yours. Anyway, I'm sorry, I didn't realize it was a secret."

Paige stiffened. "What's a secret? I don't have secrets."

"Chill, Ritualist. Consideration isn't illegal." Pepper clutched the last crown to her chest and stood up on her toes in unsuppressed glee. "Swoon-worthy, though. Do you know how long he talked to me about how to ask you to consider him? Years. Actual, literal years. It's such a tragedy you'll never be espoused now—he's been pining for you forever. I was honestly a bit jealous."

Ugh. As if the original request hadn't been horrifying enough, as if Paige hadn't had enough guilt over it in the first place.

"Well, you can have him."

Pepper laughed. "Only if he wants me to consider him instead." She paused, her wistfulness turning into something like reproachful suspicion toward Paige, and arched an eyebrow. "Do you *know* how lucky you were?"

Lucky. For what, exactly? For obtaining the affections of someone she didn't want? Pepper's tone implied that Paige should feel guilty about passing up such a brilliant opportunity as Adam, even though she hadn't had a choice either way.

What was worse—Paige *did* feel that shame.

She hated it.

No, she told herself. Not hate. Just vehement dislike.

"I guess not," she told Pepper truthfully.

Pepper opened her mouth to say something else, but at that moment the Matriarch swept in with the Pandora. Not the replica that Pepper had once nearly broken, but the actual Pandora itself, the one no one was ever supposed to touch.

"Heeeel-lo," the Matriarch crooned casually, handing the Pandora to Paige with one hand, as if she hadn't just had a conversation with her in which she'd self-identified as a sexual deviant, something that had gotten Aunt Felicity cleansed.

Something about the casual way the Matriarch presented herself now threw Paige off. Her heart burned with something sudden and strange—embarrassment? Fury? Confusion? She couldn't be sure. She could only think about that photo of Aunt Felicity from the photo album, the one where she looked so vibrant and confident and like the poster child for what New Standardites aspired to be, and felt a twinge of jealousy that Aunt Felicity had been cleansed when her week-long auditing camp had failed to edit out her same-sex compulsions, while the Matriarch was the leader of what was left of humanity and used that power to save her anonymous friend. Or—no, not friend. That was the term the Matriarch had used in veiled language. Beneath gossiping whispers, Paige had heard the term people used for Aunt Felicity's "friend": *lover.* Something that should have been good, in the vein of New Standard's commitment to love, but was somehow charred with breath-stopping shame.

The Matriarch smiled at Paige, gracefully, in that political way that Paige had apparently always mistaken for genuine but now questioned every inch of it. It was secrecy, something rotten, and if it was coming from the top, was it really isolated there? She couldn't even pretend to smile back.

The Pandora looked fragile out of its normal home in the glass case in the Council building's meditation room. Paige jerked her arms out instinctively, but they were too far away from her body, like she was holding someone else's newborn baby.

But the Matriarch seemed unperturbed. "Whoops, I should have handed it to you a little more steadily, I'm sorry. Here, wrap your fingers under the bottom, like this."

The Matriarch pressed the Pandora toward Paige, encouraging Paige's arms to relax into her body. She held the Pandora closer to her heart. The Matriarch smiled, like she was proud of Paige.

"You're going to be great," she said. "All you have to do is hold this and walk straight."

She was going to be great. The Matriarch said so. Paige made herself smile back, trying to let the confidence she wanted so badly to prove she had show through. She tried not to think about Yuri-of-2094, of how if she dropped the Pandora, his entire existence would be spattered all over the floor, forever lost—not the remains of a person, a citizen, a beloved breadmaker who'd lost his daughter, but a pile of dirt needing to be swept up.

Or it could free him, said a small voice in the back of her head. Mott's voice. A Theorist voice. A voice that didn't understand. She ignored it, focused instead on the amusing novelty of having heard the Matriarch say *whoops*. This is what it was to be the Matriarch, maybe. This was what it was to be a leader. You had to push your own feelings to the side, blend in with the energy of the group. The burning in Paige's heart subsided; the Matriarch wasn't disregarding their conversation. She was demonstrating how to put her own experience aside for the good of their people.

"EA Pepper?"

The huérfana from earlier—What was her name, again? Lily? No, Lane—approached with a bored look on her face.

"What," said Pepper.

"You're wanted." Lane pointed her thumb behind her toward the man with the glasses. "EA York says we're starting."

"Mercy," swore Pepper. "That was really quick. Anyway, Paige, good luck."

She swept Paige into another brief arm-hug before twirling around. "You know, ashes are really just a bunch of dust," Paige could hear Lane saying to Pepper as they walked away, and all of a sudden, despite the room full of people in chaotic energy, Paige ached with loneliness.

EA York and Pepper ushered people around, arranging dancers and musicians into formations. Soon they were moving, en masse, the excitement buzzing among everyone's chatter, and Paige let herself glide along with the energy, out the door and in the hallway, ready for the administrators to tell them to go.

The Matriarch stood tall and quiet, providing a calming presence that Paige echoed while she clutched onto the Pandora. Paige half-expected it to burn when she touched it: she was sure that something as sacred as the Pandora could sense her inadequacy, both as a human and the supposed spiritual emblem of her people. She waited for the fiery crawl of sinful guilt she remembered from when she was younger, but the Pandora only felt like a box.

Maybe the guilt wouldn't come. Now that she'd made the right choice—to surrender herself to the community—maybe she was vindicated.

Surrender. A delicious, seductive word that always made Paige feel like she was flying. Surrender was relief; it was the acknowledgment that someone else was in charge, not her. She didn't have to be the one making the decisions or calling the shots, because the Ancestors had already decided that long ago. New Standard was protected land, home to protected people. The Ancestors, then, were their protectors, gatekeepers of the Afterlands, and all the New Standardites had to do to show worthiness of the gift of neverending life in perfect peace and comfort was follow the rules that the Spared had used to find favor with the Ancestors back during the war.

She was doing that, she reminded herself. She was following the rules. Keeping the covenant. Earning her place.

Deep breath in.

"Are we ready?" said the administrator.

Deep breath out.

The administrator didn't wait for anyone to respond. He wiped his glasses with his shirt and glanced passively at the Procession before waving them along. All Paige had to do was walk straight. Hold the Pandora, not drop it, and walk straight.

And the rising sun and cooler, dewy morning air with the cheering crowd, the energy frantically relieved in the wake of having a new Ritualist who promised to be more dedicated than the one who abandoned them, washed over her a familiar comfort. Paige marched next to the Matriarch in the middle of the Procession, guarded by CSes all around them. The student band led the group, playing the lively patriotic song "Come Light, Healing Light"; the current sitting Council of Elders trailed in a phalanx behind Paige and the Matriarch; bringing up the rear, a group of dancers performed a traveling square dance in time with the music.

The band played the same song year after year, the audience watching on the sidelines joining in singing. Each year prior to this one, it was the one song that put Paige entirely in her happy place.

Now, she tried to resist the pleasure flooding her brain that insisted on making her feel like her normal self again. It wanted to make her happy, but she didn't deserve it. She had doubted. She hadn't fallen prey to temptation, but it wasn't because of her own resilience. It was luck that she'd been in the right circumstances.

But the Statutes were forgiving; they guided you, if you let them. The music, too, was relentless. It washed over her like a shower, the spray of comfort raining a homey heat over her hair and down her face, behind her ears and around her neck. Singing was a hot bubble bath on a cool January night; it was the blissful surrender of anxiety, the security of knowledge of the Truth. Paige sang as they marched down the citizen-lined street, one voice melding among the thousands:

"Come light, healing light, come light eternal,
Shake, shake out of me all that is carnal
I'll be a pure light, I'll lead the way
I'll show the Theorists how we behave."

The dancers marched in step and shook their hands like they were trying to get off something sticky. Like sin. And as if the universe was peering into Paige's brain, she spotted Mott in the crowd. Her dark mane of tight curls spread out from her head like a delicate brown halo; she watched Paige quietly, a rarity for Mott, but what else was there to do?

Nothing.

Paige tried to avoid Mott's gaze. Hell, she tried to avoid anyone's gaze.

She caught sight of Adam toward the front of the crowd, his lips wrinkled in what seemed like disappointment. Paige kept the polite smile on her face, unwavering. At least that was the good thing that had come from all the stressors of her childhood environment: all the times she'd had to go to Meditation after Mama had cleaned her mouth out with soap when Paige had talked back, when Paige had tried to defend unorthodox punishments—she'd had to pretend, to play the part of the obedient, devout daughter then. She'd been expected to keep her mouth shut about the soap thing, just smile and greet their neighbors. Smile and keep sweet. Smile and be polite. And smile.

She did that now. Smiled into the distance, beyond Adam, over the top of his head. He became a blur in her peripheral vision. She smiled and sang, loud and proud, all the way around Serenity Park, and she could feel the spirits of the onlookers joining with hers.

Until the dancers in front of her stopped suddenly and she nearly ran into one of them.

They were staring at something.

A crowd.

"What on earth—" murmured the Matriarch.

A gaggle of loud, gossiping citizens crowded around the Edufice; moment by moment, people stopped watching the Procession and joined the folks on the side of the building like magnets steadily building into one central attractive force.

"Hey!" shouted CS Holly. "Back away from the wall!"

The crowd obliged.

On the wall of the Edufice, a passage was scrawled in red letters, paint bleeding from their edges. It was too small to see from where they were in Procession, but as they approached the building she could see the letters more clearly; she barely caught a glimpse of the all-too-familiar distant silhouette of her brother holding a paintbrush, not even bothering to hide, before the CSes approached him in their arrest.

The wall boasted a passage from the Statutes, but chopped up and incomplete and all wrong:

we refuse to fall prey to the temptations of our ancestors

for their weakness and selfishness nearly removed us from

earth their screams echo across the desert plains surrounding

our small town because there is no one left but us but history

has taught us that peace is in our hands and i tell

you friend that the key to peace is

the key to peace is

And that was all.

Paige shivered as she stared at it.

It wasn't a passage. It was a poem.

Paige swallowed hard. Poetry wasn't illegal, and ordinarily this sort of mild vandalism would have resulted in some community service cleaning up the mess. But with a Ritualist gone, his sister the replacement, and the words on the wall taken directly from the holy book itself—it was enough to capture the attention of onlookers, to incite feelings of unrest among the crowd. It was enough, the Council would likely determine, to encourage Theorists.

If he wasn't a Theorist himself.

The tears welled up in the back of Paige's throat as she watched the awkwardly long neck, the neat, brushed-back brown hair, the smooth, bobbing way that Solomon moved, like she was seeing it all for the last time.

But the most terrifying thing Paige saw was the fierce calm on his face, forced like she'd seen him do a hundred times while he pretended that all was well in their home—

—and, layered over that, a lack of regret that reinforced how done he was with pretending.

THE COMMUNITY

a handwritten note

They gather in rows and they gather in lines. Equidistant and quick, one at a time, ants with a task under the direction of their queen. They start with the oldest, who steps into the pyramid, offers his body so they'll care for him. He walks in, his light goes out. Eyes roll back as the body slumps in the chair, two arms, ten fingers, one head. He thought the fire would lift him up but he falls into a pile of ashes. The second-oldest steps up next, offers her body, and so on, and so forth, systematic, machines. Later, the young will collect the ashes, will turn the ash into feed for the crops. And isn't this how community should be, the young caring for the old, the old making room for the young? They start the fire and the bodies recycle, the bodies burn. So long, thirty-nine billion nerves in each of the hundred-and-six separate forms; together burn two hundred twelve arms; together, two hundred twelve legs. The skin starts to flay and the young work swiftly to clean up—ashes collected, floor swept, systematic, machines. Isn't this how community should be?

LEADER

ITHOUT THINKING ABOUT IT, Paige lurched herself forward. She scrambled between the string ensemble, accidentally scraping her neck with the tip of a violin bow in the process. She hardly noticed; she had to get to Solomon. The CSes were moving too quickly. She blinked and his hands were behind his back; she blinked again and they were leading him away. Somewhere that wasn't there. Somewhere where she might never be able to see him again.

Crap. Hell. Shit.

Hands grasped her shoulders and yanked her back; her chin jutted forward with the whiplash.

"It's all right, Ritualist," said the CS holding her shoulders.

No. No, it wasn't. Paige thrashed her arms out to break herself free from the CS.

But it was no use. The CS's grip was tight and Solomon was going, going, gone. Nothing left but the sudden sound of the gasping sob that climbed out of her throat, the graffiti that Solomon left behind, and the retroactive obligatory guilt about thinking vulgar language to herself. And the wide-eyed stares of every citizen watching the Procession.

She didn't care. They'd taken her brother away. They'd taken him *away*.

She sobbed wildly, unable to believe that he wasn't right there but unable to reconcile that concept with reality. Stuff like this didn't happen. And if it did, it happened to other people, in the past, during or before the Paterazm. Her family already had one Theorist in its lineage, and her parents and their parents had done everything in their power to erase the stain Aunt Felicity had left on their blood. They couldn't afford a scandal like this. Not with their own son, the Ritualist's own brother.

They were going to cleanse him. Mercy. *Mercy.* She couldn't feel her legs.

The CS relinquished his grip only after the Matriarch approached and placed her hands on Paige's shoulder in place of his.

"The sacrifice of the individual on behalf of the whole is one of the most difficult actions our Ritualist performs," the Matriarch projected toward the carefully watching audience. She stepped directly next to Paige, her entire arm draping the top of Paige's back. She gave Paige an empathetic smile, her eyebrows pressed up in pity. This was it. Leadership in action, and it had the best of New Standard—empathy in the face of chaos. "We are *with* you, Ritualist. Mercy have you!"

The warmth that cast itself over Paige's heart only made her cry harder.

"Mercy have you! Mercy have you!" the onlookers echoed, but it was so in unison and so instant that it turned the warmth into chills.

Though that also could have been due to the Matriarch's grip tightening on her shoulder. To hold her steady, probably, because Paige couldn't stop crying.

She wanted so badly for Mott to be there next to her so she could bury her head in the crook of Mott's neck. Or for Solomon to have never painted graffiti on the Edufice in the first place. Or for any of this to have ever happened so she could return to her stupid, miserable, mundane future as Adam's spouse-turned-sex-object because at least then she wouldn't have had the grief of leaving the two most important people in her life and she could have gone on believing that everything around her was the Truth she'd been raised on.

But it wasn't, and she couldn't, and the Procession retreated quickly back to the Council building, Paige in the thick of it.

Once inside, the Matriarch kindly invited Paige to a door on the opposite end of the hallway as her room. "Our next appointment is in here," she said, at a volume that anyone around them could hear her. A sign on the door featured only one word:

EXAMINATIONS

Thank the Ancestors for this mercy. It was a cover. The Matriarch was going to give her a place to grieve.

A padded examination table waited in the center of the small room. It didn't seem comfortable. Instead, the high-necked dress the Matriarch wore looked like a far more attractive place for Paige to lay her head. She imagined the Matriarch's warmth wrapping around her like a blanket, her arms reassuring her that Solomon was going to be okay. It was all going to be okay.

As soon as the door closed, the Matriarch's smile vanished.

"You will *never* do that again."

Paige's hope dissipated in a half-second, her heart pounding.

The Matriarch was furious. Her flat face was accentuated with high cheekbones and a wide nose; objectively, she was beautiful. It was this beauty that made her seem otherworldly and magical. But now, the anger made that magicality terrifying.

It had only been a few hours ago that she'd sat on the bed next to her and she'd shared her own fears, her own past. Just a few seconds ago, she'd been the motherly presence Paige longed for.

"This *morning*, Paige. We talked about this this *morning*. I said, 'When you lead a people, they will follow you.' Did you hear me?"

Yeah. She remembered. Paige nodded miserably. The Matriarch *was* a motherly presence—her strictness rivaled Mama's.

So any warmth was either temporary or a lie.

138

"Out loud, please."

"Yes," Paige half-whispered through the phlegm in her throat.

"And did you under*stand* that implicit in that statement is that if you lead some sort of resistance, they will follow you in that resistance?"

"Yes."

"And did you understand that if they follow you in that resistance, *they will die?*"

"Yes."

"And that you will be responsible for their deaths and potentially the eradication of the human race?"

"I'm sorry," Paige croaked. Her whole body soured like a pickle. Everything was horrible.

"You don't need to be sorry. You need to be obedient."

Obedient. Yes. Paige cried her way through a nod of acceptance.

"Stop crying."

Paige nodded again, wiping her eyes. It was just as well—the Ritualist wasn't weak, she didn't cry. But tears still poured out regardless of her will.

The Matriarch sighed, relaxing her shoulders. "I don't mean to have scared you," she said. "But you're a leader of this community, now. You can't *have* emotional reactions like that."

"What kind of emotional reactions am I meant to have, then?"

The words were out before Paige could stop them. Her whole head felt fuzzy, beating in time with her pulse.

The Matriarch's neck remained rigid, the sharp angles on her face tightening again in—frustration?

Fury?

Fury.

"Let me be very clear," the Matriarch said quietly. "I know I'm asking you to put your life on the line to save the people you love, but you *will not* undo the single greatest sacrifice I have made so that you and your family could live. You and I serve the people, and they deserve to live. So you *will* let us do our job, you *will* shut your mouth, and you *will* do as you're told, or you'll find yourself on the stake burning right next to your Theorist brother."

Paige couldn't bring herself to protest that Solomon wasn't a Theorist, though she felt the words on her lips, trying to squirm their way free. She couldn't bring herself to say anything. The Matriarch grabbed something off a table and ran it under a sink on the other side of the room.

Everything was unraveling in front of her. Her brother was in captivity. She'd lunged after him in a moment of insanity. And now the image of the kind, sympathetic Matriarch who understood Paige and her plight was destroyed, replaced by one with a hypocritical traitor.

The Matriarch tossed a damp washcloth into Paige's lap.

"Clean up your neck."

And then she was gone.

—

THE BLOOD FROM PAIGE'S neck was gone but the tiny scrape still stung. She stared at the door without really looking at it, trying to fit all the puzzle pieces together in disbelief. Aunt Felicity, Papa's sister, as the Matriarch's lover—it was almost laughable, how unrealistic it was, how much of a conspiracy theory it was, but maybe that was just it: so implausible that it was real.

Taking the Matriarch's place in the room was a tall, pointy-nosed woman who seemed to be around the Matriarch's age, dressed in the uniform gray scrubs and light-blue smock of a medic. Trailing behind her was a young woman whose pigtail braids suggested that she might not be old enough for the medic smock she wore.

"I'm Council Medic Zara," said the older woman, stretching a pair of medical gloves on her hands, "and this is Council Medic Amanda."

As if Paige couldn't read the name badges pinned to their smocks.

"Hello," said Paige, trying to pretend like she was okay. "I'm—"

"I'll take that." Medic Zara reached for the washcloth, now decorated with a tiny bit of blood, and exchanged it for a thin lavender gown. "Undress completely and put this on. Garments, too. You can change back there."

Paige wanted to stand her ground, to resist having to follow orders after having been interrupted. But she thought of Aunt Felicity, of how kind and gentle she always looked, of how Papa always said she was a traitor for having taken a female lover and refusing a male spouse, and how loyal of a person Aunt Felicity really was, and whether Papa actually knew that or not—and she took the dress, resignedly, because if she was going to do anything about it, now was not the time.

She headed toward the curtained-off area in the corner of the room that Medic Zara pointed out. Normally she changed alone, no one to hear the nearly-silent-but-still-somehow-there sounds of Paige shifting her weight out of her Procession dress and her garments and into the medical gown. Even though she changed in the corner of the room and there was a curtain separating her from the medics, Paige still felt exposed as she slipped the gown over her bare body, the fabric brushing against her nipples in the same way that she'd experienced while changing before the Rite of Responsibility.

She hid behind her arms crossed over her chest when she emerged from the curtained-off area, but neither medic was paying attention to her. Medic Zara was attaching a small wooden platform on either side of the foot of the table while Medic Amanda zeroed out a scale.

"Oh, great, you're done," said Medic Amanda, offering Paige the friendliest, most genuine smile she'd seen in what felt like forever. "Come this way."

The younger medic seemed unnaturally cheerful—the very opposite of Medic Zara—her very-light skin rosier than Paige's after a run and potentially more full of freckles than Mott's. Mott would like this woman, probably. Her pigtails had wispy pieces of hair falling out and her smile lit up her face so much that it made Paige forget why she was sad. She offered Paige a hand. "Take my hand for balance and get up on the scale, there you go! Wow, you've got great balance, you don't even need me."

Paige checked Medic Amanda's face for signs of sarcasm. There were none. The kindness was genuine.

Medic Amanda turned her attention to recording Paige's height and weight while Medic Zara checked through her instruments on a small wooden table. "Routine exam today. According to my charts, your cycle is such that we should do the first NI-2 tomorrow. You do know what NI-2 is, yes?"

Non-Intercoursal Impregnation. Paige glanced down at her belly, at the straight gown on top of it, at her knees underneath. There was no way a baby could fit in there.

"I do."

Medic Amanda led Paige onto the examination table, where Medic Zara proceeded to assault Paige's mouth with a wooden depressor and her knee with a rubber triangle strapped to a metal wand.

"Lie down," said Medic Zara. "Knees apart."

Paige obliged, though hesitantly, especially because she'd heard Papa complain a billion times about young girls during the Paterazm who *just opened their legs for anybody*, that that was what had gotten them all into this mess in the first place. She'd done this a few times—ever since she'd started her cycle, and only ever with a medic—but she was familiar with the medic who normally performed her examination.

Medic Zara was a stranger.

Still, she leveraged her feet onto each respective platform and let her hips loosen, let gravity pull her knees in opposite directions. For lack of anything else to distract her, she turned her head to watch Medic Amanda scribbling furiously on the clipboard she held.

Medic Zara pressed down on her pelvis. Paige couldn't imagine what she'd be looking for—could she count the number of eggs Paige had by pressing on her skin? Medic Amanda glanced up once to watch what Medic Zara was doing, smiling at Paige with a thumbs-up when Paige accidentally caught her eye. Paige lied a smile back, keenly aware of the increased blood flow to her lower half, and shamed herself for not being able to hold back what felt like leaking from her vagina.

What she hated even more was that she both wanted and dreaded Medic Zara's touch.

Medic Zara shoved a couple of fingers briskly up between Paige's legs with her other hand, still pressing down on her pelvis with the first one. Paige inhaled sharply, part-pleasure, part-pain, and let herself wish with her conscious brain that it wasn't Medic Zara's fingers that were there, but Mott's instead. Her breathing deepened as she imagined Mott's tight curls brushing against her neck while their bare chests met and they reached their arms around each other, nothing separating them anymore, grabbing onto the skin of their backs like they were never letting go.

Paige shut her eyes so that she wouldn't look at Medic Amanda during her shameful fantasy, but that only increased her pleasure. She turned her head the other way and trained her eyes on the wall instead. It was the least-sexy wall she'd ever seen.

In the back of her mind, she thought to herself: if Medic Zara's fingers hurt there, even a little, there was no way she was going to be able to push out a whole human. How had Agatha done it? Maybe they gave her some sort of special ritual that helped. Maybe there was a salve that lured the baby out. Or maybe babies knew how to force themselves out, destroying their mothers' bodies in the process. Maybe her baby would split her open entirely and her battered genitalia would be hidden by the Ritualist gown glowing in the candlelight of the Ascension, no one the wiser.

Maybe Agatha hadn't really gotten through everything after all. Maybe that was why she'd seemed so hollow, physically and spiritually, at the Ascension.

Medic Zara removed her fingers and snapped off her gloves, turning her attention back to cleaning up her workspace. "Everything looks good, you're all done."

Good? It was horrible, lying there splayed out like the glow toads they dissected as age-sevens. Paige couldn't do this. She couldn't do any of it. She was going to wither and die like a poorly fertilized orange during a bad crop season.

"It's going to be okay," said Medic Amanda, reading her panicked expression. "You're going to be just fine."

There was that reassuring smile again. Paige wanted to believe it so much.

She wanted to believe everything, again.

—

"You're quiet," said Medic Amanda as she led Paige across the lobby and back to her room. "Can't say I blame you, though. I remember when they cleansed Yuri-of-2094—the Ritualist was dead silent after that. I would be, too, if my dad were cleansed and I had to do it."

Right. The Ritualist was an active part of the cleansing ritual. And if Sol got cleansed, she would have to do it.

"You don't—" Paige almost asked, but she closed her mouth.

"What's that?"

Paige shook her head. She couldn't ask Medic Amanda personal things. She was the Ritualist for Medic Amanda, too. Probably she should appear enigmatic or something.

"Nevermind," Paige said, doing her best to look enigmatic.

Was it working? Her face felt important. It was totally working.

"No, it's okay," said Medic Amanda. "You can ask me anything."

Or maybe she just looked terrified. Medic Amanda seemed like she would be true to her word. Hell, Paige felt like she could have even told her about how she felt about Mott and not have feared judgment.

She took a deep breath.

"You don't think the Matriarch would *actually* cleanse my brother?"

The medic, for the first time in the short time Paige had known her, didn't respond right away. A tiny, worried crease line nestled into the fair skin of her orange-freckled forehead.

"You have to understand, Ritualist," she said. "The Ritualist the Council picked *left*. At the risk of her own death with no hope for redemption, completely giving up any possibility of getting to the Afterlands. That sort of thing tends to leave people rattled. They second-guess everything. And, from a strictly empathetic-love point-of-view, I can understand why, if the savior selected by our world leader runs away, people might be a bit uncertain about their own futures. It opens up room for a whole host of possibilities, you know?"

Paige nodded, still processing. "Possibilities?"

"Of other people doing the same thing."

Oh. Right.

"So—it isn't out of the question."

Medic Amanda shrugged, darting her eyes around the room. "I couldn't say."

The way she said it didn't seem like she couldn't say because she didn't know. More like she wasn't allowed to.

Who wasn't allowing her to?

Probably the same person who was considering cleansing her brother.

Paige shuffled after Medic Amanda back down the hallway toward the Ritualist's room. She felt hopeless, helpless. Solomon had given up on everything; it was egotistical to think that her selection was the reason for it, but if the guilt Paige had been carrying around with her was correct, then Solomon definitely was feeling what Paige had understood she did: abandoned him. And with Ingrid deliberately rebelling against their whole world, he might have wondered why he had to go along with the system in the first place.

Paige was the second-most revered person in New Standard, and she couldn't help her own brother.

The Statutes said that obedience was crucial, but that loyalty and benefit of the doubt were more important. There had to be something in between passively going along with everything and actively rebelling.

"Can I talk to her?" Paige asked.

"Who? The Matriarch?"

"Yes."

"Right now?"

Paige hesitated, equal parts ashamed at the audacity of the request and terrified to face her again. Too demanding? Not reverent enough?

Yeah, she told herself, *but shame is on your side. You're the new Ritualist. They can't hurt you, or they're out two Ritualists. Unspeakable.*

She took out a deep breath and exhaled, trying to own her tentative confidence.

"Our leaders are always accessible to their people, aren't they?"

"Of course," Medic Amanda hurried to agree, "but typically we wait for visiting hours—"

"But visiting hours are for civilians to talk with the Matriarch and the Ritualist. Am I supposed to visit myself?"

Medic Amanda stopped talking and squinted sideways at Paige, like she was trying to decide what to make of her, her orange pigtail braids tilting to one side of her body under gravity's rule. She sighed, checked the hallway like she was looking for someone, then glanced at the clock. "I guess not. She should be in her office now. Follow me."

A cool thrill of hope swelled in Paige's diaphragm. She had some sort of power, however thin of a shred it was, and it was hers. Mott would have been so proud.

Mott.

Just like that, the hope sank into an anxious sweat. She had the power to save people—probably, maybe. But she didn't have the power to save her own heart from shattering into pieces.

REDEEM, REDEEMED, REDEMPTION

an excerpt from the Statutes of Equality

WE DO NOT EXPECT perfection, Friend. We ask not if we will err, but when; not whether our souls will be stained but how. We as humans will inevitably fail ourselves; therefore, we are all equal in our failures, and therefore, we do not judge each other by the error of our ways, for all have sinned and fall short of the glory of the Afterlands, and all are justified freely by the grace bestowed upon us by the Ancestors through the redemption[1] that comes through the Ritualist, our Redeemer.

Our world did not come to us by accident; we are the children of those who deliberately turned away from sin. In the Old Days all of the humans on Earth fought in the Great War of Immortality, slaughtering each other to get their hands on the famed immortality serum, and only our Ancestors refused. They stood defiant in immortality's grotesque face of greed, powerful though their numbers were small. And when they were cornered, when all hope seemed lost and vandals threatened the lives of all who refused to succumb to greed, one young Ancestor stepped forward. She begged the vandals; she pleaded that they take her in exchange for her brothers and sisters. And as she wept her tears of selfless love, the vandals

---

[1] **Redemption,** n. The process through which our souls may be cleansed from the dirtiness of humanity. We are born dirty; through our persistence in our endeavors, we shall die clean. All of the dirt that surrounds us must be swept away, removed from the human experience, collected into containment and burnt from the surface of our skin. For the only true way to purify anything is to burn it, for everything that can stand the fire, you shall pass through the fire, and it shall be clean.

accepted her offering, pulled her over, and slit her throat. Her sacrifice redeemed us; her blood has saved us all.

The vandals banished the remaining Ancestors, and those Ancestors fled to a forgotten land, dried up and destroyed already years ago by bombs that had fallen there like rain. They settled there in the forgotten land and vowed never to make the mistakes of those Immortal Vandals, for those who tried to live too long ultimately slaughtered others who tried to live too long, who slaughtered them in return. We accept our modest lives on Earth. Our Redeemer established a place for us beyond this Earth where those who have embraced modesty in all things will be free and their souls will flourish, but only the pure will be welcomed. Our Redeemer allowed the purest among us—she who, like her, loves her community so much that she would give her rights to partnership and motherhood—to enter first, and bring those she cleanses along with her. We will never be worthy of our Redeemer's sacrifice, but our continued commitment to love, to selflessness, to community will make us candidates for these Afterlands where we can find our refuge.

Fear not, Friend. We embrace you and your pursuit for purity.

Let us together be redeemed.

OPEN, SESAME

"COME IN."

Medic Amanda pushed the door open, but now that it was open Paige let her foot hover over the threshold.

"Something wrong?" asked Medic Amanda.

Now was not the time to succumb to the fear igniting in her heart. Paige took a deep breath and forced herself to step into the room.

"Thought I saw something on the floor," she lied. Lying got easier every time she did it.

The office, despite being a designated personal space for the Matriarch, held few luxuries. Basic furniture took up most of the room—a couple of chairs surrounding a small table on one side, a secretary desk in the corner on the other side centered over an oval woven rug. The desk served as the main feature, with a large hatch that displayed an impressive collection of books. Next to the edge of the hatch, framing the space in the wall above the rug, hung a window identical to the one in Paige's room with one key difference—the absence of metal leaves crawling across the glass.

The Matriarch looked up from the papers scattered across the desk.

"Ritualist," she said, lowering a pair of reading glasses. "To what do I owe the honor?"

Paige took a deep breath, doubting very much that the Matriarch felt that this interaction was an honor at all.

"I want to talk to you about my brother," she said, carefully watching for the Matriarch's reaction.

The Matriarch sucked in a slow inhale through her teeth. When she spoke again, her words were measured in their pace, patient by force. "Medic, will you kindly wait outside?"

Paige could have sworn she felt a cold sweat on the back of her neck at the reality of being again left alone with the Matriarch, but she didn't dare reach her hand up to check. Medic Amanda bowed her head in a shallow incline before scrambling for the door like some disease in the room was chasing after her.

Paige refused—against her better judgment—to give in to the sudden (self-preserving?) urge she had to follow closely behind. Instead, she trained her eyes on the book titles. *Survivors of the World, Unite!*. *Extinct Explorations: Religion*. And of course, a pristine copy of *The Statutes of Equality of the Town of New Standard*.

The door clicked shut.

"So." The Matriarch leaned back in her chair. "Your brother."

For every exam Paige had ever taken her entire life, she'd studied excessively. Flashcards, question drills, essays out loud for critical reasoning—she expected nothing less than perfection for herself. But there had been no preparing for this particular moment. Her knees felt jiggly and her arms were nothing more than bony fat-bags loosely connected to her shoulders. The ease with which the Matriarch sat back in the chair, overly casual, only emphasized the dissociation that spread across the surface of Paige's skin; still, she couldn't let the Matriarch know that. She pushed her shoulders back to fake some confidence. Her brother had a name.

"Solomon," she insisted.

"Yes, I know him," said the Matriarch, matter-of-factly. "You both look very distinct, you know. The Council is very careful to stay true to the Spared's commitment to equality by way of mixing races as much as possible."

Wait, *what?* Paige blinked at the Matriarch, trying to process her words and match them with her reality. The wide variety of looks in Paige's friends and neighbors that she'd taken for granted all her life—that was orchestrated, too? Something so trivial that she'd never even thought about it so overtly was all a big strategy for the Council?

A word hit her, like something dropping from the sky to *thunk* on her head. *Humanmade.* That was what their lives were. Not divined fragments of organic time, but deliberately woven and produced like the plastics of ages old. The fear in Paige's heart grew colder, colder, colder, until it burned hot.

"The physical mixture you and your brother have is quite specific—it's what used to be China and Mexico—and I think a bit of Spain, actually, if I remember your mother's grandfather correctly—"

"Are you going to cleanse him?"

The Matriarch's expression dropped cold at the interruption, at Paige's demanding, insistent tone. In truth, Paige had surprised herself with that tone, was terrified at the Matriarch's silence, but she forced herself to feel resolved in it. If someone was threatening her brother, to hell with *keep sweet*, to hell with politeness. And the Statutes always taught courage to do the right thing when it was tempting to do the popular thing. Integrity—crucial to being a citizen of good standing.

Though by the way the Matriarch leaned forward onto her forearms on the desk in a completely unamused fashion, Paige wondered if the Matriarch believed in integrity.

"Let's get one thing straight," she said, the corners of her mouth upturned in a smile that could only be described as threatening. "You don't talk to me like that. Ever."

Paige's heart pounded from her esophagus through her vagina. It took every ounce of strength she had to maintain her rooted posture, to lift her arms in a fold across her chest as if to say, *I just did.*

"He's just a kid," she said aloud. "He's never been in trouble before."

"I am aware of that."

"You can't cleanse him."

It burst out of Paige's mouth; she wanted to swallow it back, especially at the sight of the Matriarch's eyebrows, raised so high Paige thought they might skyrocket off her face. Paige's heart thrummed throughout her body until she was no longer a girl—a young woman—but a shimmering collection of nerves: pure, defiant energy ready to tear the world down.

The Matriarch smiled in a way that Paige felt people shouldn't be allowed to smile. "I'll tell you what," said the Matriarch, too-sweet voice like overripe figs. "You cooperate with whatever is asked of you, and your brother will have nothing to worry about."

Paige stared at the Matriarch. Her leader's words sounded friendly, but the tone didn't. Mott frequently liked to remind Paige of how dense she was, how not-great she was at reading social cues, but this moment couldn't be misread. She understood perfectly: if she stepped any further over the line, if she didn't agree to do what she was told, Solomon's life was at risk.

So she said, "Thank you." And she shut her mouth.

"And do both of us a favor: Don't mention this conversation to anyone else."

Whom would Paige even tell? The proverbial radioflies on her wall? The corners of her room? The chipping paint? The metal leaves on her window, probably. Huge gossips, those.

Still, the part of Paige that wasn't angrily resistant sent up red flags of fear in the back of her brain. The Matriarch trained a threatening gaze on Paige with enough force that she could physically feel it. If the Matriarch was trying to scare her, it was working, but Paige wasn't going to let her have the satisfaction. She forced a coolness into her voice that her body refused to feel.

"No problem."

BACK IN PAIGE'S ROOM, the leaves on the window were arranged in a way so that she couldn't squeeze out. She laughed to herself in the hollow silence of the room: she'd followed every rule her entire life, and now she was a prisoner, and her brother was, too.

She let herself fall backward on the bed, her head nestling into the pillow. Fine. She rolled over to her side and cuddled the pillow under her neck.

And her fingers made contact with the paper under the pillow. The words flickered in her mind once more:

I REFUSE.

The writing was so sure—no cracks in the letters to indicate the pen coming up for air. So definitive. Solomon had known what he wanted, had known what he was doing. He'd deliberately rejected everything he'd known, and he'd gotten arrested for it. On purpose.

She wanted to cry. He had to know he was making a choice that she couldn't protect him from. And she had to just sit back and wait? She had to save her brother by following through with being the Ritualist—the thing she'd once wanted so badly, but now saw for what it was: a punishment.

Paige was impressed by his courage. Jealous of it, too. Mad at him for putting himself in danger. She'd spent her whole life shutting up and keeping sweet. And for what? To be complicit in a sacrifice that was . . . all for show?

How sad, came her mother's voice in her head—not directed at her, but directed at someone else, someone else with the moral failings that Paige had never dared to dream she could have. *How sad it is to grow up with everything, to be given everything, and then turn your back on all of it.*

No. She still believed in it.

Didn't she?

A thin tapping noise on the window startled Paige out of her reverie. She nearly peed herself as she considered who might be looking in on her as she thumbed the illicit paper, like a guilty cockroach seeking shelter in the corner of an Edufice classroom on a sweltering day. They'd found her. Who, it didn't matter—it was They, the powers-that-were, the people who would—

What was a fate worse than death?

"Hey," a voice whispered. She caught sight of rays of tight black curls suspended in the air and then falling, then suspended again and falling, coordinated with the sound of loafers hitting concrete sidewalk.

Paige's heart leapt. She launched herself out of the bed and toward the window.

"You," she told Mott, grinning stupidly against her will. "You're *here.*" She couldn't help it, couldn't hide the thrill of seeing her. Or, well, seeing the top of her head. And her eyebrows, as Mott found a foothold on a set of planter rocks and propped herself up higher. "What is it with you and windows?"

"Windows are nice." Mott's freckled face finally appeared from behind the metal leaves, an easy smile pretending like everything was perfectly normal. Like they were headed to their last day of school. Like they were gossiping about exams and who would be considering whom and how Paige was definitely growing a unibrow, and not like they were in a reality where she'd outright acknowledged her feelings for Mott for what they were—*attraction*, desire, betrayal—and Paige had—unthinkably—rejected her proposal of running away together while Paige's brother was in prison. "Thought I'd come to check out your new digs."

"My . . . digs?" Paige blinked. "You're reading up on old-world slang again, aren't you."

"Don't be jealous, Paige. It's not a good look on you."

Paige couldn't help the laugh that burst out of her. It felt so good again to see Mott's face, her breezy smile, her blouse untucked from her tea-length skirt as usual. For a moment, Paige could almost believe that things weren't . . . well. How they were.

"You're going to get caught." Paige peered beyond Mott: no CSes in sight. They'd probably figured that if she couldn't get out, they didn't need to guard the window itself. Or maybe they were just on their break or something. Then again, this was a well-hidden corner of the Council building, covered by a broad fig tree. Shadows of real leaves cast patterns on Mott's cheeks.

Mott had come back for her. She'd come back.

"What are you really doing here?" Paige asked.

"I come bearing news."

"About Solomon?"

"Kind of. About something he's involved in."

"Involved in?"

Mott hesitated. "I'm—I'm sorry. I thought you knew."

Paige blinked at Mott, as if to say—*knew what?*

"You didn't? Really?"

"Spit it out, Mott."

"He's— um— a Theorist?"

Paige stuck her fingers in her ears to clear out the wax. Surely she hadn't heard her right.

"A what."

"A Theor—"

"Mercy sodding *shit*. I *did* hear you."

Mott shut her mouth; Paige rarely swore. Ordinarily, Mott would have asked her if she was sure her hearing was working after all, or if Paige was secretly an old woman, but she didn't now. She knew when to tease Paige, and she knew that now wasn't the time, and Paige loved that about her.

"How do you know?"

"*Tch.* I know things. I hear things. I observe things. Listen: there's been a lot of chatter around town in the last twelve hours. Everyone's panicking at the prospect of Theorists taking over the whole town, but more than that—there's some growing doubt about the whole system. People are talking about closing the work day for a period of rest to work things out."

"Closing the *work day?*"

"I know."

"That's never happened. Ever."

"I know."

Paige shivered. Could New Standard even operate without work for a full day? A period of rest was indicated as a possibility in meditation practices but never employed, only mentioned as a last-resort. Maybe things could function and it wouldn't be a big deal. Or maybe they couldn't, and it would be, and bread wouldn't get made and crops wouldn't get picked and fruit would wither and die and rot in the dirt where it fell. And New Standardites would go hungry, but they would call it 'fasting,' but didn't fasting involve some modicum of consent? Didn't you have to decide to do it? It wasn't something you did because there was no food available. People could survive on their emergency packs for a day or two, but after that . . .

"Is everyone okay?" Paige asked, mostly to shut her brain up. Unspoken, the real question lay underneath:

Are you okay?

"Everyone's fine. I'm fine."

"I didn't ask about you," Paige lied.

"Right." *Yes, you did.*

Paige gave a short laugh. Typical Mott. "I miss you."

"Miss you back, P."

"But, like." Paige imagined Mott's hand on her back, rubbing circles into it, letting herself settle her head into the crook of Mott's shoulder and breathing in the skin on her neck. She loved that. She loved that. And it was awful for her to even be thinking about that at a time like this, but it was so nice to escape into that fantasy when the world was handing her the options it was.

"I know," Mott said.

"But—"

"I know."

"Yeah."

Silence. A silence so thick that it seemed to invite every hope, want, desire of Paige's to come flying out of her mouth and into the space between them. And maybe, now that Paige's hands were tied and she was officially doomed and she could never have

Mott or risk being the death of her own brother—maybe now she could tell her. At least part of it.

"Mott, I want to tell you something."

"What?"

"Well, I can't just say it."

"Why not?"

"I don't know."

"Is it because you're afraid to?"

Yes.

"Don't be afraid." Mott said.

"It's something I want."

"It's okay to want things." *It's okay to want me.*

"But I can't have what I want. So it's like, why even bother wanting?"

Mott exhaled through her nose, pressing her lips together in a quiet smile. "Sometimes, wanting motivates us to keep going, even when everything feels like defeat."

Paige was in the right place, then. She felt like defeat.

"I want—" She couldn't say it. She tried to keep talking but nothing came out.

"It's okay. Don't be afraid."

Paige exhaled in a controlled breath. Everything was okay, now that Mott was here, talking to her. She could lie enough to herself to pretend like everything was perfectly normal. All hope was not lost.

And she could have courage. Mott gave her courage.

Paige took a deep breath. *Embrace your thoughts but restrain your bodies.* The Statutes gave her courage, too.

"I want to kiss you," Paige said, her privatest thoughts finally out loud and unhidden and unable to be swallowed back between her lips, "but I feel like that makes me a bad person."

Mott didn't move for a moment.

Mercy. Paige had broken her. Mercy mercy mercy mercy mercy mercy she'd said the wrong thing she never should have listened to herself she should have hidden it away forever why couldn't she just hide it away forever—

And then, all of a sudden, like a wind-up doll shuffling along its designated walking path, Mott grinned like she'd never paused at all, like Paige had totally imagined it.

"That's interesting," Mott said, her *ts* sparkling, delicious sound between her teeth. "Next time, I'll make sure to not let you leave without kissing me, then."

Paige's stomach fluttered at the impossible prospect, at the wild unreality of it. Her head buzzed with the surreal knowledge that Mott wanted to kiss her, too; that Mott was *talking* about kissing her, and if only this iron gate wasn't here, if only they could lean their foreheads together, if only, if only.

To have the courage to hope was to be able to live in a dream, and dreams were all she had anymore. Paige sighed and held her breath, somehow, at the same time.

"I'm going to ascend in a year," she said, not so much as an excuse as it was a problem to be solved, "and until then I'll be really closely guarded."

Mott scoffed, looking behind each of her shoulders. "Shit guards you've got."

Paige eyed the leaf detail on the window gate. "Not much reason for them to be worried here."

"Overconfidence. The worst of the sins. If we get you out, you won't be sacrificed, and that'll be poo on the guards."

Paige laughed with a side-helping of guilt that she was laughing when her brother was imprisoned, which she ignored. "And how do you propose I do that? Oh! I know. A magic trick. I'll just shrink myself up really tiny and scale the wall and jump through these leaves."

Mott's broad grin had faded into a grimace of something serious. "I was going to say through the group of Theorists in the Council building, but I guess your way works, too."

"Well, my way is certainly more realistic."

"I'm not joking. There really is a group of Theorists in there."

"Oh yeah? Who? The receptionist? That guy is *way* too jumpy to be a secret undergrounder."

"It's led by an huérfano."

An huérfano? One of the most lasting, if secretive, symbols of New Standard, in a movement to be its undoing? "I'm sorry, but have we forgotten? Huérfanos are born of Ritualists, and Theorists are evil."

"Okay, but—but why?"

"Why what?"

"Why are Theorists evil?"

"Because—" And at that moment, Paige realized that she didn't have any answer other than, *because they are.*

"Theorists are just people," said Mott.

"People who are undermining the very fabric of our society. People who could be the death of all of us." Even as she said it, she wasn't sure that she wasn't just recycling someone else's words. "People who recruited and exploited my little brother."

Mott tilted her head to the side for a moment to study Paige. "P, do you really think that there's only one way to survive?"

"Of course not. But surviving is different than thriving. The Ancients survived, Mott. We thrive."

"You're locked in a room."

"Well, I'm willingly giving myself so that everyone else can thrive."

"How is that even fair?"

It's not about fairness, she heard in her brain, but because she couldn't explain why, she said, "Keep your voice down."

"You weren't chosen."

A pang hit Paige in the corner of her shoulder.

"Yes, I was."

"Yeah—second. Ingrid was supposed to be the sacrifice, and she peaced. You can, too."

"I'm not running away with you, Mott."

"Well, no, you can't anymore. There are CSes actually by the border. None of us is going anywhere. We're trapped."

"*We* are not trapped. *I* am staying here of my own volition, as a volunteer, and you can leave anytime you want."

Not that she would. No one would. The last time someone had run away was in New Standard's fourth year, and it was stupid. A search party had gone out to go find him—the runner—and came back a week later with his corpse, half-eaten by desert creatures, maggots burying their young in his eyes.

Ingrid was stupid to run away. There was no way she'd survived. The land outside the borders was nothing but a depressing collection of rubble and dust and dead things. The only source of greenery left on the planet was in the garden that had been cultivated by New Standardites, the trees they'd managed to grow, the weeds in the lush soil that generations past had spent lifetimes reviving. At least that runner had made a good fertilizer. She opened her mouth to say as much when Mott groaned—

"Just—just open your *mind* for one goddamn *second!*"

Startled, Paige closed her mouth.

"Sol isn't evil, right?"

The sweet little boy with the long eyelashes and an unparalleled thirst for learning, for discovery, for truth? The kid who wanted nothing more than to love and be loved by the people around him?

"No. Absolutely not." But maybe she was wrong. Maybe she didn't know anything after all. "I don't think so."

"Doesn't *evil* mean you're hurting someone?"

"I guess. Yes. I don't know, this feels like a trap."

"It's not a trap."

Her face was close, her eyelashes tickling the iron leaves. Vulnerable.

"Do you trust me?" Mott asked.

Paige held her breath. With Mott's face only inches away, familiar freckles Paige had thought she'd memorized clustering on her nose and expanding across her face like the limitless stars in the sky, how could she not trust her? Of course she trusted this woman who had been there for her since she was an age-four, who'd walked her into the Edufice passing her own confidence through their palms? This woman who kept coming back again and again, chasing Paige down when she didn't deserve it, and honestly she *didn't* deserve it, not Mott's dedication, her persistence, her promise to keep trying.

Paige nodded slowly.

"Okay," said Mott, "then just listen.

"There's this book. No one knows where it came from, or how old it is, or if it's even a book at all, because it's mostly just individual papers that could eventually be assembled. But people are passing it around, and before you get super-judgey about something that seems illegitimate, trust me. It's brilliant."

Paige doubted it, but she held her tongue.

Mott looked around her shoulders again, then slipped a tightly folded piece of paper through the leaf-gate.

It looked delicate. Old, like it was an original copy of whatever it was. It was folded exactly like the paper Solomon had given her: two sides of tight folds, like a set of doors, one of the sides tucked into a pocket that the other made.

Hesitantly, Paige took it, even though it had to be some sort of sin, because—if she was really honest with herself—part of her thought that it might not be completely, one-hundred-percent wrong.

"Open it," said Mott.

So Paige did.

＝

a handwritten note

Two things exist in the world:

      1. What we perceive, and
      2. What is.

These two things are not the same.
I repeat:

These two things are not the same.

If I hit my neighbor, my neighbor might believe I harbor hate toward him, when my own perspective is that my spatial awareness is simply poor. Is my neighbor wrong for feeling that I might want to harm him? I cannot fault him for his feeling, regardless of whether it was my intention or not. He feels what he feels.

But the action remains the same: this is what is. My neighbor and my hand have collided. The difference is not in what happened, but rather in the language that we use to tell the story. My neighbor's calls the incident assault. I call it an accident. Nevertheless: we have collided. This, neither of us can deny.

In similar ways, we may fail to acknowledge the effect the filter of language has in our everyday lives. Past eras called for multiple languages to be spoken at the same time among different groups; a hunk of metal could be known by three different names, in three different writing systems. This, in turn, affects our perception. That perception, in turn, affects what we identify as fact and what we identify as fiction.

In *Holy Bible*, we see, over and over again, the phrase *God is love*. Most people interpret the main character, *God*, as human (or humanoid), since *Holy Bible* consistently insists that we humans are "made in His image." My challenge to you, dear reader, is this: what if the focus is not on *God*, or on *love*, but on *is*? What if the phrase is not to emphasize how God embodies love, and how, in order to make your spirit more Godly, you must love—what if, instead, the focus was on *is* as an equals sign?

We then run into an issue of language. Who decides which name we give that energy? Who decides which names we give anything? Who determines the order of the letters from the Roman alphabet that will represent these uniquely human constructs?

Bodies are composed of, according to our literature, "two arms and two legs and ten fingers and one head. Two eyes and a nose and a mouth with thirty-two teeth. Two ears. One tongue. And nerves, countless nerves, thirty-nine billion nerves, for sensing."

Each of these parts is nothing more than a collection of cells to which language has assigned a name. There is no good; there is no bad. Not objectively. Things simply are. And then they are whatever we call them.

Therefore: with the premise that we live in a reality that simply is, we recognize that we have arbitrarily assigned human meaning, human language, to everything that is, so that we can understand it. From this premise, I can only conclude:

The values by which we live our lives are utterly, entirely made-up.

CONTROL RESIST CONTROL RESIST CONTROL

Tʜᴀᴛ ᴘᴀꜱꜱᴀɢᴇ. Pᴀɪɢᴇ ᴋɴᴇᴡ that passage, the quoted one. It was from the Statutes, from the chapter that talked about how New Standard's predictability increased community safety and practically guaranteed life. But the mentions of *Holy Bible* in a way that made it seem as common as the Statutes suggested that the passage's speaker was of a different time. *Our literature.* Who was *our*, and why were the Statutes considered literature instead of law?

Her mind reeled with something in between curiosity and nauseated disgust. The whole concept was ludicrous, ridiculous, *preposterous*—what did the speaker mean, 'entirely made up'? It was— it was— it was nothing more than a series of lies, was what it was.

Paige scoffed at the document as a whole. "It's a miracle I can even read this," she told Mott. "The handwriting is terrible."

But Mott's expression, previously sparkling with hope, read unimpressed.

"*That's* what you got from that?"

"Okay, suspending my disbelief. This thing basically says that nothing exists." Paige rolled her eyes. "How is that even possible? Hint: it's not. Things exist."

"That's not—" Mott gave a groaning sigh. "That's not what it says."

"Okay, fine, I'm oversimplifying. Everything is 'assigned human meaning'? Our value systems are 'entirely made-up'?"

"I mean—you don't think it takes the pressure off? No good? No bad? Just—no such thing? That makes sense to me. And it's relieving."

"You can't just believe what you want to believe, Mott."

"*Why not?* Think about what it's saying—everything is just a lens. It's just a framework. You know how all the old-world religions had a massive flood? They all called it different things, but the flood itself was consistent. Now we know it for what it was—climate change—but then, they didn't have that kind of language. They just interpreted everything as a sort of other-worldly, cosmic event, because they didn't have modern science. And as our species learns, we get better language—"

"Whoa. Whoa. Slow down."

Mott's face looked relaxed, her curls soft and glittering with a copper overtone in the sun. She looked like the breath of fresh air she took in now. Reset, somehow. More alive than Paige had ever seen her, bursting with new energy.

Hopeful again.

Beautiful.

"It's just—" said Mott, breathlessly, "—just think. If this lens theory is real, think about what that means."

Paige's heart panged. If the handwritten pile of nonsense she was holding was right, all the rules around her existed for no reason. And then what would she be dying for? What would she be living for? Why shouldn't she live, then, if everything was a lie and there was no real purpose to the Ascension, because there were no Afterlands, because *everything was a mercy-filled lie?*

And if it was all a lie, then suddenly the feelings she had for Mott weren't so awful anymore. She could have them and it was *okay.*

No good. No bad. Relief.

Why *couldn't* she believe what she wanted to believe? She was going to die, anyway.

"The Theorists aren't trying to kill everyone," continued Mott. "They just want to breathe."

"To breathe," Paige repeated, not processing.

"To be free."

"Hm."

To be free.

What did that even mean, freedom? It was something the inhabitants of this land had felt they were owed prior to the war. And hadn't that freedom led to extreme capitalism? To polarized economies? To the regular oppression of marginalized groups, to slavery with a prettier name? To the global, no-bars-held pursuit of immortality. To war.

Her head hurt.

"Just look for this girl, okay?" Mott pressed—gentler, now. Like she was trying to mute her zeal now that she knew Paige was thinking about it, now that she knew she'd won and was trying to not rub it in.

Lens theory, Mott had called it. Theory, Theorists. No wonder the Council considered Theorists so dangerous: they could undo entire realities.

Paige took a deep breath. She folded the paper in half, then in half again, then in half again, and again and again and again, trying to keep with the creases already folded into it, and tucked the left side into the right side's pocket.

"Which girl?"

"The huérfano. Huérfana. The one leading the resistance."

A brief knock at the door startled both of them.

"Paige?" came a voice, slightly muffled from behind the door. "Just checking in. Are you okay?"

CS Holly. Paige whirled around, half-panicked. "Just fine," she hollered through the door. "Talking to myself, is all."

There was a short pause.

"I'm here," said CS Holly through the door, "if you need another person."

It sounded earnest. Like she pitied Paige. Or like she thought Paige was losing her mind already.

Maybe she was.

"Thanks," she called back, and then turned back to the window, ready to give Mott a piece of said mind, to ask her where she'd gotten the paper, to scold her for taking a risk like that if New Standard's political energy was really as tenuous as she said it was—

—to finally let out everything she'd been holding back, to admit that she did, in fact, want her more than she wanted the rules—

But she was gone.

"Mott?" Paige whispered to the wind, to the leaf-gate, to the tree in the distance.

She glanced back toward the door, where CS Holly undoubtedly stood on the other side. She wanted, badly, to take up CS Holly on her offer to talk. Paige laughed to herself, imagining how she might explain the situation to CS Holly—

I thought I wanted this job, and I don't; and I thought I could turn off my romantic feelings for my best friend, but I can't; and I thought I was safe from ever being lured into temptation by Theorists but apparently *I'm not and nothing makes sense anymore and I just want to go to sleep and have this all be a stupid dream.*

That wasn't a bad idea, actually. She kicked off her shoes as petulantly as possible, though it didn't feel as satisfying as she thought it might. She surrendered herself to gravity, letting it pull her back onto the bed, then curled her legs under the covers, her cold-despite-the-heat toes huddling together to warm up beneath the protection of the blankets. And she closed her eyes, nestling the pillow under her neck, shoving the folded paper in with its new friend inside the pillowcase, and let herself drift off anywhere but here.

—

A FEW HOURS LATER, she woke up.

She blinked, bleary-eyed, as the popcorn ceiling came into focus. Growing up, she'd liked to trace constellations from the random globs of paint in the ceiling—a cricket with a broken wing, a small boy going down a slide, two girls playing hopscotch. She said hello to them in the morning. She said goodnight to them at night.

But this wasn't her home, no matter how many times she tried to tell herself it was, or that it had to be. There was no Mama coaxing the kettle into whistling, no clinking metal on ceramic stirring honey into tea, no sound of Papa's slippers shuffling around on a hallway carpet, none of Solomon's bright, happy voice bidding good-mornings and chattering about whatever he was learning in school.

A pit of despair wrangled itself inside her gut. She was the Ritualist. Ingrid was gone. Sol's life was being threatened by the Matriarch herself. Mott had come back and gone again. And there were Theorists inside the Council building, just on the other side of that door.

What time was it? Her stomach grumbled unabashedly. She could see the ceiling in the cool moonlight, but not much else; it must've been the middle of the night. She'd missed two meals. Why had no one come to wake her up?

She rolled over onto her side, only to stare at a tray of food sitting in a chair in the corner of the room behind the door. They weren't going to let her starve, at least. She shivered as she wondered if the same thing had happened to Agatha. When Agatha had rolled over to get out of the bed, did she ignore the tray? Did she let the food sit there and rot? The unthinkable— did she *waste* it?

But despite her rumbling belly, the sight of the food made her sick to her stomach. To eat felt selfish, somehow. Pleasurable when nothing should have been. Like some sort of sin.

Still, it was worse to leave it there.

Paige ate the food quickly, barely tasting it. Her belly

tightened around it as it devoured, swallowing it into the depths of her gut where she would never see it again. She tried to not get any pleasure out of it, but the sheer relief of not being hungry anymore was so good. Subconsciously, she scolded herself; if she felt enough guilt, perhaps she could somehow earn the food she ate.

What to do with the tray now? It sat empty in front of her, hosting nothing but paltry crumbs. Her body felt gluttonous, soft, like the pilot from the history museum she'd seen when she was younger. The room around her dark, the noise outside her door obsolete—she was alone.

She could leave it where it was, a visitor with an unsettling stillness settled on the floor. She didn't like it there. The other side of the door seemed vacant, too—no one to collect it.

It couldn't hurt to go out and drop off the tray at the kitchen, right? Get out of the room for a bit? Wander around while all was quiet?

Then again, CS Holly was probably right outside the door, preparing to block Paige's exit.

Or was she?

Definitely couldn't hurt to check.

Holding her breath, Paige carefully wrapped her fingers around the door handle. She exhaled, counted to three, and gently pushed outward, waiting for the rebuke that would undoubtedly come in response to the loud unsticking sound the door made when separating from its frame.

But none came.

She peered around the door on one side, then the other, then wandered down the hallway, past the washroom across the small, Shaker-style hall from her room.

No one was around; in front of her was nothing but an open lobby, usually well-populated, but that now maintained a quiet, empty soliloquy of stillness. Moonlight filtered in a thin whisper through the windows like it had in her room. Further in the distance, past the vacant receptionist's desk, a CS stood watch, though his back faced the inside of the lobby.

The kitchen stood only a few feet away, next-door to a room that might have been the same one where Paige had had her medical exam. She considered her options: get the CS's attention and have him take her tray to the kitchen, or take it herself. The first option sounded less-than-exciting. She'd had enough attention already. Still, something about tiptoeing toward the kitchen with her empty tray in-hand felt dirty, even if there was nothing explicitly preventing her from doing it.

She did it anyway. She was careful about shifting her weight, careful about her balance, as she silently slipped across the pinewood floors toward the kitchen. She glanced behind her shoulder at the guard; he watched outward, none the wiser, and she was nearly there—

And then she was at the door.

Yes.

She held her breath, stabilizing the tray in one hand and reaching for the door handle with the other. She twisted it counterclockwise, and with a tiny, muffled click, the door opened.

She checked behind herself again at the noise. The guard had turned his head sideways and leaned forward to have a brief, unconcerned look, but otherwise he stayed where he was.

She'd done it. She'd successfully sneaked to the kitchen. Paige breathed out and let the tray hit the metal countertop.

Clack.

Shit.

The guard instantly whipped his torch around and shined it in the echo of where'd been before she ducked, just in time, beneath the counter. A good spot to shelter herself in the middle of an earthquake, she thought to herself out of habit. Not that any of her semi-annual emergency training would be useful if the CS found her.

She held her breath as the torchlight grew larger on the wall opposite her. There was a salt shaker on the countertop that preened its shadow over her, looming only broader as she heard the guard's footsteps draw nearer.

And then the light crept so near that it brightened the whole wall behind her.

It barely missed the countertop so far. One inch lower and he'd see her. She didn't dare breathe.

She heard him breathing, then heard him pause it to listen.

How much longer would it be until she ran out of breath? Only five seconds. Three. She couldn't outlast him. She was going to faint soon. Then he'd see her body keeled over on the ground and it wouldn't matter anyway.

Black spots started to infect her vision. Her head filled with a pressured lightness. Her eyes felt like they were vibrating in their sockets.

He got closer.

His feet were just on the other side of the counter's wall.

SMACK.

A loud crunch, a solid punch to the ground beneath rubber. Paige cringed, but she bit down hard on her lip to prevent herself from squeaking.

"I got you this time, beetle," said the guard. "Three days. Three days in a row and this time I found you."

And then the guard's footsteps retreated, the champion, leaving the guts of the beetle on the ground.

Paige waited where she was. She wanted to cry from the anxiety of it all, then from the guilt that the worst thing she'd had to deal with in her life was that she was sad that a beetle had gotten squished right next to her ear. In the stark darkness, the sheer stagnance of being the only one in a large area where no presence of life was detected other than the end of one—it weighed on her like a giant wet sponge, seeping cold responsibility over her chest.

After a few minutes there was no more evidence of light. If she didn't get out now, she risked him coming back. She lifted herself up from under the counter, pointedly ignoring the beetle's corpse on the ground, and scurried back out of the kitchen, back toward the darkness of the hallway.

But something caught her eye.

The faintest of lights, glowing from the stairwell in the hallway adjacent to the one with her room.

No, she was imagining that. She blinked twice.

No. It was real.

Paige glanced behind herself to check if the guard was near—he wasn't—then started up the stairwell, her heart pounding at the dare she knew she was presenting to fate to be staying out after such a close call. But no one should have been up at this hour. *She* shouldn't have been up at this hour. The only reason she was was to disobey, out of the restlessness of inaction, just to be able to control *some*thing, even if it was only a tray. And if she was out for disobedience, then this light . . .

There was only one way to find out.

A door stood at the end of the stairwell. The closer Paige got to the door, the brighter the light got, though still it remained incredibly dim. And another thing—

The rumble of voices.

Two of them. One she thought she'd heard before, the other unfamiliar. She paused with her hand on the doorknob, trying to make sure that the familiar voice wasn't someone who could eventually thwart her, punish her, to punish her brother, but it seemed too young to have that kind of power.

But if they were Theorists—if what Mott said was true and she really was about to open the door to the resistance within the Council building—would she, the Ritualist, be welcomed?

It wasn't too late. She could let go of the doorknob, fly back down the stairs, and cooperate with normal New Standard rules, trusting that they were there for a reason, and that reason was beyond her. Just like she had all her life.

She could let herself die and save Solomon.

But how long would that last?

Dying, she realized suddenly, on that dark staircase in the middle of the night with a faint glimmer of light on the other side of the door, wasn't going to prevent Solomon from misbehaving after she was gone. And she was stupid to not have faced that reality sooner. She could be part of the change that was already in motion, no matter how small the hope was. She could try. All she had to do was turn the knob.

So she did.

ON PUNISHMENT AND REWARD

an excerpt from the Statutes of Equality

THERE WILL BE TIMES, Friend, when you want something so much that you will feel consumed by your love for it. You will feel helpless in the state of your longing; you will feel dread when you are confronted with the reality of your desire.

Fear not! For love knows only equality. And those who enforce love know only equality. Oblige these Friends and you shall be free in your practice, free in your theory, and loving of heart. Take only that which is given to you; seek not what you do not have, and your heart will remain unspoiled.

Your unspoiled heart shall be welcomed into the Afterlands, and those who are spoiled are past their spiritual expirations. Their bodies in this life have rotted from the inside out, gangrene on their toenails, for their longing has consumed them instead, and now only silence remains.

Make haste, Friend, in rewarding Friends for their successes and punishing Friends for their shortcomings. To report on a failure is to love, for how can we claim to love our neighbors if we do not keep them safe from the dangers of potential threats? We implore you, love your neighbors. Love is talking, love is listening, love is understanding; to achieve true love is to understand the whole of one's neighbor, of one's person, of one's Friend. No Friend should be left behind in the dust of this world. No one is left here but us.

ACQUAINTED WITH GRIEF

I T'S WRONG," A VOICE said as Paige pushed open the door, and
then it shut up immediately.

Two people, surrounded by books in stacks crowding the
room. One of the people was a huérfana. The same one she'd met
while talking to Pepper. The one with the flower crowns.

Lane.

"Ritualist," said the huérfana, peering nervously out from
under the short mop of dishwater-brown hair clinging to the
sides of her face.

She sat on a woven, oval rug with a light-skinned young
man wearing glasses—probably an age-twenty, maybe an age-
nineteen; either way, old enough to be someone's spouse—in the
middle of a small pile of pages, crinkled and worn with desperately scribbled handwriting, much like the one currently hiding
in Paige's pillowcase. The man didn't seem as panicked as Lane
did; he beamed a handsome smile at Paige with straight white
teeth, his broad forehead reflecting some of the light from the
flickering lamp they'd brought in.

Paige eyed the pages hungrily. They were full of writings by
the same author as the one in her pillowcase, she was sure of it,
and her heart fluttered arrhythmically as it sensed the closeness
of hope. Lane held her elbows perfectly still, the whites of her
fingernails showing as she gripped the edges of the papers.

This could be the huérfana Mott had mentioned. This could be the Theorist resistance.

"I didn't think anyone else was up," Paige offered.

"We like the quiet of the night," said Lane, "to research."

We? Paige had only ever heard someone talk for a pair of people when they were either inviting her somewhere or they were espoused. Neither seemed to be the case here. And research seemed like a soft, vague excuse for staging a revolution inside the very building where the rules were enforced.

"I see," Paige said, though she didn't. "It was Lane, right?"

Lane nodded. "This is Moses."

"Educator Moses," said Moses. *Educator* Moses. "I teach the huérfanos everything they know."

"In the middle of the night?"

"Extra credit," Lane said, too quickly. Gone was the exasperated girl wilting the flower crowns; in her place cowered a jumpy conspirator.

"Lane here is very interested in remnant philosophies from the pre-war era," supplied Educator Moses. He was annoyingly charismatic, his charming smile laced with dimples at the corners, his hair evenly combed. Quite the opposite of Lane's brooding stillness. "Not many other students are interested in them, so I've taken it upon myself to teach her when no one else has to slog through it."

He laughed, as if there was some sort of joke that Paige was supposed to get, but all she understood was that Lane's arms were now tightly folded across her chest and that there didn't seem to be a joke in sight.

Lane didn't trust her.

But—and the thought hit Paige with the force of an unexpected crash to the ground during a round of double dutch—if Lane didn't trust her, then she had to understand enough about the darker side of the world around them to have that lack of trust in the first place. A huérfana up in the middle of the night, one who didn't trust anyone—

Mott was right.

"You *are* Theorists," Paige realized aloud. And instead of her hope rising like she thought it would, her heartbeat rose instead, her head growing fizzy with unexpected anger.

Theorists who had influenced her brother. Theorists who were using her innocent Sol as a pawn.

They said nothing to the contrary, and at their silence the rage in Paige's heart only burned harder. Something broke inside her chest, like her heart had folded in on itself beneath her ribcage. The muscles in her legs blazed so hot they felt cold, and she was afraid to move because she was sure that if she did, she would stride over there in two leaps and start choking them.

"Where are they keeping my brother?" she said, her voice shaking.

Lane and Moses only blinked at her.

"Who?" said Moses, at the same time Lane said, "How should I know?"

Bullshit. "Don't play dumb with me."

"Who's your brother?" said Lane.

"Don't *toy* with me!" Paige shouted.

"*Shhhhhh,*" said Moses, jumping up to bound across the room, his hands outstretched.

"You know perfectly well—"

Before she knew it, Moses had one hand over her mouth, the other forcing both of her arms behind her back. She'd known it. She'd known his smile was too curated to be genuine. It was a conspiracy, and they'd known when they recruited him that he would get captured and they absolutely knew where he was. They were trying to silence her, lying, lying Theorists were *always* lying. It was their fault that he was lying in wait for the Matriarch to pass unfair judgment over him, and it was their fault that she couldn't just run away, that she had to stay around here to appease a ruler who had threatened her livelihood and that of her brother's.

She wrenched at his hands on her mouth, completely losing control of her emotions at the same time. Tears forced their ways out of the edges of her stinging eyes; she flailed her arms around, trying to elbow him in the diaphragm, but he was stronger than her. His arms were shockingly taut and strong for being so skinny and bony.

His grip intensified around her forearms, pressing so hard that his thumb bone flicked the tendon over her ulna. Paige tried to scream, but it was easily muffled by his hands and the strong insulation in the walls. She sobbed, spitting against his hand in an effort to make him let go, only to have her own spit, laced with her own tears, spread across his palm and slide its way into her nostrils.

They had Sol. They had her. She was going to die either way, whether the Matriarch took her or the Theorists did.

The panic choked her and she hyperventilated while she cried. Dots of blackness swarmed into her vision and she felt her body starting to go limp, relinquishing itself to Moses's power. He was stronger than her, bigger than her, older than her. She felt, finally, like what she was: a bag of uterus-equipped flesh anointed as an offering to the Ancestors.

"Let her go, let her go," she could hear Lane calmly directing him. "She's going to collapse."

Moses let Paige go, but Paige let herself fall to the floor anyway. She sobbed there, because what did it matter anymore if she cried? It felt so good to let herself wallow in her misery. It was easier to accept that she'd lost than to get back up and fight. Especially when she was destined to lose no matter which route she picked. The world just wasn't built for people like Paige to win.

Slowly, the world blinked back into focus. When Paige finally looked up, Lane was standing in front of her, offering a handkerchief. Paige hesitated. Moses leaned against a bookshelf behind Lane, his arms folded over his chest in annoyance, one leg crossed casually over the other.

"Solomon," said Lane. "Your brother is Solomon, isn't he?"

Lane looked at Paige with something that seemed like pity. Rude. Lane must've been Sol's age, and here she was being insightful or some shit.

Of course, Sol was insightful, too. Apparently. Otherwise he wouldn't have got himself arrested, would he? Otherwise the things he'd written could have been dismissed. He could have gone to Sister Nadine for a light audit, spent an afternoon in the Conflict Resolution Center, and gone home cured from whatever temporary illness plagued his mind. Instead, he was being held Ancestors-knew-where in the Council building, close enough for Paige to feel the undercurrent of his presence, just out of reach.

Paige's eyes leaked some more. She finally grabbed the handkerchief and blew her nose into it, highly aware that she looked absolutely awful and not at all like the otherworldly leader the Ritualist was supposed to be.

"We're telling you the truth," continued Lane. "We've never met him. I'm not even allowed outside the Council building other than for special occasions; when could we have crossed paths?"

"I don't know, some . . . secret . . . *Theorist meeting*." Paige resented how dumb it sounded out loud.

Lane immediately swung her head over to share a pointed look with Moses; Moses's face bubbled from annoyance to amusement. Then they both laughed. Paige's heart flared up with anger.

"What's so funny about you— you *seducing* my little brother into your little cult?"

This made them laugh more. Only Lane had the decency to look guilty about it.

"'Theorist meeting'!" she exclaimed. She started to stack up the scraps of paper on the floor. "Like we could have that kind of organization."

"We *dream* about that kind of coordination," Moses said. "To even call it a cult is flattering in the insinuation that it actually— well—*functions* like an organization."

He spoke so calmly after nearly killing her. The skin over her ulna felt like it was forming a bruise.

"Or functions at all," added Lane. But then her face fell. "I'm sorry about your brother. I heard what he did. But I promise you, we had no hand in that."

"How am I supposed to know you're not lying to me?" Paige asked, more in defeat than in an actual challenge.

Lane was a small girl with a mouth and lips that seemed too big for her face. She looked like an age-fourteen; she talked like an age-seventeen. What had she been through to make her so jaded? "I'm sorry," Lane repeated. "But on the plus side, I like your anger. We could use that."

"He's here, isn't he?"

"What, in the building? Probably."

"Are there—" The question tripped on her fear; Paige swallowed hard and started over. "Can they hurt him?"

She could only ever ask Mott such questions, and even then Mott would have brushed it off as Paige-is-being-paranoid-again. People didn't hurt people in New Standard. Everyone was nice. No one was cruel, because everyone loved everyone. Those were the rules, and if anyone broke them, they were . . . not punished; corrected. Audited. Adjusted. These were displays of love.

"Yes," Moses said. Paige didn't like that the question seemed to not rattle him. Still, Moses didn't seem to get any pleasure out of the concept of Solomon being hurt.

"Can you get to him?" she pressed.

Lane squinted at Paige, folding her arms over her chest. Her hair, parted straight down the middle, clung to the sides of her face, making her seem even younger.

"Look," said Lane, "I don't know who you think we are, but I don't know you. And you don't know me. I'm sorry about your brother, but you need to be a good little Ritualist and get down to your room, now."

Paige felt too tall, uncomfortably out of place. It took all of our courage to speak again, her voice quivering despite her focus on keeping it steady:

"You didn't answer my question."

The Matriarch had threatened her brother. Mott had said there was a Theorist resistance within the Council building, and this had to be it. Mott wouldn't have given her bad intel. Unless this was a trap.

But what the hell kind of trap would this be? Mott wasn't stupid enough to fall for something like that.

Oh, Mott. Her face was in Paige's head; the memory of her sweat-and-laundry-and-nut-oil smell stuck in Paige's nose; the feel of her lips lingering, ghost-like, on Paige's own—

Focus. Mott was diligent. Brilliant. Beautiful. And if she'd been asking Paige to run away with her, into the vast unknown, running from everything but running to nothing, then Mott wasn't going to take any risks on sending her toward potential threats. Paige was, like, ninety-nine percent sure of that.

Maybe ninety-seven.

Eighty-four, just to be safe.

But the point was: Paige wasn't paranoid. The Matriarch *did* threaten her brother's life; Lane *wasn't* nice; Moses *had* physically assaulted Paige. She wasn't imagining cruelty. And most of all, the question didn't seem to be whether they could get to her brother, but whether they wanted to. And while Paige wasn't totally sure how she felt about the Statutes at this very point in time, they were very clear—

" '*We pledge ourselves to our community,*' " Paige recited, " '*even and especially when it is difficult, and understand how crucial we and our philosophy are to the thriving and prevention of destruction of our neighbors.*' " She took a step closer to Lane and felt Moses's eyes trained on her every movement. "Am I not your neighbor?"

Lane exchanged a nervous glance with Moses.

Paige had a sudden urge to pump her fist in the air, a sweet moment of victory in an environment of hellish tension. Mott would have been so proud of her standing up for herself, of insisting on getting what she wanted.

Or rather, she would have been so proud of Paige for deciding to give fewer shits about consequences.

"You know how to get to my brother. So tell me how to do it."

Lane blew out a controlled exhale. She gave a grim smile to Moses.

"I told you," she said.

"Told him *what?*" said Paige.

"That violence would be necessary."

Paige swallowed hard. It took all of her courage to ask, what she imagined as defiantly, "What are you going to do to me?"

"Not you." Moses pushed his glasses up his nose, only to have them fall down again as he leaned his forehead against a nearby bookshelf.

"In general," Lane said. "To make any changes at all." She glanced at Paige, arching a challenging eyebrow at her. "To get your brother out."

"*If* he's here," Moses said, "and they have him, he'll be in the holding cells. This building has a basement; they're in there. The cells. They're well-guarded. There's no way to get him out."

"Without a . . . distraction," Lane added.

"It's *wrong*," said Moses.

"Not if it means the end of all of this. Do you really think New Standard is going to go quietly?"

Paige's stomach jumped. She didn't like how Lane said *distraction*, like it was going to involve an inconvenient murder or two. She'd heard people talk about how Theorists wanted to end New Standard, to disrupt and destroy and let chaos reign, and she'd imagined that chaos and destruction over and over again. She'd played out in her head how she would grab Solomon and grab the emergency packs and hide in the corner of her closet, huddled together with her hand over his mouth even though he knew not to whimper; how they would drape a dark towel over themselves and scatter the rest of their clothes on the ground to make their place look pillaged already, in hopes that the intruders would think that the lumps under the dark towel were just more clothes. She'd never totally understood how that would throw off an intruder, but it was all she could think of, and she'd clung to the concept that that would keep her alive.

She'd always pictured Theorists as violent people, though perhaps not so young as Lane. And certainly, she'd never thought that the younger Theorists would be leading acts of violence. Surely Solomon knew what he was getting himself into when he decided to put himself and his poems out there, to expose himself for the Theorist he apparently was.

But if that was the case, did he know that he was getting himself into violence? Did he make that connection? Did he expect to be arrested?

Paige looked over at Lane. A solemn look focused her face, the image of security and seriousness, the same look Sol had given her when he'd said goodbye.

And that broke Paige's heart. She ached for Lane, she ached for Sol, for the lost childhoods that they were promised but couldn't have because they identified what was wrong with the world so early. When Paige was an age-fourteen, she'd been obsessed with brewing herbal remedies for the acne clustering on her face, with no thought for the systematic issues her neighbors faced. She wished so badly that she could go back to that place, that time when she thought that the world around her was perfect, that the system was real and functional and flawless. She missed that blindness. She was pissed that she was robbed of it.

"They deserve empathy," argued Moses. "The Statutes—"

"Heeeeeeere we go," Lane huffed.

"—the Statutes teach," Moses continued, pushing his glasses up his nose as he held up a book sitting on the ground to his left, "that we should offer empathy to everyone, including the Ancients." He turned to Paige. "I was telling Lane here that when we approach it from this empathetic standpoint, we can understand that the Ancients' sense of victimhood led to their obsession with violence."

Paige squinted at the title of the book. *Bodily Changes in Pain, Hunger, Fear and Rage,* the cover boasted in large print, with a smaller, illegible subtitle beneath it. She'd never heard of it before, but now that she studied one of the shelves near his head, she realized she'd also never heard of any of the other books in here before, either. They were relics, all of them; evidence of life from a different time.

"There was a man in the early twentieth century who coined the term 'fight-or-flight response,'" continued Moses, his eyes flickering with excitement as he shook the book like a lit torch and his voice picked up speed. "And he talks about how animals respond in emergencies—when their lives are in danger. Like the Ancients at the time of the Paterazm. In the Statutes, we acknowledge our animal instincts as humans. We discuss how to curb those instincts, since those instincts—in particular, the ones surrounding threats to the livelihood of our species—are damaging to society as a whole. In essence: sometimes, the instincts that alert us, as animals, to a threat to our individual survival are the same instincts that should be ignored when participating in a *society*, because society invites cooperation, not competition. And what I like to hypothesize—completely for academic purposes, of course, only as an exercise—is that this fight-or-flight response shouldn't be ignored, because it seems congruent with natural selection. We spend so much time trying to resist against natural selection, trying to fight against our animal instincts for the sake of a society that's essentially entirely *fabricated*, and for what? To make ourselves miserable? To survive, but not to thrive?"

"Yes," Paige found herself saying. "*Yes.*"

He was right. She was an animal.

Pain, hunger, fear, and rage—if they were all grouped together in a title like that, Paige had to wonder if they were all related base instincts. Thinking of herself as an animal made sense to her; it explained everything. She was just another biological construct, the result of life's persistence. And if she was just another animal, just another cockroach that had survived the Paterazm, just another nuclear-resistant ant working with her colony to create a home, then she couldn't be blamed, right? Not for falling in love with Mott, because if the reason for "actively practiced" homosexuality was, as the Statutes said, a way for natural selection to weed out weak genetics, then Paige's genetics were weak anyway and she *should* be weeded out. She *shouldn't* generate new spawn to survive in this regenerated world. Relief swept through her sinuses, her esophagus, her heart: there was nothing wrong with her. She just wasn't meant to survive.

So let them take her. If she was going to die by fire either way, as the Ritualist or as a Theorist, better to die in a way that resisted the approach to humanity that undermined every fiber of Sol's resistance, of her existence. If her body was going to be frayed by flames, let her heart remain intact until it melted from incineration.

"So you understand," said Lane quietly, interrupting Paige's reverie. She'd nearly forgotten that Lane was even there, but now Lane stared at her in earnest, like if she broke eye contact, the world would suddenly fall apart. "We're asking ourselves if this is worth it."

She said it like it wasn't hypothetical anymore. Like she was really trying to decide whether New Standard was worth it or not.

Paige laughed with a heavy sigh. "What are you going to do," she said, just to say it, but she didn't expect Lane to answer—

"Burn it all down."

Paige laughed. Lane and Moses didn't.

"Burn *what* down?" said Paige.

"Hypothetically," said Lane, though the look she gave Paige suggested anything but, "the whole town."

"Of New Standard?"

"Correct," said Moses, though she definitely heard an invisible, *no, the other town* from Lane.

"So are you in?" Lane said aloud.

"What would I have to do?"

Moses and Lane exchanged a nervous glance.

"You'd have to kill the Matriarch."

THE FIRST STEP IN YOUR WALK TO HAPPINESS

an excerpt from the Statutes of Equality

Walk not alone, Friend, for the path you take does not exist without your neighbors. Love cannot be achieved without others, because others are the origins of love. Humans thrive on co-dependence: without our neighbors, we cannot have schools, nor the manufacturing of goods, nor celebrations, nor safety. We cannot build. We have no common and no community. And happiness is an entity that comes from Truth and cannot be experienced alone: without common and community, there is no happiness.

We come from terror and division; in everything, we refuse to subscribe to that again. We refuse to stomp on each other. The greatest value that we hold is that of our collective existence, where everything is in us and we are all things. We submit ourselves to each other and each other to ourselves. We are many, but we are one.

The first step in your walk to happiness, Friend, is to surrender your Self to your community. Do what is best for your neighbor, for what is best for your neighbor is best for your Self. In our pursuit of the Truth we have learned that the Self cannot bear it witness alone. Truth is everything; Truth is all things. The Self has a maximum of two eyes, one mouth, one nose, ten fingers, and how can we experience All That Is with such limited resources? It is only together that we can find Truth. It is only together that we can be happy.

And of course: Truth cannot be witnessed without purity of spirit, without holiness of soul. And if we desire holiness above all else, we shall

sacrifice everything for it[1]. We sacrifice ourselves for
our neighbors; this is the holiest of all things, this is
how we can witness All That Is, this is the only path
to the Truth.

Through sacrifice, we find holiness. Through
holiness, we find Truth. Through Truth, we find
happiness. Through happiness, we can have peace.
In the old days, Friends could not find each other
in the blinding storm of warfare that weathered the
winds between neighbors; now, we are close. We stand
together. We stand firm.

Walk not alone, Friend. Walk with me. Let us
walk together.

---

[1] Originally from *Science and Health*, Chapter 1 ("Prayer"), page 11, lines
23-25. Science and Health was a religious publication by Mary Baker Eddy
of the early Americas, circa 1875. The source material lists "but" as the
starting conjunction of this phrase rather than "and"—it is a favorite line
that resonated with our founders, the Spared, who sacrificed everything for
the good of everyone around them, for the future of all of humanity. These
words compel us to continue to live by the strict code of ethics that has
saved our community; for without them, we would have nothing, and the
abence of All That Is would be the greatest human tragedy to befall us all.

COVENANT

To kill or be killed —that was the question before Paige now; the stark realization of it filled her gut with something hotly acidic. The next morning, back in the examination room, Medic Zara held a syringe full of something clear-but-a-little-milky up in the air now, and—after instructing Medic Amanda to fit Paige's feet in the unfriendly-looking metal stirrups at the foot of the examination table—she flicked the syringe expertly, the pointed end of the needle gleaming devilishly in the fluorescent lighting. Paige breathed in and out, attempting to measure her breaths as evenly as possible, lest she defecate on the table.

Somehow, that seemed even more horrifying than killing the Matriarch.

Medic Amanda smiled at Paige. "It'll be over before you know it," she said. "Just relax."

Paige appreciated the effort, but telling an anxious person to 'just relax' was like telling a blind person to 'just watch.' The open-backed gown allowed the breeze from the ceiling fan to stick to her skin.

Medic Amanda tried as delicately as she could to place Paige's limbs in uncomfortable, exposed positions. It was more difficult not to feel terrified at the small metal table of thin metal rods with an assortment of tips—pointy, rounded, hooked. No friendly wooden depressor today, no gentle rubber triangle.

Paige tried to stop wincing in anticipation.

"I haven't even touched you," said Medic Zara. "Calm your muscles, it'll be easier for the pain."

Paige kind of hated Medic Zara.

Not hate, she chastised herself automatically, but then she eyed the syringe still in Medic Zara's hand. Pain? There was going to be pain? No one had said anything about pain. Screw it, she was allowed to hate someone right now.

Someone who was putting her in a position of pain whether she wanted to be in it or not.

Whether she was the Ritualist or not.

Someone who was putting her brother in a position of pain.

She'd heard that sex would be painful. Nothing had ever been in her vagina before—would this hurt as much as a penis?

Why was she put in a position where she'd have to find out? When she didn't even want to have sex in the first place, the supposedly pleasurable violence of it that she'd heard so much about?

She held her breath. Her heart burned; her head filled with a warm fizz.

"*Hey!*"

From the hallway, muffled shouts accompanied harried footsteps. Paige sat up on instinct. And, probably, hope that she wouldn't have to go through with this.

"Lie down," said Medic Zara, with more patience than Paige had originally sensed she had. "There's nothing going on out there, just lay down, it's all sorted. Not sidew—on your back, there's a girl. Scooch down for me."

The implicit *or-I'll-scooch-you-down-for-you* convinced Paige to comply. She cringed, closed her eyes, and tried not to think about Mott as the warm breeze flowing through the window screen fell, lacy, over her clitoris.

And then there was a scream.

A distant shriek split through the air, but the medics both ignored it. Everything about this situation screamed *danger*, and yet she was expected to lay here, complicit. Or maybe she was just imagining it.

"Have you ever had an injection before?" asked Medic Amanda.

The shriek pierced down the hallway again. She was definitely not imagining it.

Paige kept her eyes trained on the ceiling, trying to trace new constellations into the popcorn paint. Why weren't they reacting to the screaming in the hallway? Why couldn't even *that* distract them from implanting her? She concentrated on her breathing: in, two, three; out, two, three. She shook her head—and instantly regretted it, thanks to the resulting dizziness.

"Never broken a bone or anything?" Medic Amanda pressed down on Paige's lower abdomen, indenting it with the tips of her fingers, and Paige felt like she was going to suffocate.

More muffled shouting from the hallway. Like someone giving instructions, but she couldn't make out the words. If there was danger, it wasn't in this room. It was somewhere removed from her, like it always had been.

"Scraped a knee or anything?"

"Yeah."

"Remember sucking in your breath when the pain first hit?"

"Maybe?"

"Do that."

Medic Zara wheeled herself on her stool over to Paige and held the needle in front of her face. "This first one's going to pinch a little, all right?"

Paige nodded through an exhale. Her voice felt completely gone by way of having to focus exclusively on breathing, on swallowing back down the panic that threatened to expel itself from her mouth and her butt. This was not what she'd thought being the Ritualist would be like. This was not at all what she'd ever wanted.

She sucked in her breath.

Medic Zara didn't say anything. Instead she handed the needle to Medic Amanda, who slid it into Paige's arm and Paige cried out for a moment, a hissing *aughhhhh*, but then it was all over. More than a pinch, and her body felt a rush of something dizzying. There was a pressing sensation inside her arm, and then the pressing turned to throbbing, and then she was suddenly exhausted and was grateful that she was already strapped in. Her body felt heavy; she wasn't sure if she could lift herself back up. The panic had subsided, but she was vaguely aware that she should have been scared when she heard the whisk of something metal being pulled from the tray, and the rolling of Medic Zara's stool over to the foot of the examination table.

"Where—where are you putting—?" tried Paige, but her mouth felt odd, like it was moving through thick, sludgey water in the sky.

"Best not to ask questions," said Medic Zara, and Paige felt a set of hands holding down her feet—not that she could have moved them anyway.

THINK RELAXING THOUGHTS, she yelled at herself in her mind.

"Keep your knees steady," said Medic Zara.

"Don't panic, it should be more scary than painful at this point," said Medic Amanda somewhere through the haze of reality. Paige felt like her vaginal walls were being pressed open, too much, they weren't meant to stretch like that, they were probably going to crack—

There was a swoosh, and some more footsteps, and a new voice, this one male.

"Sorry to interrupt," said the voice, somewhere between terrified and authoritative, "but there's been an incident."

Paige knew that voice from somewhere, didn't she? From another lifetime, maybe.

"An incident?" repeated Medic Zara. Paige thought it was Medic Zara, anyway. But the more she thought about it, the less sure she was.

She could vaguely feel something inside her—maybe panic, if she could remember what that was like—but it was dulled by the freezing-hot—blurry—

"A runner," said the voice. "We caught her, but then she stabbed herself—we tried to save her, but she passed out—"

Runner? Someone out for exercise? No, that wasn't right—everyone sounded scared.

Why were they scared? Paige felt warm, her head light and happy. No one should be scared. Everything was fine.

"How long?" said someone else, and the room was spinning, the voices weren't in the right place, she heard whimpering from somewhere far away—

"She's been completely out about five minutes."

—and then there was pain, bright and hot in the existing warmth, scarier because she couldn't feel their hands anymore, they were letting her go—no, they couldn't let her go, she wasn't happy anymore—

"Well, what're you waiting for? Get Eric."

"He's already there, he's trying to wake her up as we speak, but there's a lot of blood—"

—she was going to the Afterlands earlier than she thought. At least the runner would keep her company?—

"You said she stabbed herself?"

"Yes, Medic."

"With what?"

"Had her own blade."

Had she been happy every other day of her life?

"What, she stole one from the kitchens?"

"One of the bread knives from the bakery."

It didn't matter. Mattering is something we invent. She didn't have to fight anymore.

"How did she take it home?"

Her whole body was burning, a searing in her ears and behind her eyes and on her feet, and she couldn't get away from it, couldn't move anything, it was everywhere, strangling her or wringing her or something, she couldn't think—

"All due respect, Medic, let the civil servants worry about that, she's losing a lot of blood—she really wedged that thing in there."

"Well, Irode, I'm sorry that my pre-existing patient ran into your precious schedule. I'm almost done."

"Please, Medic, every second counts."

"You say that like I'm new to this."

—She just wanted some sort of relief, to make it go away. Popcorn ceiling, like fluffy clouds, a place to rest, some tea, honey—

"She needs at least a pint of blood."

"I'm coming. Amanda, watch her."

—Mott?—

—

SMOKE CHOKED UP THROUGH Paige's nose while she waded through the pieces of crumpled-up paper on the ground, each of them burning bright. Solomon was so close, just over there across the room, within arm's reach. She could do this. She could grab him. She could save him.

He was mouthing something, but she couldn't read his lips. His mouth stayed open, his eyebrows pressed in toward the center of his face in a desperate sort of fear, and he kept shouting, but she couldn't hear.

What? she said over and over again. *Hold on, I'll be right there!*

But gravity took his body into its clutches, pulling him up and off the ground, and Paige knew where this was going. He was going to be floating again. She was in her Afterlands cottage, and he was going to turn blue, and she knew suddenly that, behind her, Mott stood with an invitation of honey-soaked bread, with the promise of kisses and ginger cuddles and the sense that everything was completely okay, and she'd been dreaming about all of the stressful things that supposedly had been reality.

Solomon floated toward the ceiling, and Paige's heart pounded, and she pushed as hard as she could through the fiery pages licking the top of her skin, ignoring the pain, ignoring the blackened searing that she could feel on her shins, the flesh rotting away in real time. She could feel the walls of the cottage being sucked away as she kept reaching toward him, her legs working as fast as they could but held in place like molasses clung to her feet.

Sol, hold on, she shouted.

But behind him a large slab of stone connected with his back, and as she watched, the wind knocked out of him, and his eyes widened in surprise, and they didn't close anymore.

And then all of the sound around Paige disappeared and she heard Solomon's voice in the vacuum of space:

I love you.

HOW TO HEAL

an excerpt from the Statutes of Equality

THE RITUALIST IS THE bringer of tolerance, the mother of life, the healer of souls. Once selected, she must be protected at all costs. None of our lives are our own—they all belong to the community—but this is no more true for anyone as it is for the Ritualist. She shall beget a child for the community: one who will grow up with others like him or her who will later become part of our Council of Elders, those wise enough to be exposed to the horrors of our past, observe the status of our present, and advise us on the challenges of our future. Through her childbearing she will erase the sins of her past and ours—and we shall continue in faith and love and holiness, with self-control[1]

The sins of our Ancestors are visible throughout our town, rubble rushing like a tide to the remnants of ruins. The rubble breaks, up then down, like a wave over the brown dirt. It's the echo of humans left screaming; it's the dust of their nature, endured. It should be free, as particles, as atoms, as memories of that which used to be. Free to escape out of bounds,

---

[1] This phrase may seem similar to a passage in *Holy Bible*'s 1 Timothy book, chapter 2. However, the context of this original passage is entirely different: in it, Eve, who is the mother of all of the Earth according to the character God's command, must be saved through childbearing because she had become a "transgressor" when she listened to the villain character, Satan, and implies that Adam, her husband, was entirely blameless because he only listened to Eve. The illogicality of this implication is obvious: if Eve is at fault for listening to Satan, then Adam is at fault for listening to Eve, for they both fell prey to temptation. The Ancients were wrong in many ways, and inequality such as this is frequently at the core of their beliefs. But the concept of being saved by childbirth rings remarkably true to us as New Standardites: because new children born to our community mean that these children shall be raised with the beliefs of our community, and in this, our Earth will be saved; for New Standard's principles have a commitment to values that have been proven to foster happy, healthy, non-destructive life—with modesty, community, and love at their core.

**away from the town, into anarchic liberty.
Join us, Friend—in freedom.**

LOVE THY NEIGHBOR

P AIGE WOKE UP CRYING.
The physical pain wasn't so bad after all. The bruise on her forearm from Moses gripping her hurt more, although the walls of her vagina had a different sort of pain: a distant but mild ache. She could handle it. Just a feeling of lightheadedness, hotheadedness, some thin sort of pressure that made her wonder how much longer she could sit up without losing consciousness completely again.

But the emotional pain was worse than she could handle. Sweat condensed around her hairline, in the middle of her back, around the neckline of her medical gown, and Paige tried to sit up in order to sob into her knees.

She felt violated. Robbed of her own wants and wishes and will. She was a shell, a carcass for New Standard to use. They saw her as nothing else, so why did she want to be more? It only made things more painful.

"Oh, shhh-shhh-shhh-shhh-shhh," crooned Medic Amanda, "whoa, there. Don't try to get up. You've been out for a bit. Do you know your name?"

Paige opened her mouth but nothing came out except sobs.

"Deep breaths," said Medic Amanda.

She breathed in deeply and placed a hand on Paige's back. Paige followed her lead:

In, two, three.

Out, two, three.

In, two, three.

Out, two, three.

"There's a girl," said Medic Amanda. "Tell me your name."

"Paige," Paige wheezed through a focused exhale. Tears still streamed down her face, but she was no longer hyperventilating.

"Good girl. Do you know where you are?"

Not home. Not her Afterlands cottage. "Council."

Medic Amanda's forehead released its worried lines, and Paige thought she heard relief in her exhale. "You're all right," she said. "You're okay."

"What happened?"

Medic Amanda tossed her thick mane of hair over her shoulders, pressing two fingers to Paige's neck to get a pulse. "You made our hearts stop, that's what happened. Passed out in the middle of fertilization. Doesn't happen often, from what I hear, but I've only done this twice before."

Medic Amanda stepped over to the side of the bed and Paige couldn't tell if she was meant to still stare at the corner or if she could sit up to look at her, but she wanted an excuse. Any excuse to look at the hot spring rain she could hear streaking the glass window.

"Well, we'll know tomorrow whether it took," babbled on Medic Amanda, speaking very quickly, as if silence were contagious. "Always the chance it didn't, and then we'll have to try again, but we've become rather good at medicine these days, particularly with things like these. I think the Founders perfected it long before they even founded New Standard, probably most likely. But you seem fairly fertile. Agatha took a few tries, far as I can remember, but Za—Medic Zara, s'cuse me—says that every year before that was perfect, 'spitting as a tulip's blossom,' she says—can't think of what that means, but she's always on about stuff like that—"

Paige did not feel like a blooming tulip; she felt like a caterpillar trying to escape its cocoon. Please let it take. Please, so she didn't have to do it again.

"—anyway, I need to go check in with the boss lady. I'll be right back, okay?"

But Medic Amanda been getting up as she'd been talking, and by the time she finished her question, she was already out the door, leaving Paige in silence.

The silence buzzed loudly in her ears. She debated between keeping her eyes open and shutting them closed to block out the rest of the world, but the threat of the nightmare from which she'd just woken up decided the conundrum for her.

She looked to her left: a small tray of emergency equipment, things that could save her life. She shivered once, then again when she realized that she was less concerned that she was going to die and more concerned that she didn't care if she did.

She turned her head to her right, not at all expecting to find a person there on the gurney next to her.

Especially not a person she recognized.

Blond braid, face devoid of the round wire glasses she normally wore. A small mole behind her jawline. A face that normally looked far beyond the world in front of her, so much so that she couldn't see the world itself.

Chang. It clicked: the runner. It wasn't a dream; it was a real-life nightmare, Chang's chest bandaged up with tinges of red pricking the bandages, her pink skin reddened and puffy under blue eyes glazed over in a silvery gauze. She blinked up at Paige and spoke in a quiet rasp, slow but steady.

"I tried to warn everyone. They own us."

Had she been there the whole time? She was so quiet, it was creepy. No wonder Medic Amanda had dashed out so quickly.

Paige was vaguely aware that there was a person in Chang's enlarged belly. She tried to ignore that thought. If there was a person in Chang, then Paige had just had a person put in her. Someone nestled in the depths of her reproductive organs, feeding on the blood and tissue in which it was cocooned, when Paige just wanted to claw it out.

"No one owns me," Paige said, as if Chang had tried to stab Paige rather than her own heart out.

"Not just you," Chang said. "*Us*. They own our bodies, they own our lives, they own our children. Everything."

"Who's *they*?"

Chang laughed softly and shook her head. Her voice was barely above a whisper, and the longer she talked the more she gained the momentum to do so. "*Troubled*. That's what they say about me. And yet they're the ones trying to remove someone from my body. My body isn't mine, to them, to anyone. Yours isn't, either. We're all just resources to them. Things to buy and trade and sell, and not even because they want the coupons, only because they *can*."

They. A shiver crawled up Paige's spine as she realized that, for the first time, she understood Chang perfectly, because Chang was echoing her own thoughts.

"They tried to make me abort him," Chang said miserably, staring back at the ceiling again as if it was an escape. "The baby. Because he has a *hearing loss*. He's not perfect."

Paige felt a pang in her own uterus—not one of longing, but one of fear and guilt and horror, one where she imagined a little parasite gnawing away at her insides, swimming and doing flips in her, the unwilling host. Chang wanted this; Paige didn't. *They* were the Council, who ordered the medics to abort Chang's baby. The ones who would tear her open against her will.

"Wanna trade?" Paige laughed darkly.

Chang snorted in a sickly wheeze.

"This would be the third time," she said.

Three abortions. Three of them against Chang's wishes. It sounded horrific, but Paige couldn't fathom it.

And why shouldn't they? Let Chang have the baby she wanted and not to force Paige to have the baby she didn't want. To Paige, that math added up. It was simple. Instead, both of them were suffering, their bodies violated by ownership that wasn't theirs. And Paige kept running through the Statutes in her mind, one passage echoing more than the others:

—for to deny the body of feeling internally is to rip the soul from the body—

And if Paige felt that she didn't want to give birth to someone she'd never know, to lend her body to people who demanded it without even asking, then that seemed right. Her soul felt like it was being ripped from her body. Like now that they had physically taken her over, she was hollow within, a shell without personhood, but then again, why did she need to be a person when they'd put a new person in her anyway?

She cried.

It all made sense now: Chang's outburst at the Ascension. The murmurs of her sedation. Her unwillingness to abort a fetus that was very likely ill, especially when she'd already been made to abort three others.

She just wanted to have her body left alone. She just wanted it to be *hers*.

Paige could feel the crying stop gradually as she thought through the whole thing. Nothing in the Statutes was even real in the first place. And real—what did that mean? What even was real? Herself, now, in this moment? Chang, her hands tied to the gurney that cradled her? The gurney, its railing made of recycled palm wood—and was that wood even real? What even was wood?

What was a person?

What was Paige?

"Are you okay?" Chang asked, her voice seeming so far away that Paige wasn't sure if she was imagining it.

She was far away, now, as if she was looking down at herself from the ceiling. She wasn't Paige the Ritualist; she was some kind of spirit, an energy form watching down with mild interest. She felt nothing. No stakes, no sadness, no thrill of the present moment, not even the sheer relief of the absence of pain—just nothing.

"Yeah," she said to Chang, nodding her human head, but Chang didn't seem like she was really listening much, either, and she gazed right past Paige's head and up at the ceiling like it had the answers to life that you could find if only you looked hard enough. "Actually, I'm great."

The funniest part was: when Paige was out like this, disembodied and unaffected, she saw that Chang was absolutely, completely sane.

Paige's anger teetered between frustration and resignation. Everywhere she turned, she was faced with a new revelation that the world she'd trusted her whole life wasn't the world she'd always known. And it wasn't just the world around her—it was her whole way of life, her life itself. The Statutes were written by the Spared, and the Spared were nothing short of sacred, having had survived the Paterazm. But if even *they* were corrupt? If the Matriarch couldn't be trusted, and the Ritualist was fraternizing with Theorists, then what did anything even matter anymore? How could she care for the rest of the world when the world didn't care for her?

At least it made it abundantly clear: Solomon wasn't evil. Mott wasn't crazy. Paige wasn't dirty.

She was a Theorist, but she wasn't a bad person.

She tried on the label with a curious sort of confidence. Paige-of-2140, Theorist. Historical figure. Change-maker.

She had to find Lane again somehow. Find her brother. Get him out, violence or not, it was worth it. Even if it meant that she was responsible for killing the Matriarch herself.

And if Ingrid's gamble was right— if there were actually people out beyond the borders—

They could be. They *could* be.

Paige barely dared to imagine it: a place where Solomon sat writing poetry as he pleased, exposing his soul and sharing it with people who appreciated it; a place where she and Mott could sit and bask in each other's kisses for all of eternity, where they could hide in a room for several hours and trace the corners in each other's skin, and breathe with each other, and stay still where they didn't have to hide. A place where she could ignore Adam, where she didn't have to deal with her parents' constant shouting and object-throwing, where people helped each other and didn't judge. Where Paige wouldn't be expected to judge others for their choices.

The door swung open and Medic Amanda came back in, pulling off her sterile gloves and throwing them in the wastebin, and Chang shut her eyes and let her mouth fall open as if she'd been asleep the entire time.

"You're good to go," Medic Amanda chirped, reaching out to help Paige up. "Boss lady wants you to—well, rest, obviously, but she'll check in on you tomorrow, and there are a few tests she'll run to see if you're progressing along as she'd like you to be— of course, we won't be able to tell for *sure* for another few weeks, but at least tomorrow we'll know whether there's any hope. But don't worry, you should be fine. You come from a mighty fertile family, I'll be surprised if your tulip doesn't have a couple of buds in there, and if it doesn't take, it's totally okay, we can just try again! We might even just try again in a couple of days for good measure to make sure we're not wasting any time—"

Paige smiled and nodded, but her smile was thin-lipped. She was going to get out of here in a couple of days.

Or she'd die trying.

THE QUESTION

a handwritten note

to have and to hold
as long as we both shall live

they key is to live by the pledges we share
the sacrifices we make

but define living

is aching

for happiness

enough

CEDAR WOOD AND SCARLET STRING

EDIC AMANDA STAYED WITH Paige all night, supposedly to monitor her, taking her heartbeat every so often and checking her temperature incessantly. It didn't matter, Paige thought. Not when she felt nothing; nothing didn't hurt. Her heart beat more steadily than ever before. Even though she wasn't sure she could actually kill someone, even though she'd never before fathomed taking a life, she knew, resolutely, that it had to be done. Because she saw, now, the Matriarch's hypocrisy, and if the entire world was being run by hypocrisy, how was it true? How could anyone find truth, give love, feel peace?

She barely slept. Medic Amanda released her released her in the morning, babbling some excuse about the waiting list for this month's visiting hours being already too long and not being able to wait another day to re-start them. Paige suspected that Medic Amanda also didn't want to hang around an emotionally unresponsive Ritualist.

CS Holly replaced Medic Amanda. "Chop chop," she told Paige, throwing a towel at her. "Shower time."

Even in the washroom, while Paige took a shower stall, CS Holly stood right outside of the stall. Paige had never showered in the presence of other people before, and she might have found removing her clothes disgraceful if she hadn't been so busy not-caring.

She took her time getting ready after she stepped out of the shower, letting her hair drip water onto the washroom floor and wringing it out while CS Holly continually checked the watch looped around her wrist. Civil servants were always so punctual; the small rebellion of refusing to hurry warmed Paige's heart.

Still, there was only so long she could take to comb through her hair with her fingers, and sooner than she would have liked, Paige found herself being shepherded back down the hallway to her room.

"Three minutes," said CS Holly. "Dress quickly."

So this was how they controlled her: privacy only in small doses, calculated so that Paige couldn't do anything out of the ordinary. Paige smiled grimly to herself. Whatever. They could do what they wanted. The more they did what they wanted, the more the fire in her chest built up with the seething, patient anger that made her more resolute in her decision: kill the Matriarch, save Solomon, be free with Mott.

She almost missed the slip of paper almost imperceptibly hiding in the corner of her bed after she returned from the washroom:

DON'T FORGET YOUR MISSION. WE HAVEN'T.

-ML

Milliliters?

Oh. Moses and Lane. Cute.

Paige shoved the note in her bra, which honestly filled out the bra more than her actual breasts did. Like she'd forget that she'd agreed to kill the Matriarch. It unnerved her a bit that Moses and Lane had been able to somehow sneak a note into her room while she'd been in the washroom, but she shook it off. Did one of them actually come here while CS Holly supervised Paige in the shower? Also, why didn't they leave her instructions on how to kill someone?

CS Holly rapped on the door with a one-minute warning; Paige slipped on the Ritualist gown. At least the undersides of her legs weren't sticky anymore from old sweat and whatever they'd shoved up her vagina yesterday. The soft breeze from the ceiling fan over her freshly washed legs was refreshing.

She allowed CS Holly to lead her to a small room toward the front of the Council building. It was strange coming at the room from this side—like she was getting ready for one of her learning reviews at the Edufice when she was a little kid. She'd always been awed by the tapestry centered on the opposite wall, with the famous First Supper scene: New Standard's humble beginnings, the forty Spared sharing a simple dinner of bread and water on a salvaged carpet in a glass dome, explosions of light and smoke coming out of rubble behind them in the outside world.

Paige smiled at the Matriarch when she entered the room. Cooperation was the best form of deception. Mott would have been proud.

"Good day, Ritualist," said the Matriarch.

"Good day, Matriarch," returned Paige.

"Come. Sit."

The Matriarch patted the chair next to her—a simple wooden chair with a rounded back with posts supporting its arc, identical to the one in which the Matriarch sat. Paige obeyed. As a child, she'd sat across from these very chairs in the small row of chairs across from them, her parents sharing their worries for the community. It had seemed like an otherworldly experience, an opportunity to talk directly to the people she deified. She remembered how they sat, quiet and listening, always understanding, always receptive, in a way that didn't make Paige feel like she was under scrutiny. It felt genuine. Like they could really do something about the troubles that the people had. The Ritualist always gave her a grin. Paige had felt like the most special little girl in the world.

She was still special now, she figured. Now, she was the only girl in the world tasked with killing the Matriarch.

"Cross your ankles beneath your feet," said the Matriarch, demonstrating. Rage unleashed itself within Paige's diaphragm, anger burning from there through every one of her bones. It was patronizing. Matronizing, she supposed. Completely ignoring the threat she'd made to Paige literally yesterday. Completely ignoring that Paige had been inseminated by this woman's staff.

Paige crossed her ankles. Slowly, deliberately. The slower she did it, the angrier she got. If the Matriarch noticed, she didn't mention it.

"Good. Put your right hand over your left."

Paige obeyed, but the Matriarch scowled.

"Not like—like *this*." The Matriarch reached over and grabbed her hands and placed them both on top of Paige's left knee. Paige yanked her arms back on instinct, then froze.

The Matriarch stared at her.

All her life, Paige wanted the Matriarch to *see* her, but not like . . . whatever this was. Regret? Annoyance? Disbelief? She flailed inside, desperately trying to prevent herself from displaying her fear.

She put her hands back, trying her best to appear relaxed.

"Sorry," Paige said. "I'm ticklish."

The Matriarch continued to stare, like she was in a suspended state until Paige did exactly what she demanded. And maybe there was a metaphor there, but she couldn't figure it out while she was distracted by the Matriarch finally releasing her gaze and grunting at her:

"Sit. And listen." She nodded at the CS stationed at the door. "Go ahead."

The first visitor slouched in the chair opposite her in a comfortable way, as if he'd been there many times before, and talked all the way through the allotted ten minutes about how displeased he was with the unpredictability of Ingrid's disappearance. Paige expected him to stop talking at some point, or perhaps for the Matriarch to interrupt, but the Matriarch still kept her mouth shut and did nothing but raise her eyebrows when Paige looked up at her for guidance.

Right—nothing volunteered, only responded. She wondered if her silence made her seem wise.

But what had there ever been to speak up about? Chang being instructed to abort her baby? That one time that an educator washed Pepper's mouth out with soap in front of the whole class because she'd joked that the Statutes were all a conspiracy? That one time Mama held up a kitchen knife and threatened to kill herself because her fights with Papa were so bad she felt like she was already dying?

Those were all paltry things. Nothing like mass murder, like homelessness, like war. Nowhere near the human rights abuses that people suffered before New Standard and the Statutes of Equality. No one suffered here, and if they did, it wasn't worth mentioning. These visiting hours were therapeutic, cathartic, to maintain the peace—the first visitor left with his shoulders relaxed, his spine a little straighter, and he thanked them for their time, like they'd healed him.

If this all wasn't worth mentioning, was it worth killing the Matriarch? Paige realized she'd been holding her breath, her head spinning while she tried, desperately, to orient herself in the world. It was exhausting. She was exhausted. She didn't want to fight this mental battle anymore. She just wanted to rest.

The second visitor came in, a thin-nosed man with a brittle frame. He sat in the chair and stared at her through half-closed eyes, and Paige couldn't tell whether he wanted her to meditate with him or whether he expected her to ask him questions.

At one point in the very long silence, she cleared her throat and asked, in the most dignified voice she could conjure, "How can we help?"

The Matriarch said nothing, but Paige could feel her presence saying, *I told you to sit and listen.*

The man lifted his chin at them and said nothing.

Murder seemed so indelicate, Paige thought, bored with the man. She'd imagined herself performing violent acts before, but always with a sense of horror at how she could possibly do it.

Even the beetle's death the other night was too much for her. Then again, Paige had always loved insects better than people, not that she'd ever admitted it aloud to anyone else. Insects followed patterns; their social orders were much more methodical. Their commitment to their community didn't depend on how someone was feeling that day.

Paige was hyper-aware of the Matriarch as she sat in the next seven minutes of silence—an eternity—and contemplated ways she might kill her. It was more difficult than she'd thought, especially being able to hear the Matriarch's breathing next to her, like she could hear her heart pumping blood through her ventricles, through her atria. The Matriarch was being pleasant and serving the community in the way that Paige was used to, in the way that seemed to serve every visitor individually and meet them on their level; she could feel her resolve waning. Maybe the woman next to her wasn't as evil as she'd thought. Maybe no one was deserving of death—

No. *No.* Mott would get on her case for second-guessing herself. No.

This woman, kind as she was to everyone else, had threatened her brother's life. And if Paige continued to let her live, she was inviting her to kill Sol.

If the price was one life for another, and Sol had never so much as stepped a toe out of line in his life while the Matriarch had had an entire sexually deviant relationship, why should Sol have to pay that price?

There was a whole family that came in together: the young parents and two children, the boy probably no older than an Age-Four, making the girl an Age-Six. The girl was small and quiet and couldn't stop gazing at Paige with the sort of unabashed, unwavering curiosity the parents continued to apologize for, but the truth was that Paige had to remind herself that it was rude to continue staring back at the girl. She tried to tell herself to smile at the girl, to make her feel special, but the way she spread her lips to bare her teeth felt mechanical and odd.

But—as she soothed the parents' concerns that all safety in the community would continue because the Ritual would live on—she couldn't help but remember sitting in Mama's lap in that very same oversized chair. *Loveseat,* she remembered: and back when she had been small enough to fit on Mama's lap still, she'd thought of it as the place where she was most protected than anything else in the world, the sense of comfort enveloped in Mama's soft arms, in front of her soft belly, inhaling her soft scent; nowhere else did Mama let herself be so soft; everywhere else, she was strict and firm.

She could remember, distinctly now, and not just generally, how it felt to watch the Ritualist at the time, fascinated by how the Ritualist seemed so calm in every moment, as if the Ritualist had the answers about life that Paige could never find, no matter how many books she read—because she could open the portal to the Afterlands, and no one else could.

Maybe she could suffocate the Matriarch in her sleep? That seemed like the least violent way to kill someone. They'd only notice for the first few moments, and then they just . . . fell back to sleep, right?

And now, as Paige watched that family leave, the girl with one hand holding her mother's and the other hand with a finger in her mouth as she turned her head to peek over at Paige one more time before her family took her home, Paige wondered where, exactly, she was supposed to find that sureness.

So far, she hadn't found it anywhere.

And just when she thought it was all over, Mott walked into the room.

She walked steadily, one foot in front of the other. She let her arms dangle at her sides to prove how calm she was. How confident.

Too confident. Too calm.

"Matriarch, Ritualist," Mott said clearly, "I am a Theorist."

THE ANSWER

a handwritten note

ilt's never enough.

WITCH HUNT

T HE PANIC ROSE EVERYWHERE, almost lifting Paige out of her seat as if she were suspended by a vat of balloons. She might have cried.

The Matriarch stood and Paige's back tensed up against the hard seat. Whatever the Matriarch was about to say, it couldn't be good; this was the first time she'd stood since she sat down. The Matriarch placed her hands on Paige's shoulders; they were cold and almost bony. But after that stare the Matriarch had given her when she'd flinched earlier, Paige didn't dare to shiver.

"Caretaker Mott," the Matriarch said slowly, "That is an extraordinary claim."

That was distractingly weird, to hear Mott called by a title, especially one that seemed like a dream, a title she could never possibly have attached to her name.

"I'm an extraordinary person," said Mott. Was she trying not to smile?

Mott, Paige mouthed silently without knowing she was doing it, grinding her heels into the wooden floor beneath her. If the claim that she was a Theorist didn't get Mott automatically cleansed, her hubris would.

Mott raised her thick eyebrows at Paige so that her face was more open and her eyes seemed further apart from her freckled nose than they ever had been. It made her more beautiful than

Paige had ever seen her, and made her seem more innocent than she ever could be. She was trying to say something to Paige, but Paige couldn't decipher it. Was she saying, *Run out now?* Or, *Trust me?* It lingered closer to determination.

If you're going out, I'm going out with you.

Mott hadn't given up yet.

Because Mott was stupid. No one was supposed to "go out" with the Ritualist. That was the whole point. Paige was supposed to give up her remaining years so that Mott could have hers. Paige's love for Mott's life.

The Matriarch's spine sprouted up; her tone turned dangerously icy. "I'll remind you that you're speaking with your Matriarch and your Ritualist. On what do you base this claim?"

Unintimidated, Mott plopped herself into a visitors' chair and crossed one knee over the other, her shins peeking out from under her skirt. "Honestly? I'm struggling. And I don't think a auditing session with Sister Nadine is going to help."

Auditing? Rehabilitation couldn't have been Mott's real goal. Not when she'd asked Paige to run away with her three days ago. Not when she'd stood in Paige's bedroom with a bag of stolen food.

Mott had put that food back, right? She had *better* have put that food back.

"Go on," said the Matriarch.

"I love my community," she said, more methodically than Paige had ever heard her speak before. "I love my cohort. And over the past few years, I have funneled the majority of my love to one person."

Paige's hope plummeted and leapt back and forth. She wanted Mott to be talking about her with a fervor with which she hadn't wanted anything before. But not here for this, not now. Not here. Shut up.

"And now I can't have her," Mott said, turning her head directly toward Paige now, and Paige couldn't look away.

She wanted to fling herself at Mott and get lost in her lips again. She tried to look anywhere but at Mott, but the only place to look aside from the Matriarch herself was at the mural on the wall behind Mott, which featured seven representatives of New Standard and all that it was peeking out from the corners of their eyes in judgment at her.

Shut up, Mott. She forced down the panic that started to rise.

But Mott didn't shut up. She stood up. Started walking toward them, with such a slowness and sureness that Paige was terrified for her.

"You'll put me with someone else," Mott told the Matriarch, without ever taking her eyes off Paige. "Some man. I'll spend the rest of my life with him. And I'll care for him, and for our children. I'll do my work. I'll volunteer. I'll do everything you ask of me, but I won't be happy. I'll be a silent shell, dead inside, because I've spent my entire life befriending, getting to know every detail about this girl—woman—the one you've chosen to love me with her life—well. Don't I owe her the same courtesy? If she can't live the rest of her years with me? How can I without her? I love one person beyond the rest."

She smiled at Paige sadly, fondly, this was good-bye, maybe, possibly. Paige's heart fluttered with the possibility, the delicious promise of what could be freedom. Mott loved her, and her alone, as much as Paige loved her, too, and she'd figured something out. She knew something Paige didn't. She kept talking. Yes, Paige thought, relishing Mott's voice. Keep going. Yes.

"And I have chosen not to change that."

Yes.

"I am selfish, I am a Theorist. I am no longer an asset to New Standard, and unless I'm mistaken, I think that means you need to arrest me."

Yes.

Wait—

"And you're turning yourself in for the betterment of your community?" said the Matriarch.

"Something like that."

Paige's hope quickly melted into anger and she thought she might kill Mott instead of the Matriarch. She pictured herself running straight toward Mott and grasping whatever she could of her, willing herself to do it—to kiss her on the spot, to let the words tumble out of her mouth that she, Paige, loved her, too, more than she loved everyone else, and that Ingrid could go, everyone else could go but Mott, just not her, just not her—

She wanted to shout Mott's name, but she was terrified of what the Matriarch might do to her, terrified that she might make the situation worse than it already was. She tried to give Mott a *look*, something that would magically change the moment, something that would prevent Mott from getting herself arrested, because what the actual hell, Mott, the whole point was that only one of us died.

"All right, well." It only took a swift hand movement from the Matriarch that Paige caught in her peripheral vision. In an instant, CS Holly came in with another CS Paige didn't recognize, walking up behind Mott. "We'll schedule your hearing as soon as we can get a spot on the calendar—"

"Oh, no, Matriarch. You misunderstand me."

The Matriarch blinked deliberately, incredulously, at Mott. She was the *Matriarch*. She didn't *misunderstand* anything.

"I waive my right to a trial."

"*Mott*—" Paige whimpered before she could help herself, but the Matriarch held up a hand and Paige's words caught in her throat.

Mott just smiled. She threw her arms out wide, the tender insides of her elbows exposed.

"I wish to be cleansed."

THE AIR

a handwritten note

The people wish peace to each other and fare
each other good wishes as they try not to stare
at the resistance, its quiet and lonely affair.
You can taste the holes in the humid air.
The people ignore that the holes are there;

    no, no, they'd rather go 'round

       pretending their lives aren't sunk in the ground.
But those who died before them know that prayers
brought them to ashes, now part of this lair.

    They shake invisible heads and tsk invisible tongues.
    They breathe the ashy air through slick, invisible lungs.

LEVERAGE

"PUT HER IN SEVEN."

"Yes, Matriarch."

"Prepare the Pandora."

"Yes, Matriarch."

Retreating footsteps. The removal of the chairs. A click of the door. These were aspects of the life happening around Paige—she was aware of them, but she didn't understand them. She held her breath and hated that tears were escaping when she'd tried to trap them beneath her eyelids.

"I'm sorry," she heard the Matriarch say. "I truly am."

Paige didn't trust herself to open her mouth. *If you were sorry, you wouldn't be making me do this.*

"I understand that you've been through quite a lot, and that recent events can become traumatic."

Do you?

Paige didn't even want to be alive. What was the point of being alive if "living" was just a collection of days? What good were stolen kisses if they could never be had again?

"We have an extremely difficult job," said the Matriarch, whose face draped itself in a cloak of concerned resolution, as if it was *her* best-friend-slash-love-interest who was being condemned to death without salvation.

(Again.)

"We must remain steadfast and true so that the citizens of our town have hope to hold on to," she continued. "It is *easy* to forget the greater good in favor of the individual when it's our immediate friends, but *there are other people who live here.*"

Other people didn't matter.

At least her sacrifice had meant something before. Even if Sol was in trouble, Paige could have tried to save him. And Mott would live and breathe and at least be *alive.*

Now—

Now it meant nothing. Paige almost laughed to herself, but then allowed herself a few precious tears at the triggered memory: what she'd told Mott when Mott had asked her to run away with her.

The suffering of one is so much less than the suffering of the many.

What was the suffering of many if not the suffering of one, multiplied?

Were they all suffering? Was everyone having to make choices like Paige was being asked to? Was Dorothy as miserable as Paige was?

"And in order to do that," the Matriarch went on, "there are so many . . . little . . . nuances, little voices that we constantly have to push down and ignore. And just when we think they're gone, they pop back up again, louder and more insistent. And they seem to have everything to do with destroying the land which we've all collectively built."

Paige understood, now, how Ingrid could run away. She wanted to kick herself for not taking Mott up on her offer. She wanted to throw herself against a wall. To throw anything against a wall. To expel some of the energy she had somehow.

To kill the Matriarch.

But how did you kill someone?

The Matriarch heaved a deep sigh.

The source of life, Paige remembered from her biology textbook, *is kinetic energy. Most creatures within the Kingdom Animalia have a breathing mechanism and at least one organ that pumps blood throughout the body. Amphibians, for example, have gills as larvae and lungs as adults, and have a three-chambered heart that pumps the blood. At a high level, this is very much the same as what humans have—*

She could feel the invisible page under her fingertips, that image of the frog jumping vertically on the page that she'd traced over and over again, memorizing its various parts in case she ever came across one. That was where she should have been. RS Paige. Not an emotionally exhausted Theorist-Ritualist trying to figure out how to kill the leader of the only remaining faction of humanity.

Life was blood and breath.

To cause death, she had to get rid of blood and breath.

A much simpler equation.

"Ritualist."

The Matriarch meant for her to raise her head up, to pay attention to her. Hadn't she paid enough?

"Look at me, Paige. I'm old."

Obediently, Paige looked up and studied the Matriarch's face. She wasn't old—she was around Papa's age—but her eyes were sad, bags beneath them presumably from exhaustion of fighting and caretaking humanity over the years. They were the eyes of someone who had loved and lost.

Paige could see the tapestry behind her, the Matriarch superimposed in the middle of it, as if she were part of the scene of the Spared. But the longer she stared at it, the more Paige couldn't shake the thought:

It was just thread.

The Matriarch was just a person.

"I've been the Matriarch as long as you've been alive. Every day I wake up alone. I've spent my entire life in this building, growing up among dozens of brothers and sisters, and yet I am still alone. I have been alone for a long time."

There was nothing in her voice, in her face, in her body to suggest that the Matriarch was lying. Paige felt a pang of resonance in her chest—she felt that loneliness, too. But the Matriarch had felt it a lot longer.

"There were times that I felt so tortured by the loneliness," continued the Matriarch. "I was so desperate for what I had before. I wanted that intimate relationship with someone—someone who truly understood me for who I was and what I stood for and why I did everything I did; someone who knew what I was going to do next simply by virtue of having spent so much time with me— I wanted it so badly that I thought about running away. Or killing myself."

Paige's heart half-ached for the Matriarch. She wanted, so badly, to reach out and hug her, like she would for anyone who opened up to her like that, but she remembered: this woman had her brother and her best friend.

"That's awful," she said quietly.

The Matriarch smiled. "It was. But I talked to Sister Nadine. And we worked on it together. And day after day, I started looking for companionship in every citizen of New Standard. In every huérfano sitting at the dinner table. In every match I saw in the community. There have been seven unintended deaths in the last eighty-eight years. Seven. That's a record no other community in Earth's history can boast. For every time that I was lonely, I reminded myself that my leadership in selflessness—and in the community's— was keeping everyone safe, every day."

Paige's heart softened. She was afraid to hate this woman. The Matriarch was either a true believer or a really good liar.

As a child, Paige had gone to school and come back home with stories about the Paterazm in her head—that too-human craving for more, more, *more* that literally destroyed the world—overpopulation and under-regulation leading to the depletion of the Earth's resources, leading to a resource war, exacerbated by the immortality serum; half the world's eleven billion people squished into holey cardboard boxes in the middle of growing deserts or soon-to-be-underwater cities, wiped out by the "natural" disasters that the Earth's natural defenses could no longer combat. There were girls like Paige who were raped and stolen from their families and trafficked as child brides, as commonplace as stealing food from grocery stores. There were governments so corrupt due to a complete lack of morality, so focused on "growing the economy" that they did nothing to help those girls, just watched while they were impregnated, then took away their rights to get rid of the resulting babies; watched while those girls were abused and abandoned and became beggars themselves, their own daughters stolen from them in turn. They watched while the richest among them lived to be a hundred and fifty, to two hundred—old, rotting skeletons somehow still walking after two centuries, while the rest of the world—most of the world—died younger and more brutally. They watched while young boys were kidnapped and trafficked as serum mules, shipped across continents with bags stuffed up their anuses and shipped back to the wealthy and killed to maintain their silence. And Paige would come home and tell Mama and Papa and Solomon these stories, and Papa would nod wisely and read a passage from the Statutes to bring peace of mind and remind them that they didn't have to live like that anymore. Mama would tense up but try to let the words of the Statutes calm her; Solomon would listen with curious interest about what he would be studying in school soon. Papa would tuck Paige into bed and read a blessing, and Paige would feel better. The beige paint on the walls of her room then was plain, but it didn't ask for more. Every single person she had ever met had spaces like this: pillows on which they could rest their heads, satiated bellies, healthcare on demand. They weren't trafficked and had solid ethics that protected everyone around them. Then, Paige had loved tracing the constellations in her ceiling, had loved making up new ones, had loved imagining how she could eventually give back to the community that had already done so much for her.

But every time Paige looked at the ceiling now it was just blank. There was nothing to find in it. And when she closed her eyes she only saw Mott's face, so close to hers and grinning with that lively, infectious brightness that never let Paige's heart dip too low. She could almost smell the sweat under Mott's hairline, the salty-sweet musk of her skin.

"It's not like New Standard hasn't got its flaws," continued the Matriarch, her voice quiet, her face sober. "We still have a long way to go. We can broaden ourselves out. Put in new policies. Expand our numbers. Continue to clean up the air, focus on how we're really serving the people of New Standard, providing safety in their lives that they're able to embrace with looser restrictions, maybe even put in some sort of rotational program for workers who wish to learn a new skill—"

"Clean up the air?"

"What's that, now?"

"What do you mean, 'clean up the air'?"

The Matriarch frowned slightly, as if she was hearing such a phrase for the first time. "Air? I didn't say anything about air."

Paige didn't move a single muscle on her face. Her fingers wandered down to the hem of the sleeves of the nightgown she'd been provided, searching for some loose thread out of habit, but the seams on this gown were perfect. Seemed like a brand-new garment. There was a sharpness to the formerly dull air of the attic room; something out-of-place, though no new smell surfaced.

Hadn't the Matriarch said something about air? Paige was doubting herself. She could hear it in the echo of the room, but wondered if she'd just made up the memory. Her ears, though, were sure.

"I thought you said something about air," said Paige. She was careful to keep her voice inquisitive, though accusations pushed at the back of her throat, threatened to take over with her burning annoyance.

The Matriarch watched Paige for a couple of moments, seeming genuinely confused.

"Why would I say anything about air?" asked the Matriarch.

Her voice was so gentle. Perfectly innocent, perfectly ordinary, as if she had never shown any signs of cruelty before. The wrinkles between her eyebrows, upturned in concern, pushed Paige's perception of her back into the deitific.

Maybe the Matriarch *was* really earnest . . .

But Paige couldn't answer the Matriarch's question. She had no response. She was trying to work it out herself. The air, the air—cleaning up the air, of all things, why would that be a secret? Nothing was supposed to be a secret. What was in the air, aside from oh-so-faint residue from the Paterazm? Was there something more prominent in the air? A Council conspiracy? Was Paige making it up? It was all so subtle, she couldn't tell. And if even if Paige was right—even if there was something nefarious in the Matriarch's tone—she wouldn't be able to actually say anything in response. Any answer she came up with was weak at best; she would be considered a Theorist if she suggested any of the explanations that came to her brain, and questioning the Matriarch's authority if she regarded her with suspicion.

"I must have misheard," said Paige.

The Matriarch looked upon her with pity. "It's this that worries me," she said. "I'm concerned that you're lost in your own head. That the same dark thoughts that plagued me have cornered you."

In that Paige was suicidal? She could have laughed to herself. The Matriarch wasn't totally wrong.

"It's a difficult task," continued the Matriarch, squatting before Paige so that the sun shining inappropriately through the windows crept into the wrinkles on her skin, highlighted flakes of dryness and oily pores. "I know what it's like to be separated from my dearest friends. I know what it's like to banish their souls from the Afterlands."

She said this part carefully, so quietly, that Paige wasn't sure she actually heard it.

Paige would have to cleanse Mott.

If she cared about living before, she didn't now.

"I am so sorry, Paige. I want to offer you—not Matriarch-to-Ritualist, but woman-to-woman, human-to-human—my condolences. As much comfort as I can provide."

The Matriarch's hair was a little out-of-place, Paige could see. Maybe the wishes were genuine. Paige just wanted to stab her, but didn't have a way to.

She understood, now: death—as opposed to ascension—had never been a penalty, but a relief. A reward. The scrap of paper Mott had given her was right. This *was* all made-up. The whole town was nothing but a fabricated construct of wishful peace, and if she died without ascending—if ascension was even real—she could reject it all.

The light seemed too bright in the room. Paige felt her heart racing, sweat starting to bubble at her hairline, and if the Matriarch stayed there a moment or two more then she'd certainly start to see it sneak down the sides of her face. The in-between-ness of the whole scenario was overwhelming and painful and Paige could sense real emotion coming from both her and the Matriarch—powerful, moreso than the Statutes' words ever were. Powerful like feeling Mott's arms around her, like feeling Mott's hair on her shoulder— she was broken.

"You know what would provide me comfort?" Paige said slowly, as fast as she could without her voice trembling. "Seeing my brother."

The Matriarch tilted her head at Paige. "I don't think that would be wise."

"I would like to see my brother," Paige said, louder.

"Lower your voice, please."

"Take me to him." Paige didn't change her volume.

The Matriarch looked at her for a long time—so long that Paige thought the Matriarch might be considering cleansing her, too. Paige had risked her defiance on the premise that the Matriarch didn't want to have to appoint a new Ritualist.

Did she have that power?

Surely; the Matriarch needed her. To keep up a semblance of normalcy, of compliance, despite a Ritualist's escape and suicide. Right? Would the Matriarch cleanse her, too?

Did she care?

No.

No, she fucking didn't.

"CS Holly," said the Matriarch at last, her eyes never leaving Paige's even for a moment, "take the Ritualist to say goodbye to her brother."

Paige would have said *thank you*, but she didn't want to.

ON FOOLISHNESS

an excerpt from the Statutes of Equality

WE UNDERSTAND, FRIEND, THAT we are locked within our bodies. We are slaves to two arms and two legs and ten fingers and one head. Two eyes and a nose and a mouth with thirty-two teeth. Two ears. One tongue. And nerves, countless nerves, thirty-nine billion nerves, for sensing.

And what do we sense? Existence is a finicky, not-insignificant experience. We feel love when we appreciate one another; we feel pain when our skin has lacerations. We use our legs to walk through the park, to our dining hall, where we fuel their bodies. We utilize this fuel to exert effort. The effort fuels the community. The community fuels the bodies—the ears, the tongue, the nerves. We fuel for the good of us all. We fuel ourselves so that we can all continue to be fueled.

We have learned, since the War, to not trust the unpredictability of chance. We have learned that competition leads us to allow our Friends to be left behind, to submit our bodies to injustices: poverty, loneliness, hatred, hunger. We have learned to take responsibility for our own, and to ensure the rights and responsibilities of personhood to us all. We have learned that to ignore each other is to fall prey to foolishness, and that which is Outside is the predator to the fool.

Participate, Friend, in the boundaries that we have set, physically and spiritually. You'll find that these boundaries keep us all safe and guarantee life. If you give your life to us, we will keep it for you. Let us keep you, Friend. You are the light within us.

BEHOLD, THE FIRE AND THE WOOD

CS Holly LED HER toward the back of the building, not even that far away—maybe a two- or three-minute walk away from Paige's room. Two doors stood at the end of this hallway, both with small, embroidered tapestries hanging from a nail on the door. The one on the right-hand side read *AUTHORIZED PERSONNEL ONLY*; as they approached, two children, one in late-teens and the other maybe an age-five or -six, walked out of the door. They peered at CS Holly in question—*were we supposed to see this?*—who shooed them with a wave of his hand, and the children scurried off past them without so much as a *hello*.

Instead, CS Holly placed her hand on the other door's handle. This tapestry had not a label, but an adage:

PEACE CAN HAPPEN THOUGH RODS MAY BE SPARED.

They didn't want anyone to know, Paige thought.

The hinges squeaked as CS Holly pulled the door open. "You have five minutes."

Five minutes? She dared to negotiate.

"Twenty."

"Five."

"Thirty. What are you going to do if I don't comply?" It felt good to say it. Her voice didn't even waver. She had nothing left to lose; there was power in that.

CS Holly glanced at her, then away, then back at her. She ushered Paige through the door. "Ten minutes. You have *ten* minutes."

Paige's skin felt damp, the air down here somehow both wet and dusty. She thought she could hear the rattling of the old, refurbished air conditioner from the other end of the room and rubbed the prickling hairs on her arms as they stood at attention.

Ten basement cells, all empty except one. As it should have been—only extreme cases were held here, in this dank, dimly lit space, and extreme cases only came every few years. But what made Paige shiver beyond the chill in the basement was the fact that it had only been a couple of years since the last Cleansing, and now there was not one, but were three cells that were marked as *in use*, though Chang and Mott weren't there now.

But where were they? They couldn't have been cleansed already—

She tried not to wonder about Pierce and Chang's young son adjusting to life with a newly assigned mother, the Age-Twenty-Three or Age-Twenty-Four huérfana, depending on which one was female. And she tried not to picture Lane, ten years older, tiptoeing around Pierce in the space Chang once occupied—her hair stuck to Chang's pillow, her favorite tea in Chang's mug.

How easily they were all replaced.

"Paige!"

Solomon flew to his cell wall—a wire grid supported by thin wooden beams—and shoved his fingers through the holes in the wire to reach out to Paige.

"Don't be mad," he said.

"It's too late," Paige said, through half-laughing tears, "I'm mad."

Her breath blurred his face through the glass. For a moment all she saw was the outline of his head, the eyes and nose and mouth she knew so well hidden behind the fog, like he was worlds away. But then the fog was gone and he was clear again, sharper than she'd ever seen him before.

"I'm sorry, P."

"Apology not accepted. What the *hell*, Sol. You could've—you *have* gotten yourself killed."

He laughed without humor. "Not dead yet."

"*Sol.*"

"I know. I'm sorry."

Paige grasped at straws. "You could apologize."

"For what?"

"For whatever they tell you to. It's not too late."

Sol laughed, and for a moment Paige caught a glimpse of what he looked like in those rare moments when they were younger and they'd had a moment to themselves, playing hopscotch on the sidewalk or picking worms out of the strawberry patch on the front lawn of their tetriplex with Mott and Rory. Sweet summer days, blisteringly hot but that made it even more fun when the groundskeeper for their block let them run under the hose when he was watering the plants; it was their little secret. She wanted that Sol back. She wanted that time back. But was it ever really hers?

Was he?

Sol's smile faded when he realized she was even a little serious. "No."

Paige exhaled, reaching for patience. Her heart panged at the sight of her brother's curly hair, his expression open with the conviction that he had done nothing wrong, his long eyelashes blinking at her like they did when he was a baby and Papa threw a lamp on the ground and broke a lightbulb and Paige's scared, very-young self kept smiling down at Sol and he smiled back.

"They're going to make me kill you," she said.

Sol raised his eyebrows in a pained pity; Paige couldn't keep her cool anymore, not like she'd been able to for long anyway. She was crying—*again*—and the shame of it rocked her even though she told herself it shouldn't.

"I know," he repeated. "I'm sorry."

Of course he wasn't going to apologize. He shouldn't. He was older now. Almost an adult. He was a proper person, someone who didn't need her shielding anymore; his own man.

She reached through the square holes in the wire and grasped his fingers, just to feel him one last time.

"I can't," she sobbed.

"You have to."

"I know. But I can't. Please don't make me. Please."

Sol was crying, too. How badly she wanted to just hold him and reassure him and tell him everything would be okay, but it never would be again and she knew that, she knew it. He knew it. But then again, what did it matter when he would be dead?

"This isn't about you," Sol said, gently.

Paige nodded, ashamed by her self-centeredness. Of course it wasn't about her. He wanted her to know what it was about; he wanted her to know *him* when no one could anymore. She did her best to keep quiet, to actively listen.

"I just—I can't do it anymore, Paige. Please understand. You've got to understand. My heart has these words and they make me happy and when they are contained I feel like I can't breathe. So I have to write. Poetry. I've been doing it for years but I usually bury the paper when I help out at the garden. And for a while that was okay, but then they took you away, and I just felt so alone. Even if I couldn't show you my poems before, you at least understood, whether you felt okay about it or not, and I— I just want you to know that you are loved. And I feel like if you knew that, if you felt that from Mama or Papa directly, then maybe you wouldn't be so sad. I saw you and Mott kissing that morning when Ingrid ran away—escaped—"

Paige's stomach fluttered and she started to sweat.

"—and I just saw how *happy* you were. Like, you were just *happy*, and that was enough for you. And I feel like if I could put that into words and give it to someone else, then they could be happy, too, and maybe everything would be okay. And that's what the Theorists kept saying, so I believed in it. And I'm so *happy* when I let myself write. It's just letting myself be myself, and not having to please anyone else, and once you were gone I just decided that I couldn't live like this anymore, because otherwise I was going to have to watch you die—"

He collapsed into tears after that, and Paige did along with him. They stood there for a few moments, crying together; the cathartic honesty of it was everything.

"I have a question," Paige finally said, in her most non-judgmental tone: "Is this worth it?"

"Yes." Sol didn't even hesitate.

"Why?"

"It's my truth."

Paige understood, though she didn't want to.

"As much as I have to respect that, I'm—" Pissed? Depressed? Disbelieving that she would have to kill her own brother?

There was a slim chance, though. A very slim chance, but a chance nonetheless. They'd have him up on a stake, along with Chang and Mott, but if she somehow lit the Matriarch on fire instead, or herself—

She didn't know how, but she would figure out something. As long as she created some sort of chaos—

"I'm going to get you out of here."

Sol frowned. "What? How?"

She made herself say it, though the k caught in her throat.

"I'm going to kill the Matriarch."

Sol blinked at her, reflexively stepping back.

"I took this risk knowing what could happen to me," he said. "I'm part of something bigger. Don't throw away the chance to help that bigger movement by getting yourself caught for attempted murder."

"It won't be attempted if I succeed."

"And is that what you want to become? A murderer?"

"I don't have much of a choice, Sol. She's going to kill the only things I care about. If I let her do that, I'm just letting it happen. I'm culpable. And if I'm going to die anyway—"

"But you're not a murderer if you let us die."

"This isn't about principle, Solomon." She could hear her

bossy-big-sister voice taking over but couldn't stop it. "It's not about philosophy. This is about whether I can live with myself—even if it's only for another year—if I let this happen."

Sol squinted his left eye at her and pushed his lips to one side—his thinking face. And then he relaxed.

"I get that."

Hope fluttered up through Paige's lungs. "We could be free. If I kill her—if everyone is too distracted by that—"

The smile Sol gave her now was more pitying than anything else. He was humoring her. He was always the smarter one.

"Yeah," he said, resignedly. "Yeah, maybe."

The hope was slim. He knew it; she knew it. But it was there.

"But also," he added, "you can't always save me."

"I can try." The words spilled out of her mouth and she felt no regret: "Look, I *hate* this. I hate that I'm nothing but a marionette attached to strings, to them. I hate this *place*. I hate this *role*. I hate all of it."

She understood why Mama said *hate* before—because it was true, and truth was more important than anything else because it consumed everything. It was undeniable.

The truth was that New Standard was a far cry from what she'd grown up believing it was. It was so obvious now; she was so *stupid* for not having seen it years and years before. The world blurred around her, walls disappearing through her eyes' salty runoff. Still, this was better: she could see everything now.

New Standard wasn't a place of holiness and purity and light; it was a place where children were murdered and taken from their parents. She clenched her fists and dug her nails hard into her palms, hoping she would break the skin.

"I won't do it. I'll kill them first. I'll kill them all."

She could practically hug him, wire and wood the only thing that separated them. She could open the cage. She could destroy this wire. It was only wire. Only wood. She had a whole body, powerful enough to make a whole other person, or so they claimed. Surely it was powerful enough to free a whole other person, too.

There, on the left: the hinge that could unlatch the cage door. She fumbled with it even though she knew CS Tim would be here in another moment or two, but she had to try anyway, she couldn't not try. She tried to pull on it, hoping against reality that the Ancestors would see this injustice and send the lock miraculously clattering onto the ground.

"Paige, stop," Sol said.

Paige ignored him. She stepped back and tried to push it up with her foot, all the while looking around her for some sort of blunt object to kill the lock's structure. There had to be something. Anything. But the narrow walkway between all the cells was barren.

So she put her back on the cell behind her and ran forward, jamming the side of her body against the lock.

It hurt. It didn't budge. She cried not from the pain but from the lock's resistance.

"I'll kill them all," she said through gritted teeth, and kicked the lock with one leg. It didn't move, it did nothing, and she shouted a pained, wordless cry at it for its stupidity in not moving. She kicked it again, again, again.

"Paige, please," Sol said. She heard the fear in his voice, the crack in the middle where he started to cry, too, but she didn't stop; she couldn't stop; he had to get out of there and it was her job as his older sister to get him out. "Please, stop."

She kept kicking, clawing, pulling, shoving; nothing made the lock move, its structure hard and functional and tangible just like everything in New Standard, but it didn't matter, she had to keep going, she had to save Sol—

As she reeled her arm back to punch it, a hand grabbed her wrist, and Paige tried to yank her arm forward again but couldn't.

"Ritualist!" she heard CS Holly say somewhere through her thrashing as she grabbed her other wrist and tried to pull her back.

Paige flailed her legs around, kicking the air like a whisk beating pancake batter, shouting, "LET GO OF ME."

"What did you say to her?"

"I didn't—"

"Nevermind. Not like you'll tell me the truth anyway. Ritualist, I need you to calm down."

And finally Paige got so tired of pushing against CS Holly that she couldn't do anything else but let herself go limp and cry. Paige heard herself still sobbing and willed herself to stop out of sheer dignity, out of embarrassment, but she couldn't. She was mortified. This was unstately. She was too distraught to make herself care. If she cried harder, maybe the ancestors would hear and it would all go away. She collapsed onto the floor, crying and trying to breathe through it, finally looking up at Solomon and saying, over and over, "I'm sorry."

"It's okay," he said, still crying, too. She hated it when he cried. He sounded so impossibly *young*. She spent so much time trying to keep him from crying, to keep his spirits up even when everything at home seemed hopeless, like their family was falling apart after all despite their very best efforts, and now it was her fault that he was crying. His downturned mouth made his whole face spread out into ugly emotion he could no longer hide, a huge contrast against his long eyelashes that usually made him—as Mama liked to say—*such a handsome young man.*

Beauty, wasted. All because she'd failed to protect him.

"I knew I should've drawn the line at five minutes," CS Holly mumbled, hoisting Paige up onto her feet. She obeyed mechanically, the emotion drained from her whole body, and all she could do was gaze emptily at her little brother and repeat the truth in relief: "I'm sorry. I love you. I'm sorry. I love you."

———

THE PANDORA WAITED ON Paige's bed back in her empty room as a harbinger of the death to follow not a few hours from now. CS Holly locked her in the room; Paige wanted to pray, but couldn't.

Pray to whom? The Ancestors? If the Ascension wasn't real, then were the Ancestors? If the Statutes were just a collection of worldly philosophies, it was all just lip service. Just words, nothing mystical behind them. Just human, earthly, no other place to go.

There were no Afterlands. No bright-white cottage with a kitchen and honey and space for just her and Mott and kisses not-missed for the rest of not-time. There was only the bed beneath her, the carpet beneath her toes, the fabric draping her body. Human things, worldly things. Things. Objects. Pieces of matter.

Sometimes, Paige rested her head on Mott's shoulder as they huddled beneath a blanket together for comfort but not for warmth. They wondered about those stars, about the moon, about all of those things that were visible and yet so far away, that could only be described as dreams. Mott told her stories about the figures made up of stars in the sky and Paige lost herself in feeling the soft hairs on Mott's cheek and imagined reaching up to feel Mott's exposed neck, just to see if it was real, just to see if Mott would flinch away, to turn her face into hers, just like they did that night when Paige had rejected her. Mott, her alto voice murmuring names Paige did not recognize, stories that Paige could not imagine, and the soft heat of Mott's cheek against her forehead.

The insulation must have been thin in here. The sticky heat reminded her of a night when she sat outside with Mott on the porch of Paige's tetriplex, talking. She remembered sitting closer to Mott, and the shame of thinking about her—for the first time— as the only person she wanted to spend this time with. This solitary, private time, where no one else could interfere, where they could be alone with the distant noise of the night just far away enough. Paige remembered the cool heat from the summer air wrapping itself around her calves, a breeze pushing its way up her skirt and caressing her knees, the freedom that the air provided. Mott sat next to her, gazing up at the stars, wondering what was out there beyond the border. They had always known that New Standard was the only known community left after the

War, but Mott always insisted (against logic, against reason) that there was life beyond them, maybe out in the stars.

Mott talked about aliens, myths of things that existed in the fantasies of their ancestors, but that had never really interested Paige. Mott would talk on and on about the aliens like they were real, like they had some sense of tangibility. And Paige let her talk. She liked watching Mott's eyes light up as she dreamed aloud. She liked watching Mott roll up her sleeves as she cooled down after a hot afternoon. She liked just being there with Mott, comfortable, like she never was in any other situation. With Mott, she could just *be*.

She cried, letting herself collapse on the floor. Sobs rippled through her body, loudly, she didn't care. What did she need a body for if none of this was real? Why even bother trying? The only real act of resistance was letting go of that body, actively pushing it down. But Paige didn't care. This was a safer place to be: a place where she didn't—*couldn't* feel. Here, in the middle of the room on the hard ground with her arms hanging from the sides of her body and her hands draped on the floor. She stared at the grains in the floorboards, the uneven carves nature made in real wood before humans had to force nature to grow things despite them having killed its natural instincts. At this moment, she was certain: she would stay here for all eternity. Gravity would let her be here and she would finally relinquish herself to its forces. She would let it own her. At least then she would have a choice.

Or she could starve herself.

She should have shuddered at the thought, but she didn't. That was what Agatha had done, wasn't it? That was why she'd been so skinny. She was resisting by way of active self-starvation, because there was nothing else she could do, and Paige was destined to follow the same path.

Unless—

She raised her head half-heartedly to eye the windows. The metal leaves on the window were expertly crafted with no way out. Her only option would be to remove the leaves somehow, maybe with an emergency kit. There were always tools in an emergency kit, and they had to have one in the Ritualist's room, right?

But where—

The drawers. There was that pesky hope again, flooding itself through Paige's blood with enough adrenaline to get herself up off the floor. She hurled herself at the drawers, grasping the handles of the top one—clothes—and the middle one—toiletries—and then finally the bottom drawer.

Clothes. But the top one was wrinkled, not as neatly stacked as the ones in the top drawer. Paige lifted it up to find a small brown washcloth, and when she lifted it something hard and relatively heavy fell onto the clothes beneath it.

Someone had gotten here first.

A glint of silver. Long, though maybe shorter than her forearm, with a handle. She lifted it up to the light and examined it from the base of the handle to the tip of the knife's blade.

Taped to the back of it was a note:

NOW'S YOUR CHANCE.

THE WORDS

a handwritten note

Sometimes

there is

nothing

left

to

do

the Statutes guide

they say
they feel

but what do I feel

what do I

amindfulapproachtoavarice.
Lovedoesnotcreatenordestroyitispureenergy.
Weasknotwhetheroursoulswillbestainedbuthow.
Patiencegoodnesskindnessselfcontrolwhatdoesiteverdoforme

Nothingleftnoone no one none no
life no reason no words no love no thing left to do

just settle into

ashes

ashes

we all

fall

down

Nothingleftnoone no one none no
life no reason no words no love no thing left to do

PURGE ME WITH HYSSOP

PAIGE COULD GET USED to this new superpower, apathy. She met the cleansing procession—the Matriarch, the Council of Elders, and a couple of CSes to guard them—in the lobby that night, the Pandora in her hands, fully loaded with her "energy," or so they said. It felt like a cold box, dead weight in her hands.

Heavier still because of the knife inside.

"So you'll wait for my cue, okay," the Matriarch was saying as they walked in a pair in the midst of all the officials, "and then CS Taylor will hand you a torch, and you'll use that torch to light the hay. Got it?"

"Got it."

"Don't hesitate. You'll want to hesitate, because you have compassion for these people as your friends and neighbors. You *cannot* hesitate or you won't go through with it."

Mechanical advice for how to kill people.

"Got it."

There was silence for a moment, which threw Paige off. She peered up at the Matriarch, who stared in front of them at the distant crowd of gathering New Standardites, the people among whom she'd felt a belonging only a few days ago. The Matriarch held up a hand, and the procession stopped.

"Give us a minute," she said, pulling Paige off to the side.

This wasn't supposed to happen, was it? Unlikely. Hot

anxiety slashed through Paige's carefully curated apathy as she realized that she was now out of earshot of the CSes, and that if the Matriarch were to do anything to her, they'd be too far away to take any action in time. The Matriarch raised her arms toward Paige, and Paige winced, waiting for an impact—

But the Matriarch only gripped the sides of Paige's arms, something that resulted in more of a soothing comfort than anything else. The heat of the anxiety melted, wax on an extinguished candle. Despite her domineering presence, the Matriarch wasn't a large woman; as she looked at Paige eye-to-eye, Paige realized they were almost the same size. She could see reflections of herself in the Matriarch: self-doubt, age-old wounds, fear; and beneath it all, bravery for making the most difficult choice, a self-denial so that her lover could live. The Pandora in Paige's hands felt even heavier now, like she didn't deserve to be holding it at all, and she felt sick at the thought that she had maybe been too rash in her decision to take a life.

"Look, Paige, I know how hard this is," said the Matriarch. "It's tragic. To kill the one person you love more than anyone else is unthinkable, and I can't even imagine what it's like to have to do it twice in the same night."

The Matriarch's eyes were almost glistening with sympathetic pity, and Paige started to feel the tears well up in her own throat. The Matriarch understood how impossible this was for Paige, how close Paige was to crumbling on the spot. She squeezed Paige's shoulders and Paige wanted to melt into the Matriarch's arms, to let herself be *held* by the woman who'd given everything up, who'd kept her lover safe at her own peril. If Mott hadn't given herself up, maybe Paige could have done the same thing.

"But that's the sacrifice people like us have to take," the Matriarch continued. "Because we *see* it. The end goal. That was the only thing that got me through this."

Paige nodded, letting the reassurance wash over herself in a sort of hypnosis. This community could take care of her, if she let it, if she did away with all this irrational thinking. Then she paused, frowning.

"You had to do this, too?"

"Yes. Remember? My—" The Matriarch looked over her shoulder briefly, "—my *friend*? The scientist?"

"I remember," said Paige, not processing.

The Matriarch offered nothing but a sad smile and a squeeze on Paige's arms. Then tears visibly welled in her eyes, threatening to spill over their rims.

"Her. Worst day of my life."

Something in Paige clicked, and then everything went cold.

"You cleansed her." The words came out of Paige in a matter-of-fact manner but she couldn't comprehend their meaning. "I thought you said you couldn't let her die."

"And I didn't. That's what I'm trying to remind you of. I cleansed her soul. The alternative was that I let her body and her soul rot, so of course I had to cleanse her. It was excruciating, okay, you have no idea—" The Matriarch's voice cracked and now her tears flowed freely; the CSes around them pretended to be deeply engaged in conversation, conveniently not noticing any of the Matriarch's bold emotion. Half of Paige wanted to reach out and hold the Matriarch; the other half of her was afraid to touch her. "Well. You will, soon. But you won't be alone, okay. I'll be here for you. And Felicity is resting, and she didn't infect everyone else—"

But Paige wasn't listening anymore. The familiar thing she'd felt when the Matriarch had first told her about her lover had now made itself painfully obvious, the myth of the Matriarch's so-holy abstinence crumbling before her in a pile of ash. She felt stupid for not having recognized Aunt Felicity's story before, for not having seen the timeline and understood 'saving' someone for what it really was, for not having connected *scientist* with *medic*. She felt stupid for letting this woman, who was apparently hell-bent on destroying Paige's entire bloodline and happiness, convince her of anything.

The Matriarch had stopped talking and pressed her lips together in a reassuring smile.

"*Walk not alone, Friend,*" she said, by way of a question.

Paige smiled back, because now—*now,* she was truly free.

"*The path we take does not exist without our neighbors,*" she answered.

"Good girl."

The Matriarch pushed her toward the front of the procession, the warm night breeze providing a relief to endless things: to this responsibility, to this town, to the Matriarch. Paige flinched at the word *girl.* Like she could just be pushed along, like she was the simplistic Age-Sixteen she'd been a week ago.

Just a few moments. There was no going back. It would be too late for forgiveness.

It already was.

She kept an eye out for the newly espoused women around Chang's age on her way to the cleansing in the outskirts, in the rubble of the fields. A couple of bellies already ballooned under dresses, most modestly small. A few of them were greeting each other, exchanging sympathies. But the way they talked and the familiar way they cupped each others' faces, straightened out each others' head scarves—even without Chang they had each other. They would get through grief and childbirth and raise their children together, like Mama and Xenia. They would sing the same lullabies. They would tell the same stories.

She gripped the box in her hands—smooth wood, dusty smell—and tried to distance herself. She focused on the grass beneath her shoes, dry and crunchy since it had been weeks since the last rain. If she dropped the torch on the ground, on the other hand, the fire would spread wildly. Maybe that was a better bet.

Everyone was gathering at the stake, the murmurs among the crowd not the excited hush of ascension but an aggressive rumbling instead. No peaceful candles flickering between gathering neighbors, no songs of peace. She could sense the irritation, the angry righteousness, in the air—they, the people of New Standard, had lost enough. Now it was time for the Theorists who had caused their suffering to be cleansed.

"I heard her talking about what colors she'd paint the nursery walls," said an older man to the older woman walking next to him.

"Disgusting," said the woman.

"And not even color. *Colors.* It's just like the Theorists. Always wanting more, not even a thought to making sure there's enough for everyone else first."

They had arrived at the front of the crowd. Paige watched Chang as she was tied to the first wooden pole. As steeled as Paige had thought herself to be, the sight jarred her. Chang's hands were tied behind her back, her chest exposed. And then two more. One to the right of Chang, one to the left. Paige held her breath and kept her eyes trained on Chang. She didn't look at Mott and Sol. She couldn't look.

"When things are broken, you fix them," said a different nearby woman, younger this time. "I would've gotten rid of it. I don't see what the big deal is."

"Has he really been a Theorist this whole time?" said someone else as people shuffled together. "I wonder about her parents. And how tragic, the sister's the *Ritualist.*" The voice hushed on the last word, a few pairs of eyes connecting with Paige's in a guarded curiosity as she passed by. They didn't know. They couldn't know.

"Peace be with the family," said someone in response.

"May the Earth cleanse *his* dust, though," chimed in someone else.

I can hear you, Paige wanted to yell at them. *That's my little brother, and I love him.*

Almost everyone in New Standard was there already, more people flowing in each moment. Paige started to count them.

"—for everyone's safety, it's only common sense—"

"—never heard anything up until now, and now it's just like everything's crumbling at the same time—"

"—I always thought Mott was a good kid, and what a lovely sister—"

"—together? Because you never know these days, what you see isn't always what you get, there could be a few hidden germs here and there—"

"—false sense of security. It really makes you wonder about the Council—"

Fuck all of this. Fuck it all. She didn't even feel bad about thinking such vile language.

Paige felt like she was wading through a cloud, a little foggy and seen but still unseen. There were people all around her but they weren't really watching her, not this time. Now they were focused on the traitors tied to the wooden poles. No one would interfere this time.

The Ritualist was to set the Pandora down in front of the person to be cleansed, accept the torch from the CSes, light the hay, then open the box to let the evil in, where it would remain until the next cleansing. Paige had imagined how she would light the fires for several nights, tried to envision herself as Yuri-of-2094's daughter. All she remembered from that night was seeing Yuri's daughter, then Mama's fingers over her eyes, something warm and comforting in the midst of nothing more than idle curiosity and confusion.

Paige imagined herself in a cloud, now. Separate, slippery, suspended. She mentally walked herself through the practice she'd done in her room, and added the Matriarch's advice: quick draw, firm grip, don't hesitate. Breathe.

She only had one shot to create freedom, to create justice, to save everyone. This was why they'd chosen her, wasn't it? Because she could see what they couldn't. She had the strength to give them what they needed.

"Citizens of New Standard," said the Matriarch, voice muffled by the whip of wind. They had arrived at the site of the cleansing: three stakes at the top of a shallow hill, with room for the audience at the bottom to have their glowing faces warmed in witness of the fire. The Matriarch was almost shouting; her voice had a rawness to it while it battled the space and the weather. A Council worker stood halfway back in the crowd, repeating every line to those beyond the hearing threshold. "Today we grieve the loss of three former neighbors!"

The crowd cheered. Paige shook her head, startled by the sound; she stood watching their thirst for vengeance manifest in their enthusiasm for death.

Paige found calmness through stroking the smooth wood lines of the Pandora, gliding one hand on it like a sailboat, gripping it like an anchor with the other hand. She was in the middle of some vast, far-off ocean right now, no other boats around. She was not holding the box, preparing for an murder; she was circling an island, drinking in the salty heat, everything a quiet calm except the waves lapping against the boat.

Existence is a finicky, not-insignificant experience, the Statutes said. *We feel love when we appreciate one another; we feel pain when our skin has lacerations.*

They were cheering for the pain, Paige realized. They wanted Mott and Chang and Solomon to suffer.

She breathed in slowly, studying the faces in the first row of the audience. She didn't recognize most of them—but as she saw the varied ages, and Lane and Moses in the middle of them, she realized why.

They were huérfanos and Council workers in the front row. The children were all grouped in the center.

But whatever. If that was supposed to deter her from trying anything, it wouldn't. She could kill a child.

She *could*.

Except—no.

No, she couldn't.

Lane nodded at Paige when she caught her eye, daring her to disagree. Yes, she could. She had to. Everything depended on it. Sol was a child. And New Standard was killing him.

"We recognize that the legacies they might have left our community are now an absence. Today we recognize the continued importance of the community over the individual. Today we learn from these three individuals who have selfishly prioritized themselves over the community, and to that, we say, 'Good riddance!' "

In a hot jab of pain that widened the existing holes Paige's cool mental state, she wanted to stab the Matriarch right there, to make her feel sorry for ever suggesting that Paige's brother and her best friend and a mother who only loved her child, imperfect though the child might have been, should be put to death.

Breathe; wait. Too early and the CSes would see it coming. They'd stop her.

"Good riddance!" roared the community. The anger in the noise was so unfamiliar in its strength and fervor that it pushed Paige's ocean away, bringing her back to the dry grass covering the dirt under her feet.

That anger, too, was combined with joy. There was laughter speckled among them.

"We stand united!" shouted the Matriarch to the crowd, loud in Paige's ear since she was standing right next to her. "We stand for the functional legacy our ancestors created for us, their children. We stand for the path of love and equality they had forged before us! We have found glorious freedom in this love! And these *Theorists* have not, so we release them, for the benefit of us all."

The Matriarch whirled toward Paige and motioned for her to step forward. Every step was walking on water, oil, air. All the people below her were her ocean of dark faces. She was separate from it all, they couldn't even know it. It was her secret, here on the water, in the clouds: she loved them all more than any of them could know. She had to free them. She had to.

"The Box of Pandora!" bellowed the Matriarch. "May it accept the evil from you that has poisoned our community."

Feigning triumphance, Paige held the box up to thunderous applause, then placed it carefully in front of Chang, adjusting the corners so that it was as perfectly parallel to the front edge of the hay as possible. She focused anywhere but Chang—on the torch one of the CSes handed her, on the heat of the flames now just barely above her own head, of the clear arc of darker-than-darkness the torch left behind as she swept it in the air down toward the hay, and knelt in front of the blaze that climbed up in front of her, the fire that she created.

"Chang-of-2112," bellowed the Matriarch, more toward the waiting crowd than toward Chang herself, "Of your unhappiness, of your dissatisfaction, we cleanse you."

She could hear Chang crying as the fire attached itself to Chang's skirt. It was more of a whimper than a cry—anticipatory grief. Paige's heart pounded. This was it.

Come on, she thought at the Matriarch, *Say it.*

"Earth rise, Earth cleanse," said the Matriarch.

The community echoed:

> *Earth rise.*
> *Earth cleanse.*

And then the Matriarch nodded at Paige briefly before turning back to the crowd. CS Taylor handed her a torch. Her cue.

Paige accepted the torch and balanced the Pandora on her forearm, using her other hand to open the Pandora. Foolish attempts for foolish endeavors, but it didn't matter anymore; the Matriarch had decided that for them all.

Paige gripped the handle of the knife with her other hand. She was water, she was air; nothing could stop her, not New Standard and not the blisters the fire could etch into her feet. She dutifully obeyed the Matriarch.

No hesitation.

Before anyone could shriek a warning, Paige aimed for the Matriarch's ribs and thrust the knife into her, feeling the flesh resist as the tip of the blade burrowed its way through.

The Matriarch was frozen, her breath caught in her throat, her eyes stationary in shock. It gave Paige a half-second to move.

More than enough time to light the Matriarch's skirt on fire with the torch in Paige's other hand. Her breathing quickened as the flames did, and she threw the torch in the front row of the crowd, waiting for a CS to take her.

But before they could, the air cracked loudly in a gravelly burst of sound. There was a blinding light, then smoke and screaming at the same time. The ground's shaking knocked Paige off her balance and onto her back and smoke choked up her breathing, her vision, her head, and in that moment she could only feel a sense of peace.

It was over, she thought. No more pain. It was all over.

THE BODY

a handwritten note

goes
up in the
clouds

falls
down in the
ashes

they
use it to purify
the air

hoping
that one day
they'll clean

the world
but do
noble intentions

deliver us
from evil
that has permeated

the soil
in the
ground?

ONCE WAS LOST BUT NOW AM FOUND

Except it wasn't over. There was the residual smell of ammonia and a long, ringing sound, accompanied by the sudden onslaught of roaring pain in Paige's right arm.

Not dead was all the understood.

She was aware of the white-hot pain, everywhere, consuming her entire reality. Her head burned violently and she felt her body going limp, her vision blacken, and soon there was nothing at all but the thin, everlasting pitch in her head. But hopefully it wouldn't last long. Dying was excruciating, but it would end—

And then you can rest and then you'll be free it's relief

such relief

A pair of hands cradled the back of her head, pushing her shoulders forward in her dazed stupor. Even the slightest amount of movement sent a cacophony of pain through every one of Paige's nerves. A voice attached to the hands shouted something muffled she couldn't hear, though the ringing had dimmed.

She tried to sit up, some lingering survival instinct she couldn't snuff. Paige screamed, then sobbed.

"No," she whimpered, the pain everywhere all at once.

Can't breathe   *stop moving me*

"WE DON'T HAVE TIME." The voice sounded like she was hearing it through water, another dimension.

She opened her eyes in instinct and glanced at her pained shoulder—

Attached

—and then along her arm—

Red

—her forearm bloody and twisted, pieces of glass burrowed in the skin.

She looked away. The hands yanked her up by her left arm and the pain ricocheted through her chest into her shoulder and through the nerves into her other wrist. She let out another sobbing scream and the voice swore.

"COME ON."

Leave me   just let me rest

But he had her propped up on his shoulder and on her feet already. Whoever it was—some man, a voice she'd heard before—wasn't going to let her be. It was easier to obey.

"I NEED YOU TO WALK. CAN YOU WALK?"

It took every ounce of strength to start moving, ignoring the pain, but once she started the adrenaline propelled her in turn. She coughed, tried to breathe slowly, to avoid the dust particles that clung, burning, to the lining of her throat, but also because the breathing made the pain better. If she could just get the oxygen to her brain—

Come on come on come light healing light come light eternal

She felt her exhales vibrating out in long moans. Stayed still, another inhale, another exhale, another moan. Again and again.

There was a smell in the air. Half-delicious, half-disgusting, like meat on a barbecue, a rare delicacy and an acquired taste.

The man dragged her along with him. She blinked through the smoke to see the fire—everywhere. Fire in front of her, violently vibrant, making her sweat. Or melt, she couldn't be sure, but she didn't matter—Chang did, Mott did, Sol did. Maybe they had survived, it was only some smoke and shrapnel and some elevated flames—

And then Paige saw it. Chang's body, stringy blond hair streaked with blood, limply hanging on the pole as the flames licked bloody blisters into her skin and enveloped her baby bump, taking claim of both of them.

Mercy.

Mercy, she'd killed someone. Two someones.

No. No, Chang was supposed to have survived. She was supposed to have broken free. She was supposed to have run away or something in the confusion and saved herself somehow. Or Paige wasn't supposed to have watched her die, either way. Paige was supposed to have died with her, maybe. She didn't know. She hadn't thought that far ahead. She'd been so consumed by rage and now—

Now, everyone was coughing. Babies crying; shouting; people running. The CSes were lost in the smoke. But when she looked up, the person who had her wasn't a CS.

It was Moses.

"YOU GOT HER?" said another familiar voice, younger, female. Lane was running toward them with a rag tied around her nose and mouth, handing rags to both of them to do the same. Moses grabbed one and tied it around his own face, then handed the other one to Paige.

"JUST HOLD IT OVER YOUR MOUTH," he said, and then to Lane: "SHE'S ONLY GOT ONE GOOD ARM."

"ONE'S FINE," said Lane. "LET'S MOVE."

"MOVE WHERE?" Paige demanded, voice hoarse but external. Everything had to be external.

"OUT," said Moses. "FOLLOW ME."

"NOT WITHOUT THEM." Paige pointed toward the other two stakes, then looked over to find the people she knew would be attached to them, only to find that they were empty.

Shit. *Shit.* Where were they?

Did the CSes take them? Had they fallen off during the explosion? Where had the explosion come from, anyway? And

Lane, where had she gotten those rags? Why did she seem prepared for this moment?

"WE DON'T HAVE TIME FOR THIS," said Lane.

"PAIGE? PAIGE!"

Mott's voice. A surge of hope soared through Paige as she recognized Mott's voice and saw her running toward her with another figure only a few feet away.

"THEY'RE FOLLOWING, OKAY?" said Lane. "THIS WAY."

Lane started running and Moses followed her and Paige followed them now that she knew Mott and Sol saw her and would follow her, too. She didn't know what was happening, only that she was running away from what she didn't want and toward something else, anything else, something that was going to be *different*, and anything that was different had to be better. Her shoulder panged sharply with the impact of every step and it took every ounce of strength Paige had to not get distracted by the sheer unbelievability of Mott and Sol's presence in front of her at this moment; but the fantasy that they could get away, all of them, together, was so delicious.

If they were caught, they'd be slaughtered on the spot. That was the only thing she knew for certain, and she didn't believe in miracles. But Mott and Sol caught up and were running alongside them, and then Paige let herself hope.

The five of them ran down the other side of the hill, toward the town center, and with Mott and Sol right next to her it seemed easier to push her feet against the ground and pull herself farther and farther away from the fire and the screams. No footsteps behind them yet, no waggling lights searching the dirt floor. Paige's lungs were fire, filled with high-pile ash and harsh smoke.

They skated along in the wind, past Business Complex No. 2, past the bakery and its lingering smells of bread tugging her heart back home, but she wouldn't let it hold her, not when she'd just wrestled it off. None of it could touch her: not the comforting geometry of the windows in the dining hall; not the leaves she loved napping in in Serenity Park; not the catch of pristine glass, liquid in the moonlight, from the Edufice. All of it belonged somewhere else now. It was dirty in its cleanliness. Paige was cleaner than air.

They pushed together into the rubble, into the distance, into the ash, into nothingness. There was something right in this sense of togetherness, even if they were going to be dead by the end of it. Paige, for once, didn't care.

Her heart beat faster. She couldn't feel her toes even as they gripped her socks slipping around in her shoes, and she deliberately ignored the throbbing agony in her arm, made less painful temporarily by endorphins. All she could think was how they had to go faster, and faster. It was quieter here. Surely someone would be coming at this point. Surely there was someone on their heels—she looked back. No torches, no lights.

"Don't look back," Mott said.

"I'm not," Paige lied.

—

THE FURTHER OUT THEY went, the more realistic survival felt. It was like all the heat from setting Mott free was dissipating and leaving Paige in a seeping cold that bled through each vein, cooling her from the inside.

"We're almost there," said Lane.

It was then that Paige realized that Lane had a plan. Up until then, she'd been running *from* everything, but now she had a goal. *There*, wherever *there* was. It had to be better than *here*.

But wherever it was, Paige had the most important things: Mott and Sol. She reached for Sol's hand as he ran next to her, sweat dripping out of his curly hair and into his long eyelashes, but he shook his head vigorously and sprayed her with sweat.

Paige laughed wildly in delirious fear. Sol grinned at her. They were going to be okay. She'd killed Chang, but—not in vain, they were going to survive.

With five of them, they'd be able to figure out some way to survive in the wild. They could stick together, a pack of—what had those four-legged mammals been called?—wolves, hunting for prey. They could go back to their basic animal instincts and sniff out food. They could follow what used to be the river, Paige could see it now. They could figure out how to fish, how to collect resources, how to build fire.

She kept running in their pack. Past the rows of tetriplexes, empty of the families that typically warmed the windows, since they had all gathered to watch three of their own be removed from them permanently. She ran past the cold, past the air's humid heat pushing over her nostrils, sweat seeping between her breasts and in her armpits. She thought Mott might stop at any moment, but then realized that was stupid. Mott had never stopped before.

They were reaching Carnegie Avenue. Heading to the community's outskirts. There laid the abandoned storage yard across the cracked asphalt of Bullard Avenue and the arrows painted on the ground. It was the game Adam and Mott used to play—how far to the outskirts do you dare go?—only this time there was no play. They had to go. At least they'd find out what was on the other side.

The five of them raced over the arrows now, lost relics underfoot. No streetlights illuminated the long sidewalk; darkness swallowed up the sidewalk's end, but Paige had been here often enough as a child with Mott and Adam that she knew what to expect. Small circles of metal created concrete cracks in the sidewalk, the metal circles progressively rustier as they got closer to the border and the sidewalk turned from something paved to something worn and covered with dirt, weeds overgrown from the grout. The storage yard was only two blocks away from the ghosted train tracks where border expeditions usually started; the trees lining the sidewalk on this side of town became more bare the further down the sidewalk they ran.

The storage yard stretched the length of the entire street—too far to run, or at least too far to run in the little time they had. But they were close enough to the intersection just a little bit down the block. The short white gate sat, unguarded with all the CSes at the cleansing, only a few feet away. It was so close. Just a quick sprint and they'd be out of the community completely.

Two blocks. A straight shot.

They could do it.

Lane and Moses led the pack and didn't stop running. Paige's whole chest burned but she didn't dare slow down. Not with Sol and Mott flanking her, not when they were so close—one block, now—

Snap.

"Run," Lane whispered, then kicked her speed up even higher somehow, and abandoned all pretense of hiding. "Run, run, RUN!"

"HEY!" shouted a voice behind them. "STOP WHERE YOU ARE!"

"Don't look back, P," Sol said, but it was too late—Paige caught the gleam of emergency torches flickering in a faint glow behind them. The fear swept through her entire body and she started shaking, unsure if her feet were following the orders her brain was sending to them.

And they didn't—the others seemed to be moving faster than her—she was going to be left behind—

"HEY!" The footsteps behind them got louder, and there were at least two pairs.

Faster   faster

Almost there, just a few more feet—

And then a cluster of explosive popping sounds, followed by a sudden absence at her left; she turned around, and when she heard Mott shout Sol's name, she refused to associate it with the heap on the ground behind them.

THE SECOND DYNAMIC

MAY THIS FIND YOU in good health, Friend. For health matters to love, and love is at the core of all things. Without health, how can we in our right bodies and minds seek to be able to exercise this love, to practice it continuously, until Ascension do we part? And with our sound minds, we have sound bodies, and with our sound bodies, we bring forth a new generation for the betterment of the community, and when the land has healed, for the re-expansion of the world.

And if you are ill, be honest: your community shall care for you! Fear not, for honesty is love.

We hold dear the words of the god of our Ancestors which held true in their surviving of the last days of the old world:

> *Keep on loving one another as brothers and sisters. Continue to remember those in prison as if you were together with them in prison, and those who are mistreated as if you yourselves were suffering. Marriage should be honored by all, and the marriage bed kept pure, for god will judge the adulterer and all the sexually immoral. And keep your lives free from the love of money and be content with what you have*[1].

---

[1] From the book of Hebrews, chapter 13, verses 1, 3, 4, and 5, of *Holy Bible*. This is a book that our Ancestors held closely to their own hearts and lives, but with which we hold in little regard today, because the events in the book have little to no factual resonance. Some passages, like the one quoted here, have metaphorical resonance with New Standardites today, and therefore we treat it as an allegorical piece of literature that provides us a glimpse into our past. It is suspected that our Ancestors knew that this book was largely made up, and continued to believe in it anyway; however, any adoration of a false being such as this Bible god is strictly prohibited in New Standard, an offense which is punishable by cleansing.

Therefore, Friend, our bodies are vessels for new life. We hold them pure for the community to do with them as they wish, as our bodies do not belong to us, just as nothing belongs to us:

we are alive,
we are together,
we are One.

THE TASTE OF SUCCESS

S HE FELT HERSELF FALLING forward but not being allowed to fall. Mott yanked on one arm, excruciating pain rippling through her nerves and into her elbow, and Moses pulled on her other arm despite her commitment to succumb to the pain, begging for them to let her go and join Sol on the ground. It wouldn't take long. She'd die quickly—

BANG.

Another echoing explosion of sound, so loud it punctured the air all around them. It was threatening enough to jar Paige's survival reflexes: she yelped, jumped, and her body pushed her to run faster than Moses or Mott.

It was just her and the noise and the gaseous burning in her lungs and the blaze of pain throttling her arm. Everything around her blurred through the sobbing embedding itself into her panic, disappearing—except for Mott, who caught up easily and flew over the ground with her. There wasn't any time to grieve. Only time to push her muscles as far as they would go, holding the hem of her Ritualist gown in a bunch by her hip so it wouldn't catch on anything.

Pop. The epicenter of the sound was further back now; hope peeked its way around the corners from the back of her brain. She didn't dare look back, didn't dare stop running. Mott didn't have to tell her to keep going like her life depended on it—she felt it. It did.

They approached the short white gate, so close it didn't look so short anymore, not so far from the old, dry branches that littered the area. She'd always stayed further back while Adam and Mott tried to touch the gate; this was the closest she'd ever been to it, and she was only getting nearer. Lane and Moses were right in front of them at the gate now, hurdling over it like they'd done this a hundred times before, and then suddenly with just a few more bounds, it was Paige's turn.

"Jump," said Mott.

Paige jumped.

Her foot got caught on the top of the gate. It was taller than she'd expected and her other knee gave in as she tried to land on it. She tumbled, breaking her fall in a patch of spiky-leaved dandelions with the arm she'd injured in the aftermath of the cleansing. She cried out, the pain so much worse than it was before; was her toe bleeding?—the brown canvas boots she wore with her Ritualist gown were not made for rough terrain.

But Lane and Moses weren't slowing down. Only Mott paused for her. Sol might have, too, if he weren't dead—it was so *strange* that he was dead, so unbelievable that she half-thought she would wake up from this horrible nightmare tomorrow morning and everything would be back to normal.

The gauze of light she saw in the air from the CSes' battery-powered torches was getting bigger and bigger every moment she laid here.

She scrambled up, no longer in control of her own body as it scurried away as fast as it could, pain be damned. She was going to survive or die trying. And she wouldn't let Mott die, too. Not when they'd come this far.

Bang.

Paige's heart leapt every time she heard that sound. It made her run faster even when she was convinced that her legs couldn't take it anymore, when the muscles in them felt fatigued and done.

Just one more step, she told herself, and then again, and again, until that was the only thing she could think of.

And then she noticed that the light ahead of her had faded, and there were no more explosions of sound. There was only the brush of clothes and skin against the dried, overgrown grasses that had, at some point, become so tall that Paige had completely lost sight of Lane and Moses, and she realized she wasn't even telling her legs to move anymore; they moved automatically— and shakily, but they moved. If they stopped moving, Paige wasn't sure if they'd start ever again.

—

THE WEEDS WENT ON and on. They kept running, no matter how much the air stung their lungs, into the endless nothingness before them, and eventually caught up again with Lane and Moses. Paige waited for another bang, or someone calling her name, or rapidly approaching footsteps.

Nothing.

The mud got thicker. The visibility faded from slim to none. And finally, Lane and Moses stopped running and started walking, and so Mott and Paige did, too.

None of them spoke, but all of them wheezed as they tried to catch their breath. The panic was finally fading and Paige's arm and foot started screaming for attention as she realized they needed to find shelter for the night.

Or forever.

Whichever came first.

Lane chose a spot to sit in the middle of the overgrown wil-lowweed. No one complained as they all plopped on the ground, too tired to care where they landed. She didn't care if her legs ever started again. She'd made it out. That was all she could have expected.

She'd won.

She tried not to worry about what was happening to her parents. Were they being held for questioning? Would their motives be questioned because she and Sol had deviated so sharply from the path? She glanced behind herself to see if maybe that was literal, maybe he'd just taken a wrong turn. She saw nothing either way.

They'd be fine, she told herself. If she had never heard that conversation from behind her door a few days ago, she would never have guessed they were anything other than devout. Mama cross-stitched Statutes adages into pieces of fabric that Papa framed and hung on the walls. Papa was one of the most enthusiastic singers of the Anthymn.

Her heart twisted at the memories. She wished Mama were here right now, putting her arms around her, telling her how proud she was of her. That only ever happened when Mama knew no one was looking, and it was the most real Mama ever was with her. All of the fighting at home was just passion, she told herself. Because they loved each other. Because they loved her.

And Sol . . .

She tried not to think about how they would hold up in a Council hearing. Mama sitting in a chair, shifting uncomfortably as she tried to get used to the idea of all the Council members watching her every twitch. She would probably resent being stared at for so long—patience was not one of Mama's virtues; she had to work hard at it while it came so naturally to Papa. She imagined Papa sitting quietly, eyeing the clock on the wall until it was time for him to leave. He would not panic. Mama wouldn't, either. Surely the Council would see that they were harmless, and surely the Council would be forgiving to them. They would continue on—all of them would continue on without Paige and Solomon. Another year of Rituals, another year of calm, unquestioning complacency, just without children. Maybe that was better for them. The collateral damage of home life could be kept to a minimum.

Collateral damage. That was rich, considering her situation now. A fresh zing of pain electrified her arm. Maybe she'd been too harsh on New Standard. A warm bed, a blanket, water—at least it provided those things.

But no. She'd won. She'd won. She'd won.

Mott sucked in air through her teeth and exhaled a pained groan.

"You okay?" was the only thing Paige had the energy to muster. Even though if Mott had asked her the same question, Paige would have outright lied, because the acknowledgment that she was anything but was too much.

"My ankle," Mott murmured weakly, annoyed. "Ow ow ow ow. I twisted it, I think I stepped on something."

"Probably willowweed," Lane helped.

Mott clicked her tongue. "Well, why didn't I think of that?" There was a rustle, a groan, and then more rustling. "None of you happened to pack a torch in your extra-spacious cleansing outfits, didja?"

Paige allowed herself a small smile. It was so good to have Mott back, even if she was struggling so hard to pretend her spirits were up; so good to hear her voice as lighthearted as it was now, even though everything else in the world had fallen apart. The only thing that would have made it better was Sol—

Her eyes watered and her whole body threatened to collapse where it was. A shudder of a sob rippled through her body and she told herself *no*. She couldn't think about that. Maybe she'd hallucinated him making his way out with them. Maybe it didn't happen. Maybe she was hallucinating this whole thing. She'd wake up tomorrow morning in that warm bed and tell Mama she was sick, and Mama would bring her tea.

There was a small *click* and a soft *thunk*, and then Mott stated an extremely practical, "Ow."

A brief pause. Then, Mott, again—

"Where did you get this?"

Get what?

"I plan ahead," said Lane, as if that explained everything.

"What is it?" asked Paige. Her voice didn't waver. She didn't let it. She had control.

But she quickly found out, as a small light erupted in the middle of the blackness and revealed—

"*Mercy*," said Paige.

—a small emergency kit. Where had Lane even hidden that? Mott had lit a match from it. Meager resources nestled in a small, zippered bag attached to a stretchy piece of fabric that Lane had somehow attached to her person. It held some medical supplies, a candle, maybe a few days' worth of rations for one person, and a single canteen pouch that Paige wanted to unleash down her entire throat in hopes of restoring some of the fluids in her body that the massive amount of sweat stuck everywhere had released.

Mott lit the candle and handed it to Paige. She took out a fabric bandage roll and started to unravel it, but then stopped and handed that to Paige, too.

"You need this more than me."

"I need more than that for my arm," Paige said. Good. She could focus on this. Logistics, mechanics. "Unless there's extra skin in there, it won't do much. Just use it."

"Your dress could be good for a sling," Moses said, half-heartedly. He unbuttoned his shirt and bunched it up, then laid his head on top of it. His underclothes looked much the same as hers, with the same markings, but his had no sleeves. Paige averted her eyes as soon as she looked.

Fat lot of good a sling would do her, with no additional medical care. Her foot's damage seemed superficial, but it was only a matter of time before her arm got infected. Paige wondered if that would kill her before the dehydration did.

"You're right," she told Moses, "thanks."

Because that was what it came down to now: how she would die, not whether she would. She realized, with a shiver, that this was why the CSes hadn't followed them much further out. It was basic biology: why risk their own lives when the elements would kill their prey? The funny thing was—back in the Council building she wanted to die. Now that she was in a place that would kill her within a day, she didn't.

Candle wax dripped onto her hand; if it was hot, she hardly felt it. But the light itself was beautiful. And Mott looked stunning in its glow.

If she was going to die, this was how she wanted to—on her own terms, with someone she loved.

But she wasn't going to die, she told herself. She just needed to rest. They'd made it this far, and that was all she'd wanted. If this was all life was, and no Afterlands existed, then Paige wanted to suck out every last drop of happiness it provided, wherever she could find it. Even if she was hallucinating the whole thing.

"We should be okay here for the night," Lane said. "Get some rest. We'll start walking again in the morning."

She was so authoritative for someone so young. Like she had everything together despite being Sol's age—

Paige could delude herself, still, into believing that he was right behind them, that he'd still catch up somehow. The heap of human on the ground she'd witnessed had been nothing more than her imagination. And the glimpse she'd caught of it was so short anyway that she could have been confabulating the whole thing—

The adrenaline was wearing off and Paige let the earth hold her up. She could feel it supporting her head, her neck, her arms; the willowweed she laid on provided enough comfort that she felt she could lie there forever. Or howeverlong she lasted. Or howeverlong it took for Sol to catch up.

She had time. She could wait. And for now, she could sleep. He'd be there in the morning.

ON THE DANGERS OF THE EXCLUSIVITY OF LOVE

an excerpt from the Statutes of Equality

W E STRIVE FOR EQUALITY, Friend. We are not perfect, and cannot pretend to be, and when we fail we correct each other on our mistakes. For how can we love each other when we allow one among us to be exempt from acknowledgment of error? How can we allow the spread of wrongness into the veins of our happiness? Should we allow this, we allow ourselves to be infected. We allow our neighbors to be infected, our friends to be unclean, ourselves to spread disease. And the result of disease is that which our Ancestors allowed to be rampant: we tier ourselves into those of us who are better and those of us who are worse. We recreate the inequality that nearly succeeded in undoing us all.

And the answer to equality is this: one is not worth more than another. We cannot treat one of us as better than another; we cannot love one of us more than another. We are all one and the same: we are all bound to this earth by body, bound to each other by blood. We belong to each other. We do not belong to ourselves.

But when we focus only on what we think we want (and hardly does what we need ever actually match what we think we want!), we too easily allow each other to fall onto the wayside. We forget about some. They become alone.

Therefore we are convicted of the truth that what we do with our bodies must be best to serve our community. Our bodies—our lives—are not ours, but bestowed upon us by our parents, delivered to us by our mothers, nurtured for us by our friends. When we provide them in service to each other, we gain a collective power: we can feed each other. We can house each other. We can ensure that no one—not one soul—goes unloved.

WE ALL FALL DOWN

Paige was surprised to wake up. She blinked her eyes open through a frown only to have the sun's already-too-hot blaze shoot directly into her pupils. For a moment she was confused to be here on the floor, in a field of overgrown weeds, Mott lying next to her with no silk wrap in her hair, her black curls smushed under her face instead. Even turning her head to the side to watch the soft rise and fall of Mott's chest made Paige want to cry out, but in comparison to her arm, it was nothing.

Her limbs were splayed out at odd angles—she could feel it in the lethargy of her joints and the faint bruise feeling from where her foot had hit the gate. The tendon over her hip strained in soreness from both overuse and having not moved all night, but when she tried to shift her legs in another direction, the inescapable ache of every piece of muscle and bone made her groan nonsensical sounds:

"Muuuuuhhhhhhmmmmmmmmmnnnnn."

And when she rolled over, something poked her in her neck. She reached underneath her neck and slapped at it, half-asleep, finally pulling out a small ball attached to a clump of . . . extra-thin hay?

It wasn't crinkly like hay. It was tangled and thin and soft and dirty all at the same time. And upon further inspection, the small ball was actually a tiny head.

It spooked her at first, but soon fascinated her. The head was made of some sort of unbreakable, smooth-edged, shiny material she'd never seen before. The face was painted blue between the doll's eyes and eyebrows and red on the cheeks, but the most horrifying part was the bright, static smile painted on in permanence. The head was doomed to smile at everything—at its face ground in the dirt, at its head being removed from its body.

And suddenly, everything came rushing back: the fire. The cleansing. Stabbing the Matriarch. Shrapnel everywhere. Chang hanging limply onto the stake. Running as far and as fast as she could. Mott. Sol.

Guilt pooled itself into Paige's gut like a fresh batch of tar, sticky and unmoving and hot and cold.

What had she been *thinking?*

This wasn't her. Lying, stealing, running from problems . . . it was everything she wasn't supposed to be. Everything that would have disappointed Mama.

And Sol.

The guilt morphed into fear, anger, horror—the more she stared at the severed doll head, the more it disturbed her. It was just a remnant now, alone, and so was Sol. Had they taken *his* body?

His *body.* Not him, but his body.

Not that he was—he wasn't dead—

Except he was. And she was out here, in the middle of the desert with her best friend and two near-strangers, holding on for survival while her baby brother was nothing but a heap on the ground.

And she'd abandoned him.

She couldn't cry. She could only feel miserable in the knowledge that he was gone. She tried to cry, but it felt inauthentic, and that only added to her own self-disgust. Why couldn't she cry for her dead brother?

Dead. Dead. He was dead. The more she thought the word in her head, the less it meant anything. She barely felt it. Maybe she didn't need to grieve.

And then suddenly, in emotional vertigo, Paige involuntarily uttered a crazed whimper, and then stopped it. No. She was not doing this. Sol was right behind them. He wasn't dead.

"Mott," tried Paige.

Mott frowned, eyes still closed, crinkling up the corner of her mouth. She groggily draped one arm over her eyes.

Mott grunted. "Five more minutes."

"They haven't come after us," Paige said.

"Which is why I have five more minutes."

"Mott, I need to talk to you."

"Okay, four minutes. Just four. Give me that much."

It seemed like such a normal thing for Mott to say. For a fleeting moment, instead of panic and sadness and pain, there was a sense of fresh delight: no obligations, nowhere to be, nothing to recite, no expectations to live up to. The world ahead of them. An ant crawled on Paige's good arm and she blew it off. And then a loud rumble from the depths of her belly.

The world ahead of them—as long as they survived.

They weren't going to survive.

They were.

They weren't.

They were.

"Fine," Mott groaned, sitting up with her eyes closed, normally-poufy hair half-matted against her face. "I'm here, I'm awake. What's wrong?"

Paige held up the doll head. Mott opened her eyes and yelped.

"Give a girl a warning first! What the hey?"

"Not hay. Hair."

"I didn't mean—" Mott sighed, taking the doll from Paige. She squinted at it. "Creepy."

"I did this," Paige said. She couldn't control it anymore and her voice cracked horribly. "To Sol."

She barely got his name out before she let out an enormous, gross sob. And then another one, and another one. The tears spilled out and she inhaled a raggedy, mucous-filled breath, and then she let herself be swallowed up by the grief that sucked up all of her senses.

"Oh. Oh, P." Mott tossed the doll head behind her into the tall weeds and pulled Paige into her arms, squeezing her tight. Paige felt like she didn't deserve the comfort, at first, and then she decided that she couldn't live without it. She relaxed into Mott's shoulder, drinking in her warm scent. There was the smell of her hair oil again, nutty and sweet, combined with caked-on sweat and dirt (a familiar smell from their childhood) and stale breath.

Mott didn't say anything. There was nothing to say. Paige responded by burying her face into Mott's armpit, moist and still Mott, familiar and warm.

She didn't tell Paige it was going to be okay; it wouldn't be. Paige sobbed harder, letting herself sink into her new reality: Sol was dead. He was gone. It was her fault.

"It's not your fault," Mott murmured into her ear. But Paige could hear Mott crying, too, just more silently. "I know what you're telling yourself, and it isn't your fault."

How couldn't it be her fault?

"And I know you don't believe me," continued Mott, "but he made choices he was comfortable with. He knew that would get him cleansed. Escaping was just a bonus. It was never the goal."

Paige knew that. It made sense. And yet she cried harder and harder, unable to shake the feeling that, if she'd been better, Sol would still be here.

She let herself fall into grief; she let it surround her. She cried endlessly: when she thought she was out of tears she somehow generated more, and more, until the tears dried up and she was nothing but a pile of dry sobs and salty mucous.

She felt a hand on her back in addition to Mott's arm around her shoulder. Then another hand, this one different. It was calming to have people there, to feel like she could breathe with others who were also breathing. And when she looked up at last, she found Lane and Moses sitting around her, their eyes closed in meditation.

After a moment, they opened their eyes.

"You okay?" Lane asked.

"No," said Paige.

"Good," said Lane. "You shouldn't be, yet."

As non-comforting as that sounded, Paige found it reassuring.

"It was a gun, right?" said Moses. "It had to be a gun."

"I think so," said Mott.

"I didn't even know guns still existed," said Lane. "I thought they were all destroyed."

"There were a couple in the history museum," said Moses. "They were technically still functional, but how could they have gotten them out so fast . . . ?"

They were all silent for a moment. Then Mott spoke up.

"There's a simple answer for that."

No one asked what it was. Probably because they all knew. But Paige marveled it aloud anyway in answer.

"They carry guns. Regularly."

A stunned hush fell over them all while they pushed through the grasses. The willowweed seemed to have faded away now, leaving the terrain mostly full of shorter, scratchier weeds, something more like Paige had seen in history books that described seemingly impossible, long-ago realities like giant feathered reptiles roaming the planet—this was more that style. Large aloe plants seemed to domineer the ground here, even if they were few and far in between. They looked spiky on the edges, like they could slice her chest completely open. But those spikes didn't carry a candle to the dangerousness of CSes carrying guns in secret.

"How are they manufacturing new bullets?" Lane asked.

"*Why* are they manufacturing new bullets," Paige said, but she didn't want an answer.

"Maybe they're not," said Mott. "Maybe they're using old relics that they—I don't know, saved up and—"

"—scouted," Moses finished for her, suddenly looking around themselves a bit more. They could see further now and the distance ahead of them seemed daunting in its lack of borders. Paige shivered at the implication: all those expeditions that scouts took, always officials working closely with CSes—they were supposed to bring back materials to re-use. Things to rebuild the community. Not things to destroy.

Had the Matriarch asked for this?

Lane pulled out a silver bag and tore it open with her teeth. It was a ration of disaster foods: fish jerky, dried strawberries, preserved soyballs. As a child, Paige had imagined eating these foods with Mott's family and her family and their downstairs neighbors huddled up in their tetriplex's basement; mercy knew there had been enough practice drills that she'd envisioned eating this food plenty of times. During the drills, she fancied what she would be like in an actual disaster—the brave, resilient daughter who had a good attitude the whole time and was helpful and caring for those who needed someone, with a tough enough exterior to trust but a sensitive enough demeanor to cry on. Here and now, she felt so small in this vast, unkempt space of nature, a far cry from anything that younger version of herself had ever imagined. How her younger self would have laughed. Or been horribly embarrassed. Or hoped so, so hard that she would never grow up to be destined to this hell.

"We only have one of these," Lane said.

There was a stunned silence. Paige started to calculate how long until they died of starvation, and whether it would be before or after they were burned up by the sun. The food would last them all maybe four days if rationed well. With one canteen for the four of them, dehydration would probably kill them first. Mostly, Paige was surprised to find that she actually cared.

She wasn't scared; she wanted to plan. The whole world was literally ahead of her: she was free of New Standard, and even out here with no resources, no brother, no form of accessible livelihood, and near-certain death, Paige wanted, more than ever, to explore it.

"I'm impressed that you have any at all," Mott said.

Mott was also avoiding looking at Paige's arm. Paige suspected that was because Mott knew that Paige would eventually develop an infection, and it would happen quickly.

They wouldn't need the extra water.

"We need to be strategic about this," Paige said, trying to regroup herself. Sol was dead and the surreal, aching fact of it made her feel compelled to do something with it or else she'd completely collapse. "What's our goal here? To last as long as possible? To die comfortably?"

"The first one," Mott said. "I'll take that one, please."

"I'm personally leaning that way, too," said Lane.

"Well, it's not much," Moses said, "but one of the things Lane and I were studying was the potential of other civilizations out here."

Mott laughed—a terrifying noise, considering the hysteria embedded within it.

"Wait, wait, wait. I'm sorry. First of all, *who* are you? And—" Mott pointed at Lane. "—and you?"

"I'm Lane, former huérfana, and this is Moses."

"*Educator* Moses," said Moses.

"Go fuck yourself," said Mott, still smiling, though it didn't reach her eyes. But Paige could feel a smile starting to crack its way into the grief all over her own face. "A huérfana? Interesting. A huérfana with an emergency pack of food, who created a pipe bomb and exploded it in a cleansing."

A pipe bomb? Was that what the explosion had been? The smoke, the pieces of glass everywhere? How had Lane even smuggled that in? How did she know how to make one?

Lane just shrugged. "And you're a lesbian who turned herself into the Matriarch. So what?"

"Mott," Paige said, "this is *her*. The huérfana for the Theorists."

Mott blinked twice.

"Wait, really?"

Lane raised her eyebrows briefly and pursed her lips to the side of her face, like this was to be expected. "Guilty as charged."

"She's so *young*."

"Standing right here."

"You're so young."

"Maybe you're just old."

"And who are you?" Moses cut in. "The spouse-wannabe, I assume?"

Paige blushed maddeningly. She loved the sound of that, and what was stopping them from being spouses in this desert wasteland?

"The spouse-gonnabe," Mott sassed back. "They call me Mott."

Paige's stomach flipped itself over thirty times in a row. This was not what she was supposed to be thinking about right now, but it was such a delicious concept that the hope within her soared sky-high. Beyond the sky, past the atmosphere containing Earth.

Paige had *missed* Mott. So badly. She loved her.

"Now," Mott continued, "*Moses*. Tell me about your . . ." She wiggled her fingers in the air. " . . . theory."

Moses looked like he wanted to say something back to Mott, but he seemed to shake it off, dismissing it as unimportant. "The Council has their fair share of secrets," he said. "One of them is that not all of the huérfanos who come into New Standard are born here."

Paige would have asked the obvious question—*where are they born, then?*—but she wanted to hear him say it out loud.

"They wander into our borders, and they're captured."

Mott exhaled audibly. "I wish that surprised me."

Paige could barely grasp the shock of it, but then again so many things had shocked her in the past forty-eight hours that this somehow seemed perfectly normal at the same time.

"Other civilizations," Paige breathed.

"Right," said Moses. "And they can't be too far, if they've wandered multiple times into our borders."

"How many times?" said Mott.

"So far, four," said Lane. "Two that I've seen, and two that I've heard of."

"But how would the rest of the citizens not know about this?" Paige asked. "We would have known—"

"Would you?" said Lane. "Did you even know *my* name before I met you in the Council building? Do you know the names of any of the other huérfanos? Do you ever identify them as individual people, or are they all one big group to you?"

Paige closed her mouth, ashamed. Lane was right. She didn't know their names. She had always thought of them as huérfanos, as *them*. As future Councilmembers, as future Matriarchs, not much more than people with a role to play. But she didn't know their names until they joined the ranks of the Council of Elders.

"That's what I thought."

"I'm so sorry," Paige said quietly.

Lane gave a long sigh, then turned her attention to breaking two of the soyballs from the silver bag each in half. "Look, the point is, you couldn't have known. The Council didn't want anyone to know that there was anything else out there."

"You really are the leader of the Theorists," Mott said, impressed.

Lane shrugged and handed Mott a piece of soyball. "Here. Breakfast."

"So you think there are civilizations," Paige said as Lane handed out a soyball piece to her and Moses, "and they're nearby, and we— you think we can survive?"

"Yeah." Moses popped the food in his mouth and chewed. "Maybe. If we find them fast enough."

"Not like we have much water," Lane added.

"But if there are other civilizations," said Mott, "if there are other *survivors of the Paterazm*—"

"—there should be water somewhere," Paige finished.

"I heard something about water," Moses said, excitement sparking up his posture. "Ka-we-uh. Ka-way-uh. I'm not sure how to pronounce it, but it's a lake. Southeast."

"How southeast?" Lane asked.

"I don't know."

The pain in her arm seemed negligible now. It was hope against hope, positivity that she'd never thought she'd see in the collapse of her world, reason to push forward. It was a way to make Sol's death count. To make Chang's death count. To make Ingrid's—

Wait.

"Ingrid could be out there," she said to Mott.

"That's our theory," said Lane.

"And if she's alive," said Paige, "she's had to have found water by now."

"Or know about Kaweah," said Moses.

"Didn't you say that was a lake?" asked Mott.

Moses smiled. "A lake town where the lake hasn't dried out. A free society with resources but no Statutes. A whole other civilization."

A far-fetched dream.

Regardless of whether Kaweah really existed, water was around. It had to be. It couldn't not be. Paige swallowed her food, and though she knew it would only keep part of the nausea of hunger from making its way, full-force into her stomach bile, it was enough, for now, to go on.

"Then let's keep walking," Paige said. "I'll follow your lead." And even though her legs were still sore and her whole body felt like a barely functional skeleton, muscles loosely attached, she stood up like she didn't notice.

—

THEY WADED OVER CRUMBLED asphalt in tall weeds, the path lined with dilapidated metal gates on their left, a weed-infested set of train tracks on their right. Tall metal structures stood rusted with wires dangling from their tops like oily hair; old signposts laid on their sides. And when she looked back, in a curious glance at the world they'd left behind, the land of safety and sameness, Paige found that she relaxed now that she could no longer see it.

Sol did not walk with them. He wasn't there. But determination overtook Paige as she walked: she walked with purpose. She'd completely cried herself out; she was fine now. She was moving through to making Sol's death matter.

Lane and Moses chatted amongst themselves every now and then, though Paige, walking behind them, couldn't hear much of the specifics. Not that she cared much—not with Mott walking alongside her, her 'spouse-gonnabe.'

The pain, hunger, and thirst that nagged at Paige seemed irrelevant in this surreal moment where Mott walked next to her. She felt better as they moved, and she was hyper-aware of Mott getting progressively closer to her, of her hand brushing Paige's good arm, at first accidentally and then it was so frequent that it couldn't be anything but intentional.

And then, finally, their pinkies hovered around each other, and Mott's caught grasp of Paige's and it stayed there. Paige couldn't help but smile despite everything.

It took another few minutes before she worked up the courage to ask, "Did you mean what you said?"

"About me being a Theorist?"

"That was stupid, by the way. Just—really dumb."

"Well, love makes you do stupid things."

"Not according to the Statutes."

Mott groaned. "You can take the girl away from the Statutes, but you can't take the Statutes out of the girl."

Paige laughed. A small laugh, but a laugh nonetheless, and it felt so freeing. She loved the pain, the uncertainty, the threat of death—it allowed her to *live*. To not hide. To be the most honest she'd ever been.

"I mean, I love you," Mott said, more seriously. "I always have."

Paige's heart skipped three beats. Mott stopped walking for a moment, there in the nothingness and under the blazing sun, and intertwined all of Paige's fingers in her good hand. Paige's head filled with airy heat; she had to remind herself to breathe.

Mott grabbed Paige's arm and Paige winced at the splitting-pain touch, sucking in air through her teeth.

"Oh, sorry." Mott lessened her touch.

Paige laughed. "It's fine."

Because it was. There was something beautiful about this life of nothingness: it let her be.

It let *them* be.

Mott cupped Paige's jaw and pulled her into her, letting their lips meet in a tentative inhale.

It was like the moment would never end. It was delicious, a moment of suspended animation, tandem breathing. The togetherness they never thought they'd truly have. Paige loved how tender Mott's lips felt, though they were chapped by the sun and lack of water. It was Mott's face, Mott's cheeks, Mott's mouth, and she had it all to herself. Mott deepened the kiss, her tongue prodding at Paige's lips, and then, as she parted them, her teeth, and when the tips of their tongues met Paige thought she might die from sheer pleasure. Paige melted into Mott, pulling herself in closer to her body, and let their chests meet, their stomachs meet, their hips not too far away—

And then Mott pulled back, and Paige instantly missed the feel of her face. Mott's face was serious.

"Do you love me?"

Paige blinked at Mott, letting out a little helpless laugh. "I think I've loved you for a long time," she said, and then she pressed her lips back to Mott's.

She stayed there for a good, long moment, drinking in the texture of Mott's mouth and her scent and her sheer existence there with Paige. Her whole body was liquid joy, and as she felt Mott's mouth smile under her own, Paige smiled, too.

Sol would have been proud of her. She started to cry while kissing her. Mott broke apart.

"Are you okay? I'm not a bad kisser, am I?"

But Paige couldn't do anything but shake her head and lean into Mott's shoulder, sobbing at last.

"Sol," she managed through one of the sobs, and Mott wrapped her arms around Paige and held her tight, and Paige's bad arm hurt but not nearly as badly as her heart.

They broke apart after Paige's sobs had softened to deep breaths—how long, she wasn't really certain, but by the time she looked up, Lane and Moses were several yards ahead. Mott squeezed Paige's hand and nudged her head toward their companions. "Come on. We gotta go."

They had little food and even less water and their bodies were dirty and smelled ripe. And despite all of this, Mott was here, suffering beside her with her goodnatured grin and her freckles and her light heart. They were homeless, but—and Paige solidified this thought when Mott reached out to brush the dirt off her nose and kissed her again, there in the open daylight with no one to stop them and only an opportunity to kiss her right back—they were home.

———

After walking for so long, though, distance became a constant rather than a goal. Reality became wandering curiosity: watching the echoes of the world-that-was appear more frequently along their path, following them into the forgotten past.

They didn't talk. They stopped only to rest the blisters that popped inside their shoes, to wrap them with the precious bits of gauze from Lane's pouch, and then trekked on. Don't stop, don't stop. Everything hurt, but the elation from knowing that Mott was hers for as long as they liked was enough to keep her spirits up.

Everything was unrecognizable now except her companions. Every step was painful enough to make her want to slow down; every thought of going back made her go faster. The objects they passed grew larger with every step—half of an air-conditioning unit; an old, paint-stripped door. Piles of remnants of books. Metal gates. Everything old, weathered, ruined. She had to think about every object to remember what it was or could have been. All her life she'd been so curious about the rubble, and now here it was: dirty.

But beautiful, even through the haze of exhaustion—each piece an artifact, something that had been used by a human standing exactly where she walked now, hundreds of years ago. She wanted to examine them, to hold them and turn them around in her hands and feel every hollow of chipped paint, every interrupted jutting edge. She wished she could have seen the lives of the people who had lived there, if anyone had even lived here at all.

The further they walked, the larger the amount of old rubbish, disintegrated pieces of lives that once were from forever ago, things she'd only read in books here and solid and under her feet—empty bullet casings, pieces of flayed tire. Ash, mostly— dirt everywhere, covering everything, including a much-larger object they passed, a crusty, box-shaped automobile lying on its side with the word GOTTSCHALKS on it, and right underneath: *We're your store!*

"Oh, mercy, my ankle," Mott whined at one point. She paused to hold on to Paige's good shoulder for balance and roll her ankle out.

"We can take a break, if you want," Paige said, mostly because *she* wanted a break.

But Mott shook out her leg one final time and continued on. "Take a break, my ass."

"All right," Moses announced loudly, "I'm just gonna woman up and say it: *I* need a break."

"Oh, thank the Spared," Lane said, fearless in demonstrating her exhaustion. They were in the middle of nowhere, old asphalt prevalent on this road that had once been a place where cars drove quickly and murdered people by accident. Pieces of auto junk sat nearby as if to serve as proof of this; Lane found something tattered and rubber and used it as a pillow.

For laying on asphalt, it seemed pretty comfy.

There was an odd, boxy sort of thing sticking up in the field only a few feet away—something metal, with four dials up toward the top. Paige sat on top of it, rolling her ankles around gingerly to air out her feet.

Halfway through the day, pain jabbed both sides of her ribs. Their group passed a piece of metal half-buried in the ground that read WELCOME TO FOWLER, but she hardly noticed as her stomach churned from hunger and her skin stung from sunburn. Even Mott, whose sunburn was less visible through the denser amounts of melanin on her skin, showed a red flush on her cheeks. Paige kept willing her legs forward, her knees forward, and she could hardly tell she was walking, or sweating, or breathing.

She was too tired to think, too tired to talk. She could only gaze in wonder at the world around her, the dilapidated nothingness that was everywhere around her now.

She wasn't sure what else she'd expected.

How far? How much longer? Was it tomorrow yet so she could have another morsel of food? During the Paterazm, people had survived for weeks without food; she felt pathetic for wanting some now when she'd just eaten this morning.

The sun finally started fading, blazing orange casting a comforting blanket of light over the back of Paige's neck. Too comforting. She could take a nap in that warmth. She'd been taking a nap, this whole time, her whole life, and now it was time to stay awake. Keep momentum. Never stop moving.

The night promised acidic rain. They would find a nice tree somewhere, right? Or a nice spot of soft grass. Like their ancestors'-ancestors'-ancestors did, long, long ago, when caves were still considered suitable living conditions.

When they finally stopped for the night, Paige collapsed on the ground. She barely noticed that she'd fallen in the first place, and it took her a few moments to register how much her knees hurt from the impact of the earth coming up to meet her. She'd been an idiot for thinking this grass and its weeds were so scratchy before; now it felt so soft, so cradling and accommodating of every one of her sore limbs.

She was hungry and had no food. She was thirsty and had no water. But when Mott laid down beside her then rolled onto her side to face Paige, draping an arm over her shoulders, it didn't seem to matter whether she died here right now or lived to see tomorrow. They were nose-to-nose now, Mott's beautiful, long eyelashes making her eyes seem more open and deep than Paige had ever seen them before, but maybe she hadn't been looking hard enough before. Maybe she hadn't let herself look.

She draped her arm over Mott's shoulders in response and rested her forehead against Mott's, too. Before she closed her eyes, not knowing if it would be for the last time, she thought, *I'm looking now. I see you.*

You're everything.

ATONEMENT

an excerpt from the Statutes of Equality

THERE ARE TWO METHODS to civilization, Friend: collaboration and competition. We have seen how conquerers, driven by a thirst for power and an obsession with self-importance, have succeeded in obtaining power—but at what cost? In a world where there were more humans, where they were dispensable, perhaps we may allow this strategy merit; the deaths of millions of human beings may have been an acceptable price for the erasure of cultures, the unification of language, the "re-education" of a conquered people.

We do not have such luxuries now. We stand firmly in this place, in this spot in history, as today's chosen people, not chosen by a specific deity but Spared by the energy of the Universe itself. We have been chosen to live because the Earth recognized that our values were superior for evolution; like the great floods recorded in various historically religious texts, the war that our Founders survived by way of collaboration provided a cleansing of evolutionary inadequacy. By the decisions of our Mother, Earth, and the energy of the humans who once resided here and saw the errors of civilizations past, who have now turned to ask as we are all destined to do—these humans have become pieces of energy in our air, in our lungs, who encourage us—*require* us—to not stumble. They are our Ancestors, and as their children we must repent for the mistakes of our past. They demand that we sacrifice one Mother of our own to remind us that we are not powerful, and they hold us responsible for not repeating history's mistakes. And in this repentance for all of humanity and history we are the only ones who can earn our Mother Earth's trust again, so that

She might remind us that we are guests of Her body, and in kind we beg our own humility.

We bow our heads and meditate so that we can listen to our Mother Earth. We hear Her cries of the past; we atone for the faults of our species.

RING IT, RING IT WELL

T HE NEXT MORNING, SOL was still dead, and Paige was still alive Red streaks drew thin riverbeds under her bandage and along her arm. Ahead of them, the road yawned alongside the dry riverbed, which stretched on for years. Her head felt hot and the world spun around her; she was almost disappointed not to be dead.

But Paige didn't know when they would stop walking, and she was afraid that she wouldn't ever know, or that she would find out by dropping dead. And as worried as she was about it, the thought still brought an accompanying sense of relief: at least she'd join Sol soon. The pain of losing him would leave her forever.

The four of them got up and walked and didn't talk because they were almost out of water. Paige was so hungry and thirsty and tired that even the elation of finally being with Mott was wearing thin and she could only focus on specifics: her bad arm being too warm, searing with heat on the open wound, and the small bit of gauze in their emergency packs that Mott wrapped around it had crusted with sand.

This riverbed must have had water at one point before all the horrendous droughts in this place that used to be California. She supposed they were only following it because it was a path to follow. She tried to imagine water flowing there, tried to remember the sound of it, but the only sound she heard after a day was the loud smacking of her dry tongue against the roof of her mouth as she tried to conjure up more saliva. Her throat was scratchy from the heat and what moisture she had in her mouth felt like glue; every moment she breathed in air she felt microscopic granules of sand thickening her tongue. She wanted water so badly that she'd dreamed about it. But even in her dreams the water was silent, no cool trickling of a river, no drip-drip-drip from a faucet.

They'd never make it, but then again there was nowhere to make it to. The promise of Lake Kaweah was most likely a myth to keep people going beyond the borders when there was no realistic goal in mind, something to keep the spirits up. But still she moved on forward in pursuit of it, and Moses told them stories—when he had enough breath, when his own throat wasn't too sore—of the impossible promises it held. Freedom. Beauty. Safety. Happiness. Everything a human could want.

She had been wrong. She knew that now. There was nothing beyond their community except this dirt. It was moist and fresh and she loved it.

Ashes to ashes, dust to—

Halfway through the day, Paige wished for a bow and arrow to slice her through so that she wouldn't have to breathe anymore. Even the group letting her drink the last of the water had not soothed her, not when the sun drained every drop she tried to put into her body. She was almost fine for a moment, one sweet, blissful moment, and then everything was dry again and she wanted something sharp and quick to end it all. This must have been how the Ancients felt: a wish for something violent because the suffering was so great. She understood now: the violence wasn't destruction. It was relief.

She barely heard her own footsteps anymore. The only thing keeping her going was that Mott was still going beside her. If they could keep going, if they could keep walking, if they could find water, or food, or anything . . .

Maybe they could be happy.

She tried to push her ragged body further—the ache crunching in her ankles, the shaking in her thighs.

Maybe.

Her feet dragged on and the blisters never healed like they'd promised to and every step was unbearable. But she kept on, without thought, without purpose. Right foot, left foot. Right foot, left. Right—

Why are we still here? she wondered to herself as the sun reached its peak. Left foot. Right foot, left. Her body no longer responded to anything. She and Mott were both silent: if they opened their mouths, a pile of dirt might fall out from their throats. It scratched around, exfoliated the skin that wasn't there, probably bloodying her larynx. Left . . . left . . .

The rocks in the road got in the way, and she tripped. It didn't matter, she could barely register her surroundings anymore, anyway. She'd tasted freedom for a day, and she could die knowing that.

"Paige?" Mott croaked.

"Mm?"

She didn't look up from studying the ground ahead of her, which she watched carefully to see if it would change as she walked. It was hot against her back and the smallest of shadows hit the ground by her face. She remembered the light that streamed through a window in the safe dining hall in the safe community that had sentenced her to lose forty-three of her years on Earth. There was no safety here and she had lost those years, anyway. It didn't matter. It had never actually mattered.

It was so *hot.*

Firetruck red, firetruck red, you're too late to help—

"Paige," said Mott again.

"What," Paige said, looking up at last.

"Is that—?" said Lane.

Paige forced her head up and blinked. She blinked again. She kept blinking until she knew for sure that her eyes weren't playing tricks on her, that the structure in front of them wasn't merely a mirage. But she wouldn't know for sure until she felt it with her own two hands.

"No way," said Mott.

She pulled Paige up and together they practically ran toward the structure, propelled by a fresh surge of adrenaline.

It was nothing like the white cottage of Paige's Afterlands; this place barely held four walls, and it was essentially nothing more than a long rectangle of refuge from the sun. At first glance, the inside was horrible, scattered pieces of broken furniture and a blanket of dust covering the whole place; there was blood, too, staining the edges of the sofa. But there was something delicate and shining in the cracks of the wall where sunlight seeped through, something Paige had never seen in person before but always scoured textbooks for old images or drawings of this beautiful, mysterious construction—

—a spiderweb.

"How far out are we?" she asked.

"Further than most expeditions," Moses said.

"Did you see the plants outside?" said Mott.

"What, the weeds?" Lane snorted.

"No, *plants.*" Mott's face lit up, her cheeks glowing from where they met her nose and spreading out toward her ears. "Actual *plants.* That are *growing.*"

Paige frowned. "But how can they grow without—"

Mott just stood there, grinning stupidly, while Paige put it all together.

Impossible.

Water. There had to be water nearby.

And a spiderweb.

Which meant, if these spiders, were still alive, insects.

Life. A *system* of *naturally occurring* life.

Paige laughed giddily, unable to control herself. "*Mott,*" was all she could think to say.

"I know." Mott couldn't stop smiling.

"Mott."

"I *know.*"

"Show me. Show me show me show me show me show me show me."

But Mott was already dragging Paige by the good arm around the corner to the back of the shack, behind a dead tree or two or three, where the willowweed wasn't as overgrown. The terrain had evened out; the grass was lower here, and less brown—no, there were patches of actual green in there, it wasn't just the light playing tricks on her eyes. And over a piece of broken concrete, little vines wrapped themselves in intricate patterns, ones that suggested that they would never let each other go. They were there to stay.

"Are those—?" Mott started.

"—grapevines," Paige finished. "Yeah. Yeah, I think so."

And Paige couldn't help it: she was grinning so widely her face couldn't contain her happiness, her relief. She launched her body into Mott, threw her arm around her sweaty, sticky neck, and—even with her own ripe body odor mixing with Mott's in the too-hot air caught between their faces—kissed her with everything she had, pressing her nose right into Mott's eyelashes. If Mott cared, she didn't show it. She was too busy gripping Paige's hips and, as they stayed there longer, sliding her hands onto Paige's lower back, which thrilled Paige and terrified her at the same time. Mott played with the fabric on the back of Paige's dress and scrunched it up, inch by inch, into her hands, and all Paige could think was how much more she wanted her to keep doing it, and how desperately she wanted Mott's hands on every piece of her skin.

Paige only broke away to look around herself, purely on instinct, to make sure no one was looking. Mott laughed.

"It's okay. We're not there anymore. We're vagabonds."

Paige kissed her again, and again. "I love you," she said easily, simply, and it felt so good through the kisses that she couldn't stop giving and hungrily ate up. *I love you, and we're alive.*

—

THAT NIGHT, INSIDE THE shack, Paige laid down next to Mott and leaned against Mott's chest. How she had missed this warmth. Despite that Mott had been gone and that they had fought and they'd both been angry for so long, Mott was here now. She was hers, now.

She'd spent the afternoon with renewed energy, clearing the floor with her good arm. Her stomach felt like it was tearing itself from the inside out, but the adrenaline from having a shelter, a place to sleep with a floor and a semi-functional roof, was enough to keep her optimistic. And water, they'd found water. The smallest of streams, but a stream nonetheless, and it took thirty minutes, but they managed to refill the canteen. And it was only a ten-minute walk from the grapevines they'd found around the shack.

But now as she laid down on the floor next to Mott, Lane and Moses sleeping a little further away (together, which was extremely disturbing given their age difference, but Paige was in no position to judge anyone right now), Paige gazed up at the sky through the hole in the ceiling. It was peaceful. And peace was strange. Peace seemed darker than she'd thought it would be.

It was so quiet. So quiet that she could hear, through the rhythm of the crickets that hummed outside the shack, familiar words etched inside her brain:

When your body tells you it would prefer not to wake up, you command it to rise; when it tells you it would rather love another of the same sex, you remind it that is not wise. The best method for survival is logic and calculation—and the love that supports it. That love is selfless and kind. The pleasure of selfishness is irrelevant and must be ignored.

She hadn't ignored it. She wasn't ignoring it now. Sol was dead, and she had been selfish, and the painful pleasure of her current existence felt like it was the cause.

Because it was.

It seemed, in the stark darkness, like a truth so obvious that she couldn't believe she'd ever thought otherwise. She felt helpless in her happiness, ashamed that she'd ignored everything she'd been raised on.

"I don't deserve this," she whispered to Mott.

Mott must have been nearly asleep, because she groaned and rolled over so that she was nose-to-nose with Paige again, groggily blinking her eyes open. Paige loved being in this position with Mott, so close and delicious and she felt herself longing for Mott's skin again, and instantly felt sick for feeling it.

We have learned that competition leads us to allow our Friends to be left behind, to submit our bodies to injustices: poverty, loneliness, hatred, hunger.

"You're thinking," said Mott, half-asleep. "Why are you thinking."

We ask not if we will err, but when; not whether our souls will be stained but how. Her soul was stained. It was so very stained, and the stain was never coming out. There was no laundry out here.

Through her childbearing she will erase the sins of her past and ours. She wasn't going to have a child. Unless the implantation had worked, and she was pregnant—but if she was, how could it survive when she didn't even know if she could?

She thought of the Spared. *They gave up the seductive comforts of the world that destroyed nearly everyone; they surrendered their desires for the benefit of humanity's survival.*

"P?" Mott sounded more awake now. Paige couldn't see her; her eyes were clouded with tears she didn't know she could produce. She mostly dry-sobbed in the space and let Mott put her hand on her cheek until she calmed down, and was able to say:

"I was so afraid and I didn't want to be."

"Oh, P." Mott pressed her forehead to Paige's, then pulled back to kiss it. "You don't have to be, anymore."

"And I was so selfish, and I killed Sol—"

"You didn't."

"I know. I know. But I feel like I did."

"Listen to me. It's not your fault."

"I know. I *know*, okay? And that—" she almost didn't want

to say it. Mott would be angry, or annoyed, or exasperated. But she steeled up the wretched courage inside herself and forced herself to speak. "That's what terrifies me."

"What does?"

"Freedom."

"Why?"

"Because I feel like I'm responsible. And I feel like I can't get the Statutes out of my head. And I kind of don't want to, because I feel like I don't know who I am without New Standard. I don't feel like a— like a person. I feel like my— my soul is . . . I don't know. Lost. Forever."

Mott tilted her head at her, staring at her for a long time.

"You haven't gone anywhere, you know," she said after a while. "It doesn't matter where your soul is *going*. Right now, it's right here."

"Where?"

"You can't see it?"

"What are you talking about?"

Mott sighed. "Close your eyes."

Paige did.

"Picture your soul. Maybe it's white and wispy, or maybe it takes the shape of a tree, I don't care. But picture it close to your body. Now picture someone cutting that string. Where does it go?"

"Up," said Paige. "It floats."

Mott laughed. "Whenever I picture this, my soul just kind of dissipates into thin air."

"Well, we always knew your soul was fragile." Paige could feel herself smiling and opened her eyes as Mott poked her in the side.

"I like to think of it as *delicate*," said Mott.

Paige stared at the side of Mott's face, wanting to kiss it but afraid to lean in even though they'd already kissed so many times today. *There's no one out here,* she reminded herself. *Just us.* And she leaned in, feeling better from having taken a few breaths, and kissed her delicate cheek, and Mott didn't flinch away; she smiled from Paige's touch.

"It's beautiful," Paige murmured into Mott's ear, then she leaned her head onto Mott's shoulder and stared at their surroundings. There was a rising dawn and willowweed and open sky as far as she could see. And Mott. Mostly Mott.

The new and the familiar, all in one spot.

Mott was right: she couldn't ignore her old beliefs. But she couldn't ignore her new truth, either. Her soul was her soul, independent of everything, independent of life itself, whether it was going to go to the Afterlands or not.

She might decide, in the morning, that she couldn't live with this. She might wrestle with the warring thoughts in her head for another week, or until she died in a day or two from the infection in her arm that was starting to burn a fever in her head. But if she was going to die overnight, she wanted to be here, next to Mott, claiming her independence and herself, dying on her own terms. She decided to like it.

THE NURSERY RHYME

origin: folk, cir. 2140

Firetruck red, firetruck red, sound the warning bell
Send Dispatch to help the dead 'cause down and down they fell

Come on, Mama, come on, Papa, if you want to stay,
Speak your mind but I think you'll find that Theorists hold the blame

The sky was blue, the trees were green, and all our lips were red,
But a mushroom cloud cried blackened rain and now we make our beds

Firetruck red, firetruck red, you're too late to help
But the bell is there and you're still here so ring it, ring it well.

ACKNOWLEDGEMENTS

I started writing this book in 2012 (or was it 2011?), back when I was an entirely different person. In so many ways, it feels like finally publishing it allows that past self of mine to rest. All of the identity stuff, the dystopic analysis, the spiritual and familial trauma and healing: this book is a really lovely reflection of all of that processing, and I'm at a point in my life when it feels good to not have to hunt, anymore, for a publisher or an agent to accept and embrace that. I'm done editing that past version of me. She's in this book, and she's whole now.

I've avoided writing these acknowledgements for a long, long time solely because I'm worried I'm going to forget everyone who helped me throughout the years. This book has been the embodiment of my young-adulthood and there have been so many people who have led me and guided me and challenged me and supported me. It's inevitable that I'm going to forget to mention someone here, and there are people who have been amazing and supportive of me who aren't mentioned below (e.g., Kevna and the Stellburgsons) but I want to give my thank-yous to a bunch of people and groups in particular who have been instrumental in getting this particular work finished and developed through at least six full revisions, so here we go:

To my readers on FictionPress: who even knows if any of you are going to see this? In case you do, I want you to know how invaluable it was to wake up in the morning after I had posted a chapter and to see that some of you had posted comments on this (back when it was titled Ritual Girl). To this day I still can't believe how many total strangers read this story, and it was the feedback and encouragement you provided that helped me actually finish this thing.

To my VH community: thanks for letting me play with you, and thanks for embracing me. It's wild how so much history is there, and how intricately that community supported my own personal character development. You all created an environment where I could be myself—and in the process of becoming myself, try on various versions of myself to make sure I knew which one fit right. That journey—and therefore this book—wouldn't exist without that. In particular, thank you to my constant collaborators: Ollie!Rebecca, Curtis, Julianna, Chris, Natasha, Football!Samantha, Beth, Ellie, Jeni, Leslie.

To Ms Swick, Mrs Mar, and Dr Torrance: thank you. For pushing me, for encouraging me, for believing in me, for tolerating me.

Thank you to all of the people in my university journey who provided so much knowledge and encouragement—Ben Miller for encouraging me in my veeeeery early work and telling me to read something other than *Harry Potter*; Michelle Latiolais for your warmth and welcoming into my first advanced writers' community and for telling me to not go into debt for an MFA. To all my critique buddies from the MFA at EWU: thank you for your critique letters and your support and analysis and your murder of my darlings. In particular, thank you to Kati Stunkard for your four-page (!) critique letter and for your continued enthusiasm for this book, and Chas Holden for giving me a chance to write and publish something new. And of course also thanks to my biggest supporters from the program, Mike Pankratz and Brent Lewis, for their friendship and literary know-how and support.

Thank you to my awesome NaNo community: Kiran, Kristen, Jay, Andrew, Joel, Scott, Katy, Sarah, and others I'm surely forgetting. Y'all are fantastic and this book would not exist without all of our speed writes.

To Shawn Vestal, the best thesis advisor I could have asked for: thank you for your mentorship throughout the years, for being able to see what this book could be beyond the *Giver* knockoff it originally was, and mostly for giving me an A-minus in your class. I think if you'd given me an A I wouldn't have felt you believed in my potential so much.

To Rosie Jonker, who believed in this enough to give it a shot and get it in front of Big-Five editors: thank you. Even though you ditched me (ha!) for S&S, the confidence I got from you believing in my work and the stories I wanted to tell was massive and wonderful. To Casey Dunn, in the trenches with me since 2020 and never without an encouraging word: thank you for everything. Having you in all of this has been grounding and motivating and all in all, delightful.

To Stacey Clark, who read so many drafts of this and spent so much time nudging it in different directions without ever telling me outright that it stunk: thank you. Gone are the days of yore when we stayed up late over IM and talked about who-even-knows-what-anymore, exchanging sleep for roleplays (which rightfully sounds dirtier than it actually is). Thank you for the years of critiques, especially on this book, and your neverending patience for my incessant use of interrobangs.

To Willcarter Huffman, I can't even believe how many times you've (willingly) read this book in so many different formats. I will always remember talking about it with you while walking at JPL and the sheer, genuine excitement you had every single time I sent you a new chapter: it kept me going, and was the best kind of reception a writer could ask for. Thank you for loving this book as much as (and maybe even more than) I did.

To Dree Redditt-Rodriguez, thank you for tolerating me making fun of you when we were 10. I'm fully convinced that our in-person, lined-paper RPs were a major catalyst for my current writing career, because it was. You spent years writing with me and more years reading my work, and this book wouldn't exist without you.

Massive appreciation to my community of incredible women who have gone through so many similar things and been there constantly with emotional support: Alex, Lauren, Marla, Lizardbreath, Celestine, Shelby, Cheyenne, Davita. Grace and Hank, you've been there for the entire journey, thank you for being my family through everything.

To my kiddos and puppy: thank you for sleeping every now and then so I could actually get this out the door. Also, I love you. I hope you never have to live this life, and I hope you always know who you are. Especially you, Bubbles. Know thyself, etc. Miss you, friend.

And finally, to Jon: this is the first time you're reading this all the way through, and even as I'm writing this right next to you right now I'm not even sure you'll ever see this, muahaha. You're the worst, but actually the best, and I love you. Thank you for everything.

ABOUT THE AUTHOR

RIE LEE (she/her/hers) is a recovering true believer. She's a little too obsessed with cults and almost definitely on some kind of FBI watchlist for researching pipe bombs. She holds an MFA in Creative Writing from Eastern Washington University and is currently working on her MLIS. Originally from Fresno, California, she now spends most of her free time at multiple libraries and coffee shops in the occupied native lands of what is now known as the Los Angeles area, writing books or working on civic engagement initiatives (votingstudyparty.org). Find more of her work at riewrites.org or follow her on Instagram (@yesrielee).